WHISPERING PINES

DAVID BOLTON

WHISPERING PINES

DAVID BOLTON

THIS IS A GENUINE RARE BIRD BOOK

Rare Bird Books
6044 North Figueroa Street
Los Angeles, California 90042
rarebirdbooks.com

This book is a work of fiction. The characters, incidents, and dialogue are products of the author's imagination and are not to be construed as real. Any resemblance to actual persons, living or dead, or to actual events is entirely coincidental.

FIRST HARDCOVER EDITION

ISBN-13: 9781644285565

For more information, address:
Rare Bird Books Subsidiary Rights Department
6044 North Figueroa Street
Los Angeles, California 90042

Set in Minion Pro
Printed in the United States

10 9 8 7 6 5 4 3 2 1

Library of Congress Cataloging-in-Publication Data
available upon request

In memory of Sean Kokochuruk

1971–1977

The child is the father of the man.
—William Wordsworth

TALES OF WHISPERING PINES

STREETCAR MAN

On a warm October evening, L. Wayne Sheer headed home from the Towson Courthouse, last stop on the Catonsville-Towson electric line for the Number 8. After a day of doling out change, chasing kids off the back, and rolling up and down York Road a half-dozen times, he strolled the streets to the apartment. Maybe the wife would surprise him with an actual hot meal, made from scratch: biscuits dipped in gravy, fluffy mashed potatoes, and a juicy slab from the broiler. A man's meal—not that crap heated on aluminum foil.

Amber was fading on the treetops. Wayne extended his walk, wandering through Towson High, his alma mater. He checked out football practice and did a quick sprint 'round the track. On the edge of campus, three coeds were passing on the plaza. Cradling their books, the redhead, brunette and blonde were singing to "Peggy Sue" on the transistor radio. Such joy. Cute, too. None, however, matched his Margo, a raven-haired Italian with emerald eyes and curves that would not stop. Of all the boys that pursued her, even twelfth graders with cars, Margo Catalano had picked him in the tenth grade as her boyfriend. Him, a kid with arms too long for his skeleton frame and an Adam's apple that went up and down like a yo-yo. Took great courage to ask her to dance.

He and Margo were engaged after graduation, with a big wedding planned after he finished vocational school. Margo became a college girl, going to Towson State, where she majored in elementary education. She wanted to teach children and have five of her own, three boys and two girls, each two years apart. He had visions of being an airline mechanic, a good union job at Friendship Airport. Instead, he was drafted into the infantry and spent eighteen months as an ambulance driver in a conflict he didn't understand. Only thing kept him going was her picture in his wallet. When he came home, he was a different person, harder on the inside…had a taste for liquor that he had to watch. Wasn't like the World War II vets. No parades for a stalemate.

Margo married him anyway, ghosts and all.

He stopped at the penny candy store and bought six chocolate strawberries. Bag in hand, he turned down Burke, passing the Tudor frame houses, tidy gardens, and front porches. Maybe he and Margo could still have a child. They would need more space. What if they moved here? He could plant a rose garden, put a sandbox in the back. Dream on, Sheer. Last night Margo told him she would understand if he had an affair, said she wasn't being a good wife, he deserved better. Why's she trying to chase him off? Nothing's been the same since the miscarriage, this time nearly five months along. She was beginning to show. Cruel.

A pair of tykes were playing football on the front lawn.

"I know you," said the boy with mud-caked knees. "You're the streetcar man."

"That I am," he replied. "And I know you. Last time I saw you and your ma, you were crying."

"Hate getting shots."

"So do I."

At the basement pharmacy on the corner of Burke and Knollwood, he bought an arrangement for the dining room vase. Holding the yellow mums in one hand and the brown bag in the other, he crossed Burke and entered the Whispering Pines complex, eight quadrangles of two-story brick apartments built after the war. His quadrangle bordered Knollwood Road and Garden Drive. He pressed his shoulder into the heavy green door of the North Building. In the foyer, he heard loud and clear the voice of Garry Moore, a Baltimore kid who had made good on *I've Got a Secret.* The television was blasting from his first-floor apartment. The door was cracked open…have to talk to her about that. Things happen, even at Whispering Pines.

He put the flowers in the vase and the bag of chocolate strawberries in the fridge, a nice surprise for dessert. In the TV room, Margo looked cozy in the rocking chair with her legs curled up. On the tray: the greasy remains of a Salisbury-steak TV dinner.

No home-cooked meal tonight.

"Chicken pot pie in the oven," she said, lighting a Tareyton. Her eyes did not stray from the screen.

"Are you a baseball player?" asked Jayne Meadows.

"Yes," said Moore.

"Are you Joe DiMaggio?" Meadows asked.

"Yes!" cried Moore. The audience erupted as the former center fielder stepped from the curtain. Look at that suit, probably made on Savile Row. What a smile. Some men just ooze with class.

"Finally," Margo said, blowing a smoke ring, "I knew it was DiMag from the beginning. Marilyn never should've left him."

"How was kindergarten?"

"Rough. Broke up three fights. One even bit me." She showed him the punctures on her forearm, and he caught a whiff of her lavender perfume. He wanted to bend over and kiss those ruby lips, as sweet as strawberries. He couldn't remember the last time they had kissed. They could make love, but without the intimacy of lips. French kissing was their favorite sport in high school, a prequel to "going all the way."

That didn't occur until graduation night—when he proposed to her.

"You should do something about that," he said.

"Don't fret. I put mercurochrome on it. I've had my tetanus shot. How was your day, streetcar man? Meet any pretty girls?"

"Why keep asking that?" he said sharply.

"I have my reasons…"

How could she say it? Margo thought. She didn't love him anymore. Each time his solicitous, hound-dog eyes fell upon her, she felt suffocated...three strikes and you're out...not his fault. She put the blame for the miscarriages on herself.

"You know," she said, "there's a hurricane coming. Barreling up the coast."

"Maybe I'll get a rainy day off, like a snow day."

Not likely. Too many depended on streetcars, especially in a storm.

Anyway, truth be told, aside from the snotty high school kids, he enjoyed his job. Kept the mind occupied. He'd had many a rich chat with strangers in the front seats. With his back to them, they'd tell him the darndest things—sickness, loss of a job, somebody done someone wrong—and he came to know them not as passing strangers, but friends. Everyone had a story. And he liked helping people, especially those old gals who appreciated an encouraging word on a rainy afternoon. Back in high school, Margo said she was drawn to him because he had "kind eyes." He wondered if that were still true.

In the kitchen—not exactly hungry, not for Mrs. Paul the third time this week—he clipped the mums and arranged them in a vase, a recent purchase at a flea market. He wanted the old Margo back, the one that kissed him on the lips and made marinara sauce using a recipe her grandmother had brought from the old country. Opening the cabinet, he reached for the fifth of Seagram's VO in the back, wedged among the canned goods and spices. Out of sight, out of mind. He poured himself a double and drank it neat. "You want a whiskey and water?" he asked, pouring another shot.

"No, thanks."

He made it anyway. Loosen things up.

"Told you I didn't want a drink."

"I think you do," he replied, turning off the television. The screen shrunk to a small white dot.

"Damnit, Wayne, turn it back on. I've had a tough day."

"Why do you talk to me about having an affair?"

"Because I'm a bad wife."

"No, you're not. You're a beautiful person."

"Hardly...I cheated on you."

"You're joking."

"I'm serious as sin."

He stared at his wife as if she were a stranger. "You fucked someone?"

"Yes," Margo replied, taking a sip of whiskey. "I fucked someone."

"Who?"

"Does it matter?"

"Are you in love with him?"

"Stop it! No more questions."

He came near and pointed a finger under her nose. "I have a right to know," he said through his teeth. "You're my wife!"

"You don't own me!"

He snarled and drew back his fist; the fright in Margo's eyes shamed him. What was he planning to do? Give her the old right hook? Had to get out of here before the Devil claimed him. He grabbed his jacket and keys. The slam of the door sent a tremor through the building.

How he longed to spin the Studebaker out of the parking lot, running through the gear box, but the chance of a child on a bicycle eased his foot off the pedal. Last Sunday that boy from the West building nearly bought the farm on Knollwood. Word spread fast in the quadrangle.

Miller, what were you thinking?

Obviously, he wasn't.

In Towson he parked in front of the Penn Hotel, where he had worked as a dishwasher in high school. It was a slow night with no Irish music or drunken lawyers from the courthouse. Just him and

Babs the bartender, who served him his first drink when he was sixteen and still had the same Clairol blonde hair and dark roots. Suited him fine. As she drew his lager, he asked if he might have one of her smokes. She shook one from the pack and handed him the cigarette. Hadn't had one in more than a year, let alone a Pall Mall.

"Bless you, Babs"

"I can tell when a man's in pain," she said, lighting his smoke. "You have a bad day on Number 8?"

"Something like that."

He slid eight quarters, change from the streetcar, into the jukebox, selecting the Platters, Mathis, and Elvis, as well as Baltimore's best, Billie Holliday. Sure could sing about tough times.

As the music played, he stared at his reflection in the mirror, questioning where he had gone wrong. Wasn't that bad looking, was he? Certainly better than that gawky kid Margo had fallen for. If only they had a child—too much grief between them now. Was that why she went looking for love? *Yes, I fucked someone.* Who? A teacher at school? An old flame from the war years? Maybe she wasn't so true blue when he was in Korea. Her bitter tone sounded as if she was trying to hurt him, didn't make sense. Maybe he had let her down somehow. But what the hell did that mean? He was in mourning too! For the son they wouldn't have.

Near midnight, he paid the tab, leaving a twenty on the bar for Babs. "You okay to drive?" she asked.

"I'm a professional," he said with a slight slur.

"Go slow."

"I'll be fine." He weaved into the thick humid night. A glimpse of the county police car idling across Pennsylvania Avenue stiffened his posture. With great deliberation, he opened the Studebaker door, making sure the key went in without a hitch. He rolled down the windows and started the engine, cursing when he slipped a gear and the car lurched forward. Now he had the full attention of the cop; he looked vaguely familiar, maybe someone from Towson High. Wayne started the car a second time. The cop stayed on his rear down York to Burke Avenue. Whistling Dixie, Wayne kept the speed between twenty and twenty-five. Maybe the man would turn off at Towson State, but, no, the law followed him all the way to Whispering Pines.

Wayne sighed with relief when the cop continued down Knollwood. He turned into the parking lot. Sweat soaked the back of his shirt.

A storm was coming—yes, indeed.

Margo had already left for school when he awoke from a restless night on the couch. He called in sick and drove to the Towson Diner. An idea came to him on his third cup of coffee. The Cadillac dealership was right down the street. He found what he was looking for in the front row, a pearl white Coupe de Ville, 5,000 pounds of crafted steel, a V8 with three hundred horses and a pair of four-barrel carburetors. Those fins and grill, works of art. This would cause a stir in the neighborhood. Every time someone bought a new car, it was an event.

Why are you doing this? To make a statement? If she could have a fling, he'd buy any damn car he wished. Maybe he could tempt her into taking a ride, just like in the old days when they rode around Towson in his jalopy. A flicker of hope. Against his will, he pictured them tooling down Highway 301 in the Caddy, bound for Florida for a Christmas vacation. Maybe they would make love on the beach, like Lancaster and Kerr. Nice fantasy, Corporal Sheer, but get real.

Yes, I fucked someone…

Beneath heavy purple clouds, he haggled with a lean and shifty-eyed salesman for nearly a half-hour before they settled for $4,449, two hundred below sticker price. The Studebaker brought it down to four grand. They shook hands. "Don't you go and sell this beauty while I'm away," said Wayne.

"Wouldn't think of it," said the salesman.

The car was his.

Wayne whistled an old show tune as he drove to First National Bank, across the street from the courthouse. He withdrew most of the money from their joint account in the form of a cashier's check. Back at the lot, he handed over the check after perusing the paperwork and signing off on the sale. The salesman pressed the keys into Wayne's palm and offered his congratulations. Was this a dream? Neither he nor Margo had owned a new car. Almost forgot. He opened the Studebaker trunk and pulled out his tool kit. He put it on the floor behind the driver's seat, careful not to smudge the Corinthian leather.

It started to rain, big fat drops beading on the hood. He drove out Joppa Road, taking his time, enjoying the power steering, the quiet motor, the sweep of wipers across the broad windshield, the feel of luxury at his fingertips. No smoking in this car. He wanted that new-car smell to last.

The rain intensified and the wind had picked up when he pulled into Whispering Pines parking lot off Knollwood. He waited for someone to notice the car. See, the streetcar man knows how to live! No one lingered in the rain to look at the new addition.

No matter. Only had to impress one person, and she'd be home any minute.

At two on the nose, he spotted the green Plymouth Fury pulling up to the curb. Margo did not get out of the car right away. It appeared that she and the bearded man were having an intimate conversation, with the man nodding his head in agreement. Were they talking about him? Could this be her lover? He wore a tweed sports jacket, looked like some sort of intellectual, maybe a professor at Hopkins, way beyond Wayne's high school education. She touched the man's shoulder before opening the door. In the thirty-knot wind, she fought to get the umbrella open.

Wayne stepped out of the car, closed the door, and shouted: "Need help with that?"

“What’re you doing here?” she asked, coming toward him with the open umbrella. “Why aren’t you working?”

“Took the day off! I want to show you something.” Extending his hand, he presented the car.

“What’s this?”

“Our new car.”

“What!”

“Want to take a spin around the block?”

“Are you crazy? How much did you pay for this?”

“Four grand, along with the Studebaker.”

“That was supposed to be a down payment on a house.”

“I know, but—”

“But what?”

“Is that man your lover? I saw the way you touched him.”

“Shove it up your ass, Wayne.”

“The car or the marriage?”

“Both, I’m done.”

“Wait, babe, maybe we can work this out.”

“I’m not your babe anymore.”

“But—”

“I want out!” A gust of wind ripped the black umbrella from her fingers; it flew across the parking lot and rolled up the slope, snagging on a box bush. Ignoring the umbrella, his wife trudged through the downpour. The green door closed behind her.

Her mean words sank into his bones. Sorrow and regret churned into rage. So much for saving the marriage, you lovesick fool! Be a pleasure to rearrange the face of that pointy-head prof. Why not sample this fine piece of American technology and style before returning it to the dealer? The trade-in for the Studebaker could cost them plenty. Who gives a shit!

Wayne pushed through the storm, heading north on York Road, ignoring the tears, paying little attention to anything beyond the pavement. The two-and-half ton Caddy with whitewall tires handled the rivulets well. He stopped at a liquor store in Timonium, one of the few establishments open, and purchased a pint of VO. At a red light, sheets of rain blocked prying eyes; he took a nip from the paper bag. The whiskey went down easy, smoothing the edges, warming the insides. By the time he reached Cockeysville, the pint was half gone, and he was wallowing in self-pity. How could he live without his babe? She had made him whole after he came back from Korea.

Approaching the Cockeysville tunnel, he slowed the car. On a beautiful afternoon last June, he and Margo rode through this tunnel on their way to horse country, My Lady's Manor. A train was crossing over it at the time. Driving into the maw of bedrock felt like entering the funhouse, a funhouse with a significant dip in the middle. Naturally, he and Margo did what most people did when they drove through the two-lane passage: They screamed and honked the horn. The echoes were deafening. His heart felt like it had been crushed by an anvil.

He parked the car before the sawhorses that blocked the tunnel entrance. He stepped into the downpour. Not a soul on the road or on the sidewalks. He took a swig, swirling the whiskey around his mouth. Screwing the cap back on, Wayne peered into the tunnel. From the other side, he heard the roar of Beaverdam Run—didn't mean the tunnel was flooded. The lights of the car showed the pavement for a good bit. If it became a problem, he could always back out. He needed to keep driving north. Maybe he'd find a saloon open in Maryland Line, a country dive that sold moonshine. Flossy couldn't stop him. He was driving a Cadillac! He moved the sawhorses aside.

The water rose to the lights as he inched down the slope. Hoping that was the worst of it, he pressed on for another few feet. Now the water was coming up to his door and rising quickly. Backing up, the car shorted out and the engine died. Plunged into darkness, he listened to the water trickle into the vehicle. Impossible to open the door, too much weight on the other side. The shorted-out electric windows were useless. Past his knees the water rose. He kicked at the window several times with both legs. No luck. The window was as thick as they come, part of that luxurious, quiet ride. With water rising to his waist, the fight went out of him; he sank into the seat, trying to accept his impending demise. The world would go on without him, and the ghosts he carried would vanish.

But what about Margo? Being a good Catholic girl, she'd probably blame herself. What if they ruled it suicide? She might not get any insurance money from the streetcar company. She'd be destitute, with a 4,000-dollar car totaled because of her husband's stupidity.

"Let me out!" he cried, bloodying his knuckles on the window. "I didn't die in Korea, and I won't die here!" The water had reached his chest. There had to be—yes, you fool, the toolbox! Holding his breath, he fished about in the watery blackness and found the latch. He grabbed the hammer and gasped as he rose above the water, which was now to his chin. He slammed the hammer against the window. Cracks formed. The second hit shattered a good portion of glass and in rushed the current. One last breath before being submerged…

Shaking off his loafers, he slipped through the broken window, cutting his heel as he freed himself from the watery tomb. He swam toward the surface, lungs bursting with pain.

♦♦♦

L. Wayne Sheer didn't consider himself a religious man. He had witnessed too many random deaths in Korea to have faith in a higher power or old man MacArthur. When he limped from the tunnel to face the blinding lights of the police, he was in a different space than the man who had driven the Cadillac into the torrent. He'd been granted a second chance—by design or luck, he couldn't determine.

The cops ignored his bloody heel and cuffed him hard, steel digging into wrists. He was tossed into the back of the patrol car like a sack of potatoes, on his way to the pokey, to be charged with reckless and drunk driving. Had but one phone call. Couldn't call Margo. She'd likely let him rot. Best to call his neighbor upstairs, Mr. Eckert; the attorney would know what to do. With his foot bandaged, Wayne spent two days waiting for the gears of justice to move. You meet the most interesting people in jail. Wasn't his first time in the brig. He knew how to get by.

Released on a blustery morning, he hitchhiked down York Road, from Cockeysville to Towson. His rumpled clothes and jail slippers repelled drivers. Took three miserable hours and the kindness of a negro junk dealer to get him to Whispering Pines. Power was still out in places. Branches littered side streets. The damage to the North Building from the big oak shocked him. He raced into the building, praying to find Margo safe, smoking up a cloud, watching *Sky King*, everything back to normal. He wanted to tell her she was the reason he had survived.

For once she had locked the door. Shouting her name, he fiddled with the lock. At last, it gave way, and he confronted an apartment devoid of chairs, tables, ashtrays, rugs, the bed, television, radio, as well as the photos and art on the walls. Only the wedding photo of his mother and father remained. No goodbye note on the floor or go-to-hell message taped to the refrigerator, only a drooping philodendron by the window, a couple of dirty plates in the sink and his Hopalong Cassidy coffee cup. How dare she! Guess the lover helped her move out.

Watering the plant, he screamed at the ceiling: "Go ahead, Lord! Pile it on!"

THE TRESTLE

KNEELING ON HIS BED, nine-year-old Miller Nowaki cut out the date on the front page of the *Baltimore Sun*, October 8, 1956, marking the eighth day since his brush with the Grim Reaper. He pasted it to the bedroom wall, alongside the seven other dates. Miller viewed the passage of time like the planets circling the sun. It varied, sometimes short, sometimes long. How long was a year on Jupiter? Glenn called him "dumb" for messing up the wall. Miller ignored Big Brother. He'd do what he wanted with time.

Wish it was still summer. He would be in his usual shady position, cross-legged on the grass, hunched over the chess board, playing beneath the branches of Big Guy, his name for the oak ruling the quadrangle of two-story, brick apartment buildings. Dad had introduced him to chess at Christmas. Miller had become a master at maneuvering knights, thinking five to ten moves ahead. Now Dad couldn't touch him. Sweet!

Funny, he saw himself as a windy boy, an anxious boy, but no fidgeting playing chess. Sometimes he'd be so deep into a conflict that he couldn't hear Mom calling him home for dinner. Like a gunslinger, he took on all comers in the quad: the Chowder boys, Gill and Tag in the East Building, three of the six Eckert kids in the North Building, even Mr. Sheer, known as "Streetcar Man," who saluted him as "Little Napoleon" after several losses. Preening like a peacock around that big-ass oak, Miller drew a rare laugh from this sad-face man. Dad said that sadness had something to do with the Korean War.

Miller loved Whispering Pines, home to steelworkers, cab drivers, cops, lawyers, teachers and vets like Dad, who ran

Marines to shore in the South Pacific. Best of all, it was home to lots of kids.

He went to the bathroom, closed the door, and stared out the window. He mourned the fallen giant, dead as a doornail. Not good seeing those chain saws slicing up the tree, home for bugs and birds. The quad now seemed naked. Big Guy left a hole in the North Building, not far from Apartment 3C, where Rusty, his number-one friend, lived with five sisters. Hurricane Flossy ripped Big Guy from the ground, tossing the oak through the brick wall with a sound that Dad likened to "incoming." Betcha they were scared! Why'd they name hurricanes after girls?

Why not name one after him?

Hurricane Miller. How cool would that be!

Miller zipped up his fly. On the tiles, he spotted a black ant. Where'd it come from? Where's it going? He picked up the ant, dropped it into the yellow water, and pulled the flush. 'round and 'round the creature spun. *What'd you do that for?* Ant never did anything to him. Wasn't that a venial sin, another smudge in the Baltimore Catechism milk bottle?

Banging on the door. "What you doin'?" yelled Big Brother Glenn. Miller opened the door and tried to escape his paws, but Glenn caught him by the arm and spun him around, tapping out a tune with his knuckles on Miller's bushy red hair. "Hello to Earth!"

"Stop it."

"Hey, pisser," he said with a shove. "Take a look at the bedroom. Cross the line and..." He ran his finger across his neck.

Yep, Glenn had most definitely laid down the law. Miller eyed the chalk running down the middle of the red rug, dividing the bedroom into separate kingdoms. Everything had a place in Glenn's world; Miller's, not so much. Longingly he looked at the orderly space, the 45-record player with the spindle holding the latest hits. Didn't mean to get fingerprints on the records. No more Jerry Lee Lewis, Buddy Holly, Elvis, or Little Richard

—'cept when Glenn's out. Then he'd have to be careful and put everything back where it was, 'specially the harmonica and turtle.

Monday had dawned clear and cool, a keen day for horsing around, playing army, Nazis versus Yanks, or king of the mountain on the grassy hill out front, or racing bikes across the country club golf course. Lots of choices, even watching a praying mantis lay eggs on the screen would do. Any place but that stuffy classroom, trapped with thirty-three other kids under Sister Clementine, dedicated to making his life miserable by calling on him whenever he gazed out the window, wishing to be a crow so he could fly away. Kids on the playground called him Squirmy. *What's up, Squirmy? Pissing your pants?* They didn't know he was chess champion. Sitting at his desk in stuffy Room 4A was the worst, especially when he had to pee. Sister Clementine had him doing jumping jacks in the back of class instead of letting him go to the lavatory for the second time in an hour…led to an accident…shouldn't have drunk those cartons of chocolate milk after First Friday communion.

He clipped on his brown tie. Might as well be handcuffs. He checked his nails for crud. Ready for inspection. Per the routine, breakfast dishes soaking in the sink, clock radio playing big band music, Mom behind the easel with her oil paints. Wasn't fair, he wanted to stay home and paint too.

"Okay, let me see you," she said.

The big band music ended. "Folks," said the WITH disc jockey, Johnny Dark, "that was Baltimore's own Cab Calloway singing 'St. James Infirmary.' Uh oh, looks like Flossy did a number on Immaculate Conception elementary. It's closed for the day due to flooding."

Glenn and Miller hopped about the living room.

"Yay, Flossy!" Miller whooped, rubbing his arms over his starched white shirt till they burned.

"Miller's washing his clothes again," Glenn teased.

So what. He was free this Monday. Why couldn't life be like kindergarten? You made friends, listened to stories, took naps, and played on the monkey bars. Finger-painting was boss. It was okay to make a mess.

Miller traded his school shoes for PF flyers and khakis for dungarees; off went the shirt and tie; he threw on a faded blue sweatshirt, a hand-me-down from Glenn. He announced that he was going outside.

"Watch for cars," his mother said from behind the easel. "No running out in the street between cars. If that man—"

"I know, Mom. I'll be careful."

Smoke curled up from the glass ashtray, her first Tiparillo of the day. He liked that his mom smoked Tiparillos; it set her apart. She slid away from the easel so she could give him what he called her "bad-ass eye," her Dundalk eye. She was a big woman—not fat, just big—with muscular forearms from working in the steel mill during the War. "You better, young man. Understand what I'm saying? You look distracted. Miller, you can't be distracted when you cross a street. Look both ways. Promise?"

"Promise," he said, closing the door, glad to be free of her glare. Mom did have a point. A week ago, after Sunday mass, he ran across Knollwood without looking, didn't see the sports car. "What!" shrieked the driver. In slow motion, Miller watched himself fall backward—no time for an Act of Contrition—yet it seemed like minutes before that MG came to a screeching halt, inches from his face. Too stunned to move from the smoking tires, Miller saw his elongated reflection on the silver bumper. "You hurt?" the driver asked in a high-pitched voice. The car door swung open. Out plopped a black engineer boot. Miller scrambled to his feet, raced to the other side of the road, and ducked around an apartment building. Returning home later (this time he did look both ways), he found the MG driver on the edge of the sofa, holding his leather cap. Miller recognized the goateed face: Mr. Turnbaugh, English teacher at Towson Catholic High. Lived in the South Building. He apologized for "disturbing their Sunday."

Mom thanked him for letting them know.

That was a long night. Dad's spanking was bad enough, a few stinging swats with the hairbrush; Mom's tears when she tucked him in hurt more. Worst was the dream of a car racing down a very wide road, coming right at him. Woke up in a cold sweat.

Miller bounded down the steps and trotted to the quadrangle in the back, his high tops sliding over acorns. Rusty appeared at the second-story window and said he'd be right down, soon as he combed his hair. That could take minutes. On the stump, Miller sniffed the scent of cut wood. *Wonder if the roots in the ground are dead. Be weird not having Big Guy's shade on hot days.*

Rusty's hand pounded Miller's back. "Howdy, pardner!" he said, a perfect imitation of Chester in *Gunsmoke*. He had a gift for voicing TV characters. "What you say we mosey up to Towson, hang out with the drapes?" Rusty's sole ambition in life was to be a drape, comb his hair like Elvis, and ride a motorcycle. Mr. Eckert, who worked in the state's attorney office, wasn't thrilled with this direction, particularly the Vitalis haircut that came to a perfect ducktail, said it made him look like a "hoodlum."

At ten and a half, Rusty Eckert, Jr., was the tallest and oldest member of Sister Clementine's fourth-grade class. He flunked second grade and had trouble reading. Miller did what he could to help his buddy. Rusty, in turn, protected him from the bullies in the neighborhood. A skinny kid with coke-bottle glasses was easy prey.

"What do you say we walk the tracks to Towson and grab the latest issue of *Mad* at Read's drugstore?"

"You mean lift it?"

"I got coin today," Rusty said, shaking the quarters in his pocket.

"Kazaam!" said Miller in agreement.

The railroad tracks, part of the MaPa line, ran a meandering seventy-seven miles from Baltimore to York. They started at the Black & Decker plant off Joppa Road. Aware of the possibility of a train, the boys quickly crossed the riverbed, stepping on the brown ties with little hesitation. They had taken this route before. They would end up above York Road in Towson, where the trestle stood, a barrier they had yet to conquer. Today felt different; they were ready for the trestle. Just had to concentrate, one step at a time…like playing chess. You always want to know your best move before you take it.

Not far from their destination, they paused to observe the colored kids playing in the schoolyard. East Towson Elementary, three stories of a white cement at the end of Susquehanna Avenue, sported big windows and a rooftop garden. Looked more inviting than Immaculate Prison. "Bet they get a longer recess," Miller said.

A glass bottle exploded on the rail a few feet behind them. "Jesus!" cried Rusty. They took off, taking two ties at a time. Out of range, they slowed their pace.

"Someone's having a bad day," said Miller.

"No shit."

Ahead, the trestle loomed, supported by pre–Civil War rocks and cement on both sides of York Road. They built them to last in the olden days. Fear trickled down Miller's back, slowing his walk. The black iron walls encasing the track made him squeamish. There was a slight chance that Miller's skinny body could slip between those planks. But spaces between ties didn't scare him. He had conquered the Black & Decker trestle, longer and higher across the valley. It also was more open, which, for some reason, seemed safer. Here you felt trapped, closed in. Plus, a west wind whistled through the trestle—not good for balance. Below, four-lane traffic rumbled. Miller couldn't help but think of his encounter with that MG. Another foot and he wouldn't be standing here. Forget that! Deal with Number 6, a black beast chugging back and forth from Black & Decker, not to mention the occasional train loaded with slate, marble, or coal. Halfway across would be the point of no return. Don't want to be rushed by a whistle.

The boys stood at the foot of the trestle. Cars and trucks were passing underneath. No sign of Number 6 at Towson Station.

"Ready?" Rusty asked.

"I think so..." said Miller.

Rusty's steps were sure; Miller froze at the edge. "You coming?" Rusty asked halfway across. Miller wavered. He really wanted to do this. Think of it as a game, like chess. Clear the mind and make your move. He stepped onto the trestle and began his slow walk, face down, concentrating on the next tie. Near the center, a yellow jacket buzzed his ear. Bees scared him, allergic. Messed with a hive when he was a toddler.

Miller waved off the invader. "Go...a...way!"

Must be the bubblegum. He spat out the gob; it fell to the street. Swatting at the bee, his finger caught the edge of his glasses. Off they flew, bouncing along the trestle. Below his feet, the yellow streetcar shook the ties. He fell to his knees to search for his glasses.

From the other side, Rusty shouted over the traffic, "What's wrong!"

"Lost my glasses!"

"I'll come get you."

What if he slipped, got smushed by a Mack truck?

Miller planned his funeral. He hoped his friends would say nice things about him.

"Do you see my glasses?"

"No."

Wonder what Mom would say now? She worried about him. Had to get off this trestle alive. Grasping Miller's trembling arm,

Rusty raised his friend to his feet and led him across the trestle. The whistle of Engine 6 tooted. It was pulling away from Towson Station! With seconds to spare, they stepped off the ties and slid down the slope to the sidewalk, just like in the movies. The coal train rumbled overhead. *Click! Clack! Click Clack!* During a break in traffic, Rusty searched for those glasses, finding them no worse for wear between streetcar tracks as the light turned green. Snatching the glasses, he raised them in triumph and scampered to the curb. "You owe me a hot fudge sundae!"

MONICA & WALTER

RAIN POUNDED THE TIN roof of Blue Valley central. Requests for cabs were flooding the switchboard. Monica Jones, the dispatcher, enjoyed the action: the calls, the drivers, her litany of addresses through the mike. "Blue Valley at Seminary and York, Knollwood and Burke, Weatherbee and Stevenson..." She could recognize the voices of regulars, cab drivers and riders, as she juggled thirteen addresses and took responses from sixty-five drivers out on the road.

"1213 at Weatherbee and Knollwood," came the response.

"1213, Walter," she replied, "911 Weatherbee..."

Something about 1213's scholarly lilt intrigued Monica. Walter McGrady didn't act like a cab driver. He didn't dress like a cab driver. A diminutive man with a David Niven mustache, he favored sleek driving gloves, a leather vest, and bow ties—green on Wednesday, yellow on Thursday, Friday red, and Saturday black. She could see him in a classy downtown bar, serving up dry martinis and bad advice to the patrons. He always left a fin for the dispatcher, coming and going, even on slow nights.

While she took pride in her work as a dispatcher, at times the walls, yellowed from thousands of cigarettes and cigars, could close in. For relief, she taped above the switchboard a *Look* magazine photo of a blue-water paradise. Monica liked to put herself on that white sand beach, 173 pounds of love waiting in a designer bathing suit. A partner would complete the picture.

The rain eased and the clouds parted; moonlight penetrated the smudged glass. Almost time. Monica was ready for a Gunther or two. Maybe there'd be a good flick on the late show, a John Ford western. Sometimes it was hard shaking off those voices in the head. That black and white idiot box was the perfect tranquilizer.

At midnight, Gentleman Frank took over the switchboard. Frank had a voice smooth as silk, perfect for the graveyard shift. "Good evening, all…" Monica lingered in the office, puffing on one last Kent. In shambled Walter McGrady. Monica stubbed the cigarette and greeted him at the window. He said hello and slid a sawbuck for gates under the bullet-proof glass; next came the fin, a crisp Abraham Lincoln. She put it in Gentleman Frank's jar.

"Turning in early for a Friday night, aren't you?"

He slid the waybill through the slot. "The drunks can get home without me," he said with a smile. Judging from the salt-and-pepper hair parted in the middle, she guessed him to be in his late thirties, close to her age. He'd gone through some tread, for sure. Be nice to take him home, fix the man a Manhattan and a raw beef sandwich. Looked like he could use a little red meat. Maybe they could watch a movie. She could do for some intelligent conversation.

He started to turn away; she asked how his night had been.

"Productive, two airports and a ride to DC."

"Wow, that *is* a good night."

"Especially on a full moon. It can bring out the loonies."

"Isn't that a fact. Want a ride home? Going your way…" Her halting invitation seemed stuck like chewing gum on the glass between them. From his file she knew McGrady lived two blocks from Whispering Pines. Made no sense for him to pay for a cab home. But he might wonder how she knew where he lived. Too anxious, bordering on needy. She'd heard the words: *"Easy Monica,"* good for a one-night stand and little else. Her torso stiffened, anticipating a polite rejection. Yeah, she was great to hang around with, good for a raunchy joke and a stone-cold game of pool (she was the Blue Valley champion), but romance?

Forget it. At forty-eight pounds over her high school playing weight, she wasn't exactly a catch.

"Why, that would be delightful," he replied.

Monica cupped her ear. "Did you say delightful?"

McGrady nodded.

"Be right out, love," she said, grabbing her purse. "Have to powder my nose. Don't go anywhere!"

In the restroom, she gave her bleached blonde hair a quick tease and added a fresh layer of rouge over pock marks, remnants of pimples that rendered her life a living hell in high school, when she was known as "Pizza Face." She freshened her metallic eye shadow, setting off nicely her brown eyes and long eyelashes. Along with the scarf matching her complexion, she felt close to pretty. Monica had no problem attracting men, just the wrong kind. She found him by the gas tanks, gazing at the silvery moon, perched above the Blue Valley antenna. He compared it to a beach ball.

"Even makes this dump look good," said Monica.

His hyena laugh startled her. Sounded as if he hadn't laughed in a long time. All sorts of strays drifted through Blue Valley Taxi, veterans still fighting the war, guys out of the slammer.

So he's odd. So's the world.

She led him to her car, a 1947 Woodie. "Nice," Water said, running his gloved hand along the polished oak panel.

"My baby," Monica said, starting the engine. "I work on it myself. Won't let anyone else touch the engine."

"How good to be mechanically inclined. I'm on the opposite end of the spectrum. I have trouble tying my shoes."

"My dad was an airplane mechanic at Friendship, taught me everything you want to know about a car."

"Is that why you're in the cab business?"

"I found it more interesting than being a secretary. Here, for eight hours, I run the ship."

The drive to his house, where he rented a room, lasted precious few minutes. He thanked her for the ride and opened the door. "Hey," she said. "Could we talk a little longer?"

"What do you want to talk about?" he asked, sliding back into the seat.

She blurted the first thing that came to mind: "Who you think is going to win the election?"

"I like Ike."

"What about the heart attack?'

"He's recovered."

"I don't like Nixon. Too slimy."

"Agreed, but..." As he catalogued the reasons to vote for Eisenhower, Monica slung her arm over the seat and studied his Spencer Tracy face in the moonlight. She guessed their height difference at six or seven inches. His upper body was nearly long as hers, but his legs were short, with puny feet. His lower body belonged on a child, not a man on the edge of middle age.

From politics they discovered a mutual interest: baseball, "a sport for poets," Walter stated. They rehashed the recent World Series, won by the damn Yankees. "Rooting for Mantle, Berra and Ford is like rooting for GM," said Walter, though he did like Casey Stengel, the manager.

"Agree," chimed Monica, "I like Casey too, especially the ears...never seen such lobes."

Inevitably, the conversation veered toward their place of work—the "steel ballet," as she called it. She told him about the recent robbery at the barn, when two punks with Halloween masks confronted her and demanded cash. She scooped out a few twenties and tens from the gate receipts in the drawer. She suspected that the robbery was an inside job when the guy in a Frankenstein mask asked about the safe in the closet, not common knowledge. Only she, Frank, and the owner knew the combination. She couldn't place that voice, but she'd heard it before. The masked men knew the routine, picking a time when she was alone on a slow Wednesday night. Had to be an inside job. She opened the safe and handed over twelve-hundred bucks.

"You must have been traumatized," Walter said.

"Wasn't my money," she said, lighting a smoke. Flicking the Zippo closed, she blew the smoke out the window. "I knew they weren't going to shoot me. They were junkies hard up for cash."

"Here's my full-moon ride," Walter said. "My last was naked."

"No, not one of those!"

"I was sitting at a light not far from the courthouse when this fellow in his birthday suit jumped in the back, thin as a refugee, not a day over twenty...said he had to get to the airport. 'You got a wallet, pal?' I asked. The boy didn't answer, so I drove him over to Sheppard Pratt, the main hospital building. Place looked dark.

"'This don't look like an airport,' said the boy. I got out of the Impala, opened the door and took him by the stringy arm. This kid needed a meal! He didn't resist when I walked him to the big front doors. 'This don't look like an airport,' he repeated.

"'They're expecting you, son.' I pressed the doorbell for a good twenty seconds. When the lights came on, I took off."

"I admire your compassion. I would've kicked him in the nuts and shoved him into the gutter." Another laugh erupted from him, this one more like a donkey's. "It's different for a woman," she added.

The dash clock read 2:32. They'd been talking for two hours in front of the rooming house. "Oh dear," Monica said. "I've kept you way too long. Thanks for the conversation."

"Enjoyed it, Monica." He stepped from the Woodie. Through the window, she asked if he'd be driving tomorrow. "Wouldn't miss a Saturday night," he responded.

"Pick you up at three-five-o?"

"That would be wonderful. *Adios*, Monica!" He did a bow as if she were royalty.

Driving off, she felt like a schoolgirl, flushed and enamored. She knew how it would end. Enjoy it while it lasts.

Thus it began, rides to and from Whispering Pines, late night-meals in her apartment. She appreciated McGrady's intellect, attention, and his stylish attire. So different from the James Dean look prevalent in the garage. He treated her like a lady, and she anticipated their first kiss—on tippy-toes or on the couch? Could also be in the car. Yet, as the weeks flew by, the kiss did not come. Maybe he just wanted to be friends. *Hope not.* She was tired of sleeping alone.

One night they were cuddled on the sofa, watching *Moulin Rouge.* As Toulouse Lautrec trundled over cobblestones to the nightclub, Walter, a bit into his cups, mocked his own legs. He could see himself having a race with Lautrec. "First one falling flat on his face loses."

"Not funny, McGrady. Skip the pity party, okay?" Fuck, she was enamored with what she saw above those limbs: shapely arms, barrel chest, and a memorable face. What a chin.

"Don't you find me a little grotesque? I mean, my legs—"

"Stop!" She turned, found his lips, giving him a big, sloppy kiss.

He pulled away and caught his breath.

"You taste good," she said.

Walter chuckled. "You're pretty sweet yourself, Monica."

She led him to the bedroom. "Please take your clothes off."

"You sure you want to see this body?"

"Stop it! Strip. You're under arrest."

"Oooh! I like being under arrest." Walter removed his loafers, socks, pants, shirt, and underwear. How carefully he folded his creased slacks, laying them over the back of her chair. Removing his ivory cufflinks and red tie (it was Friday), he hung the starched black shirt on the bedpost. She liked a well-dressed man, especially with no clothes on.

She put *Bolero* on the record player and drifted about the shadows; she wasn't exactly light on her feet, but what did it matter? Each time she came close, she tossed a garment at her avid audience. Last to fly was the slip, which landed on his head. Amidst their laughter, the rhythm intensified as the horns joined the melody. Naked, they came together.

He asked her to roll over. He straddled her back and placed his hands on her shoulders. His touch was luscious. His supple fingers kneading the knots in her back, shoulders and neck.

She moaned in pleasure. "I'm a puddle."

"Such globules!" he lilted, kissing each check. He rolled her over and explored her nipples and undulations on her soft belly. "Ahh," he said, spreading her legs, "the promised land." Muttering Latin, he lowered his big Irish head. Who was this man? After a succession of fumbling lovers, Walter's slow love was heaven. The tip of his tongue carried her to a crescendo, too much to bear. She screamed through the instrumental climax. The music ceased; pounding from above, Apartment 4B. Walter brayed with laughter.

Something, however, was missing in the second act: his penis, flaccid as a rubber band. She wanted him inside and dedicated herself to achieving that goal. His member refused to rise to the occasion. Monica collapsed; she patted his thigh to let him know it didn't matter. Maybe he was tired. Who wouldn't be after ten hours of driving? Catch him next time.

"So, McGrady, what did you do before you were a cab driver?"

"I was a priest."

"I'm shocked, a man of the cloth. This is a first. Bless me, Father, for I have sinned."

"Haven't we all?"

She snuggled against him and slipped into sleep. She didn't dare ask why he left the priesthood. All things in due time.

As oak leaves turned golden, their lovemaking swung between ecstasy and disappointment. She hesitated, probing deeper into Walter's past, fearing what she might find. Must be frustrating for the man, ever the gentleman. He apologized for his performance.

Live the days, she thought to herself. Time seemed to quicken when they were together, whether it be at a Colt game, the Baltimore Museum of Art, or just lying around the apartment watching the Three Stooges. He introduced her to his favorite author, Nicolas Kazantzakis. Monica's tastes gravitated more toward pulp, mostly detective novels. Loved Humphrey Bogart in the *Maltese Falcon.* Anyway, she would give this Greek writer a try. Over a rainy weekend, Monica read from front to back the *Last Temptation of Christ,* hardly leaving the couch. Over a delicious bottle of rose from Provence—didn't know wine could be this good!—they discussed the humanity of Jesus. Walter quoted, "I hope for nothing. I fear nothing. I am free."

One Indian summer day, out at Rocky Point, she demonstrated the rudiments of sailing in Papa's twenty-foot sloop, a gift to her when he retired. Walter did get seasick on the choppy waters near the shipyards, but what the hey. He was a good sport, even when he banged his head on the boom. She had never fallen for someone like him. Whenever the weekend came to an end and Walter departed, she had the blues, her bed empty without him.

Walter landed a day job as a bookkeeper for Hutzler's department store and now only drove on Friday nights. He spent more time at her place than his own; by Thanksgiving, they agreed he should move in. So he couldn't get it up. She could live with that...long as he could. Whenever she alluded to his previous calling, he would change the subject.

His secretive past gnawed at her. Before they shacked up, she had to know what she was getting into. "Please tell me," she said over drinks one evening.

"Tell you what?"

"Tell me why you stopped being a man of the cloth," she said.

"I was an army chaplain in Korea. I saw things during the retreat that made me question my faith."

"Retreat?"

"Not a religious retreat, but the U.S. Army retreat from the Chinese border. Near the front line, I was serving as chaplain in an infantry brigade of 1,200 GIs, part of the second infantry division trying to hold off a hundred thousand Reds pouring across the border." He had asked the bishop for this assignment. Wanted to prove his mettle as a man and priest…had no idea what he was getting into…frozen bodies piled around foxholes…endless days of dealing with death in the battlefield…Hellfire Valley, how fitting…a seventy-mile, bloody retreat down a winding, icy road…ran out of oil for last rites, Extreme Unction…"Lost two toes to frostbite."

"God, Walter, why did you tell me it was a lawn mower that did it?"

"I wasn't ready to talk about Korea."

"And now you are. I'm so sorry I called you three-toed, like the sloth. How crass of me."

"Hey, I enjoy your twisted sense of humor. It's therapeutic. Before I met you, I had forgotten how to laugh."

"Tell me more."

After Korea, the bishop assigned him to Mission Dolores in San Francisco. "Being a priest is like being in the military: you go where you're told. Maybe they wanted to reward me with this cushy post after serving on the front. Felt like a hypocrite mouthing platitudes to those Italians, Mexicans and Anglos. If they only knew…"

"Knew what?"

"Let's switch the subject."

"Why Towson?"

"I grew up here. I was an altar boy at Immaculate Conception. No place else to go. I knew the streets and could be close to Mother, who's in an old folks' home on Stevenson Lane."

"Pretty big move from the collar to the tie. Had to leave scars."

"Haven't told her I'm no longer a priest. It would break her heart. She said I was the answer to her prayers."

Monica let the matter rest. She had learned enough. Nothing like having a man again in her life. A good man who cleaned, such a bonus! Monica wasn't exactly a domestic girl. Her idea of tidying up was emptying the ashtray. She loved walking through the door and picking up the scent of Murphy's oil soap on the hardwood floors. Plus, she had her very own Irish chef who made rashers and eggs for Sunday breakfast and shepherd's pies, beef stews, and succulent rockfish. If he went to bed early on her worknight, he left a note scotch-taped to the refrigerator door. "Made meatloaf. Baked potato in oven. Love you." Gestures like that made her all gooey inside.

Days before Christmas, on her thirty-sixth birthday, she went into the basement and opened her locker, a cage of chicken wire. In the center stood a huge black chest coated with dust and loaded with kitsch. There were a few treasures, among them: letters from generations past, wedding pictures, photo albums, hotel brochures, menus of her parents' favorite restaurants, winning tickets, cartoons, old *Time Magazines*. Guess Papa wanted a fresh start in Florida. Where'd that leave her, last of the brood? She wished she had a brother or sister, someone to share this stuff with.

She rummaged through the pile, pausing here and there to inspect a keepsake. It had been a while. Somewhere in this mess had to be ornaments…but first she had to check out her diploma from St. Patrick's elementary, then the photo of her eighth grade class; there she stood in the back row with the boys, smiling through grillwork, a total beanpole. She came across her yellow and green basketball uniform and held it up to the light. The stains of a bloody nose were still flecked across the chest, caused by the Dunbar center's elbow in the championship game. Coach Higgins plugged up Monica with cotton and sent her back in. Lost by a point, missing a layup with two seconds left, rats! Monica flipped through the Western High yearbook, stopping at page forty-three. There she was, number fourteen, in that frumpy uniform, driving for a layup, legs long and lean.

In the cardboard box, she found the ornaments…hadn't gotten around to trimming past seasons. Now she had a reason. Walter had brought home a beautiful tree, a Frazier fir that nearly touched the living room ceiling. Humming "Silent Night," she selected her childhood favorites, favoring fruit and vegetables, carrots, apples, pears, and berries. For the treetop, she found the Christ child in a flowing white gown that Mama had knitted. She also included a red ornament with her baby picture.

Closing the chest, she spotted in the corner, behind the folding chairs, a canvas sack, something a sailor might tote. Papa had a similar sack from his days as a waterman on the Chesapeake. She couldn't recall him putting the sack there. Must be Walter's stuff. She had given him the combination to the padlock when he moved in. Be small of her to peek. But it might give her some clues to his past.

She put down the box of ornaments and undid the draw rope, reaching inside. Out came a Playtex brassiere, one with pointed cones, then a girdle, nylons, rouge makeup, and a blonde wig. And what about this sequin dress with a slit up the side? It carried the scent of Red, Monica's perfume.

At the bottom, she found the Roman collar, frayed about the edges. She opened a metal chair and sat down. Fingering the collar, she speculated on the man who'd worn it. No way could she get around this one. It was over. Un…fuckin'…believable! How could she have been so off? She flicked open the Zippo and lit the starched end of the collar. Perhaps she should pack her bags, jump in the Woodie, and drive somewhere warm, like Papa's bungalow in Sarasota, only a mile from the gulf. They'd take her in for a week or two, wouldn't they? She could walk the white sands of Longboat Key and "wash that man out of her hair." Another fantasy. With three dogs and a monkey, the place was too cramped. Let's not forget Flo, his new babe, only a decade older than Monica. Did the Pigtown girl marry Papa for his pension? Sure looked like it. Flo treated her as an intruder during her brief visit last Christmas. Last thing she needed was a cat fight.

She waited for Walter's arrival, chain smoking Kents and watching ridiculous game shows. Her emotions veered between anger and self-flagellation. How could she have been so dumb? She had asked herself that question too many times. It was a theme in her life. Too bad she wasn't a lesbian. She'd probably have better luck.

At five fifty-five, "triple nickel" in the cab business, she heard the click of the lock. He entered carrying a bag of Food Fair groceries and a dozen roses.

"Sweet of you," she said dryly. He put aside the roses and bag and came for a kiss, his lips puckering. Monica rose from the sofa and avoided his mouth. Towering over him, she dropped at his feet, one by one, the items in the sack, beginning with the bra and ending with the sequin dress.

Walter's face turned ashen. "I'm sorry you found this."

"I thought I knew you. Maybe you wanted me to find it. Pray tell you're not one of those creeps preying on altar boys. Is that why they threw you out? By the way, I burned your collar." Out of the sack she pulled the ashen remains of the collar and dropped it on the pile. "I'm done with you, McGrady"

"Believe me, I—"

"Stop! I may act tough, but I'm not. Such a sucker...always pickin' losers." She stomped into the bedroom and slammed the door.

"Monica," he said at the door, "let me explain."

"Please leave! Scram, I'm sick of men!"

"I shall, but please understand, I'm not a pervert...just a pathetic human being." He waited for a response. None to be had. With resignation, he told her he'd let her be. He promised to be out by morning.

As she lay on the double bed, Monica heard Walter moving about the house, probably getting his things together or doing a final cleaning. Be just like him to leave the place spotless. Going to miss the maid service. Back to sleeping alone, girl. Well, at least she could smoke in bed. Man was fussy about cigarette smoke. She cracked open the door and listened to Walter fiddling around the kitchen. Happy fucking birthday, Monica. She wiped away tears. No point in being hysterical.

Monica stretched out on the sofa in the living room. Walter was washing the breakfast dishes. Then he clipped the roses and arranged them in a nineteenth-century crystal vase recently picked up for a buck at an estate sale. Man was a genius at finding good stuff. She lit a Salem. Time for menthol, good for the throat. "How long you been up to this?" she asked, sucking a trail of smoke into her nostrils.

He stepped back and assessed the arrangement. "Up to what?"

"You know, this crossdressing, you being a queen."

He placed the roses on the dining room table. "Upon entering the seminary at the tender age of eighteen, I aspired to be a bishop. They live in grand houses. Think of the decorations I could do."

"Ha ha, not funny. Spill the beans, tell me your story. In the cab world, everybody's got a story. Get drivers together, and that's all they talk about: stories of people on the move. What's yours?"

"It started in the seminary. May I?"

She drew up her legs. He settled at the end of the sofa and reached for her foot out of habit. The thought of a deep foot massage was appealing, but she kicked away his fingers. "Tell me your story, Father McGrady."

"As mentioned, I was eighteen, a straight-A student from Loyola. In September, I entered Ave Maria Seminary and College..."

He had "an obligation," an obligation passing from one generation to the next. The McGrady lineage of religious stretched back to the old country. From his First Communion on, Granny, the matriarch, called Walter "the Chosen One," put on God's green earth to make his family proud, in this life and the next. Bound for Heaven this boy. Maybe he would bring a few souls with him.

"I was the youngest seminarian by three years." In some ways, Ave Maria felt like high school: lots of cliques that excluded the devout youngster, who turned to Jesus for solace. After months of isolation, a compulsion to hurt himself arose. On Good Friday, after Stations of the Cross, he cut his palm with a straight razor. He would have preferred a nail.

"You told me that scar was an accident."

"I lied."

"Where did you do it?"

"In the sacristy…dug a little too deep with the blade. Had to see the nurse. When the director, Monsignor McManus, asked why I did it, I told him I wanted to experience the pain of Christ."

"What did he do?"

"He said I would grow out of it."

"That was it?"

"That was it."

A few days later, Father Thomas, his Latin instructor, asked for a word with the young seminarian after class. He wanted to inspect the wound. "You've caused quite a stir," he said, running his finger along the stitches.

"I apologize, Father."

He released the hand. "Don't worry yourself, son. A Good Friday cutting is nothing to be ashamed of. Rather, it shows your love for the Lord. You enacted an old tradition. Followers of Christ have been scourging themselves for centuries. Just don't do it again. You have a gift for language, son. I'd hate to lose you."

Starved for affection, Walter lapped up the praise. The following week he was invited to Father Thomas's study for a whiskey at the end of the day. He entered a spacious room crammed with religious sculptures, paintings of saints, and shelves of books in various languages. They sat around the fireplace discussing the life of a priest; Father said everyone here was on a spiritual journey. "I envy you, Walter. Yours is just starting." During the second drink, Walter began hiccupping. "That won't do," Father Thomas said lightly. He poured a glass of water, handed it to the boy, and instructed him to bend over and drink the water upside down. Father's hand rested on Walter's lower back as the boy drank. The hiccups ended.

Whiskey with Father Thomas became a weekly routine. They usually met on Wednesday evenings and had what Father Thomas called "the dialectic," the pursuit of truth. Sometimes they spoke in Latin. He gave Walter books to read on Saint Thomas Aquinas and Aristotle. Walter craved these intellectual exchanges. Father Thomas asked a lot of questions and valued Walter's opinion. Now and then he would stray into the personal, asking Walter if he ever had a girlfriend. "Only in kindergarten." He did not mind the man's affection, the pats on the ass, the kisses on the cheek. Made him feel special.

Slowly, the affair evolved into something more intimate. They were having "special sessions" with the door locked. One evening when he was unsteady on his feet, he let Father Thomas do what he desired.

"He raped you," said Monica.

"You could call it that. At the same time, I did not resist. I feared losing his friendship."

"Are you queer?"

"The very opposite."

"Yet you had sex with an older man."

"That was the one and only time. It screwed me up. I became asexual...wasn't attracted to anyone. Maybe that was a good thing for a priest. Don't get me wrong, I did adore women...but only as a fantasy."

"This gets stranger by the minute."

"Stay with me. Allow me to talk through this."

"I'm all ears."

"I told you that when I returned from Korea, I was stationed in San Francisco. There's a place in North Beach called Finoccios, famous for female impersonators. I became aroused watching them, a rare sensation. It wasn't the performers that aroused me, but the clothes they were wearing, the gowns and undergarments, the nylons and pumps—the more audacious, the better.

"I started prowling second-hand stores and purchasing women's clothes. I favored the flapper look. At first I only wore them behind my locked bedroom door in the rectory. Once I had the clothes on, I would imagine a woman wearing these clothes, her figure, hair and face, her lips and breasts…I would become aroused. The clothes made me feel alive, and I became bolder, wearing them on the city streets. I'd change somewhere in North Beach before making my entrance into Finoccios. I loved sitting in the shadows, watching them sing, dance, and preen."

"You ever approach the performers?"

"Didn't have to. They just added to the fantasy. I was in the skin of the woman I had fantasized."

"Technically, you're a virgin."

"You could say that."

"Put 'em on."

"What?"

"Put on the garments. I want to see you as a woman. Use my makeup if you like. Make yourself pretty. Help yourself to the Red. Go on, the bedroom is yours."

Monica pulled down the blinds and turned off the lights, save one in the kitchen. Then she put Coltrane on the hi-fi—blues, slow and deep.

"I'm ready," said Walter.

By the lamp, he was posing in the black sequin dress, hands on hips, the cones of the bra prominent like light bulbs beneath the sequins. An amazing sight, she had to admit. The blonde wig was slightly askew. Too much lipstick had been applied, making him look like Bozo the clown. And the perfume—*whew!* Could knock down a horse. Took every ounce of fortitude not to laugh. Embrace Walter's fantasy. *Become the fantasy.*

She switched off the light. There, that's better. She whispered for him to close his eyes, not to say a word. She ran her fingers over that Spencer Tracy face, tracing the strong contour, the cheeks and chin. The tip of her finger slid along his lower lip…on to the neck and the throb of the carotid artery, then those strong arms and spindly legs, all good. Up through the slit came her hand, feathering his buttocks. Unlike a lot of men, Walter had a great ass. He had chosen not to wear the girdle. Good man. Something was hardening on the other side.

She unclasped that ridiculous bra, removed the wig, and lifted off the dress. She wiped some of the lipstick off his lips before leading the nude man to bed. She settled next to him, running her fingers through his wavy hair. He turned toward her, and they had a long, long kiss, the kind she didn't want to end. Then came the luscious journey down his body. At the final destination stood a beautiful sight: Walter's cock saluting her lips. Straddling his hips, she guided him into her and soon they were rocking and rolling, good golly Miss Molly!

Six weeks later, on the white sands of Barbados, Monica and Walter exchanged vows, promising to love one another for the rest of their days.

LENA MINNOW

FRESH FROM THE HAIR salon, Lena Minnow paused before a full-length mirror in Read's drugstore. Curly gray locks framed her broad cheeks, accentuating her creamy white skin. Hadn't done a thing to her hair since the death of Beau…turned into a rat's nest, reflecting her state of mind. In the Towson Courthouse, she knew people were talking, from judges to bailiffs. The court reporter was letting herself go.

For the first time in a long time, she was wearing makeup. Hands on hips, she twisted from side to side to catch the angles of her new doo. Now if she could only get rid of that bench in the rear! Turning into a regular pear, she was—bruised and brown on the outside, mushy in the interior.

In aisle three, she couldn't decide on a toothpaste. What about Stripe, with "germ-fighting red"; Crest, "with flouristan"; Gleem, "for people who can't brush after every meal"; there's even a smoker's toothpaste. Too many choices. Leaning on her rubber-tipped cane, she came to a solution. Along the aisle she shuffled, tossing toothpaste into her string shopping bag, twelve brands in all.

Outside the store appeared several colored teenagers, eighteen or nineteen at most. One boy opened the door for the two girls. Another boy trailed behind. Judging from their proper attire—ties and slacks for the boys, knee-length skirts and dress shoes for the girls—Lena figured them to be Morgan State students. Recently, there'd been a Morgan sit-in at Read's downtown. Maybe these youngsters had participated. Lena could see them in a choir, singing in Calvary Methodist in East Towson—Coloredtown, as it was known, as opposed to Towsontown.

They selected seats in the middle of the counter and asked for cheeseburgers, cokes, a chocolate shake, and a hot fudge sundae with a cherry on top. Tight lipped, Kaseris, the Greek owner, frowned but took their orders. Lena despised the Jim Crow culture in the so-called "Free State," the separate entrances and refusals of service. In the South, the Montgomery bus boycott was in its tenth month. Colored folks here could ride the buses and streetcars and sit where they liked. And *Brown v. Board of Education* helped. Thurgood Marshall was one of her heroes. But what about the sign last summer at Beaver Springs? The flooded quarry was owned by the Slater family, fine old Cockeysville money. The message on the sign was clear: "No Negroes. No Jews. No dogs."

So shameful to walk past.

Perusing the aisles, Lena dropped into the string bag three bottles of shampoo, six bars of soap, four pairs of nylons, and three cans of hair spray for the price of two. Couldn't pass up that deal. Also had to have that percolator, fifty percent off. By the time she reached the register, her bag was bulging and hard to carry.

Half dragging it across the sidewalk, she hailed a Blue Valley cab. Rough getting her big butt into the back seat. "7903 Knollwood," she said breathlessly. Had to roll down the window. Love the crispness of the season, but this "chunky" lady doesn't do well in Baltimore's stinking humidity.

At the curb, she paid the driver, half hoping he would offer to take her bag. Should have asked, she thought, lugging it to the front steps.

A freckled boy with glasses spilled past the green door. His quick leap made her cringe…just did clear those concrete steps. Next to the bag, he landed like a cat. "It's a bird!" he cried, spinning round.

"It's a plane," she responded.

"Hiya, Mrs. Minnow. Need help with that sack?"

"I could use you, Superman."

Each grabbed a side and hauled the bag up the steps and into the hallway; they ascended the checkered steps one by one, first the bag, then the cane, last her thick legs. At Apartment 3C, she handed Miller a fifty-cent Benjamin Franklin coin, good for two flicks at the Towson Theater. "Thank you, Superman…couldn't have done it without you. Tell Alice I haven't forgotten that recipe for sweet potato pie."

"You want me to help you inside?"

"I'll be fine. Thanks again."

"See ya!" Miller slid down the banister and spun off near the bottom, landing with his back to the wall. Boy was an accident waiting to happen.

In the apartment she was met by Orange Lightning, Soul Cat, and Sweet Potato. Their whiskers tickled her ankles. Careful not to crush a paw, she slid the bag toward the kitchen, sidling past chairs, an oak chest, a powder blue settee, a matching hassock, and a cherry table for eight. Hadn't changed much since his passing, could still envision Beau at that clunky black desk, marking papers with a red ballpoint. It were as if time stood still. She clung to the memory of Beau stretched out on that settee, listening to the opera, a man in a state of bliss. What to make of the dream last night? Beau in the mirror, chopsticks moving in sequence to the orchestra, directing a dirge from Verdi's *Otello*. Was he sending a message from the other side of the looking glass? Or was she going out of her mind?

Odd how life turned out. Had she not accepted a random invitation to the Friday social at the Lion's Club, she never would have met Beau. Usually she went straight home on Fridays, exhausted from the day in court. For some reason, that afternoon she accepted an invitation from her Whispering Pines neighbor in the North Building, Assistant State's Attorney Rusty Eckert, Sr. Had a voice like a bullhorn. Used it well in the courtroom. "I'll put you on the list," said Eckert. "Just give them your name. You may not like the conversations, but you'll love the chow."

At the social, Lena had scant interest in chit chatting, particularly with the lawyers she knew; they congregated like grackles on a wire, sharing gossip and tales of courtroom drama. Holding court in the center was Eckert, known as "Wide Body" in the DA office. His meaty hand waved as she passed. After six hours of recording testimony, she wanted nothing to do with the law and sidled toward the seafood table, which proved difficult, if not impossible, to reach, given the crush of people yakking away. "The key to reaching your goal," shouted a melodic voice over the roar, "is to find an opening." Easy as butter, the straw-haired man in the patched corduroy jacket slipped past a pair of well-fed judges, returning with two crab cake sandwiches. They found a place among the potted plants, away from hubbub. "You don't look like a lawyer," said Lena.

"I'm not," he said with a mouthful of crab, "I'm a math teacher at Towson High."

"Really. Are you a Lion?"

"No, I just wandered in."

"You mean you don't know anyone?"

"I try to stay away from lawyers. I thought this was a political gathering...always good food at those events."

This middle-aged math teacher may not have been much to look at—bumpy nose, hairy ear lobes, Einstein hair—but so what, his casual audacity humored her. Plus, he had a drop-dead, fall-in-love Southern accent, as sweet as maple syrup.

They had a couple of drinks and the talk between them flowed. She learned that he hailed from a tobacco farm on the Eastern Shore, that he had gone to the University of Maryland originally to study agriculture but, to the disappointment of his parents, switched to math his junior year.

His favorite writer? James Joyce, who combined math and language in his novels. Lena was vague about her background, saying she had grown up in Towson—not East Towson, but Towson. Said her Daddy worked at Towson State, didn't mention that he was a janitor. When asked about her favorite writer, she nixed James Baldwin, instead throwing out the first name that came to mind: Ernest Hemingway. "Mostly I read newspapers," she explained. "*The News American*, *New York Times*..."

"Surprised a woman would favor Papa Hemingway."

Now she was in for it. Didn't know much about the Nobel Prize winner, except that he was a drunk and cruel to his wives. Learned that in *Look* magazine. Taking a glass of wine from the passing waiter, she shifted the conversation: "Did you know my daddy is one fine piano player?"

"How could I?"

"Played with Cab Calloway a while back."

"Is your dad in the music department at Towson?"

"Kind of..." Engrossed in the moment, Lena lost track of the time. Here was a man who seemed genuinely interested in what she had to say. She asked about the impact of *Brown v. Board of Education* at Towson High. "How are the kids from East Towson getting along?"

"I can only speak from my own experience. I have three in my ninth-grade algebra class: Carrie, Flip, and Willie, nice, but on the shy side..." They'd huddle in the back row, not a peep out of them unless asked. In the first quarter, each had to endure an awkward moment at the blackboard, done in by an equation. He felt for them. They were in over their heads. He offered to tutor them three days a week, a half hour after school, going over what was done in class.

"Did the students accept your offer?" She figured kids would rather hang out with their friends. "Frankly, I found math boring. Too bad I didn't have you as a teacher."

"I'm proud to say that each accepted my offer, haven't missed a session. They're even raising their hands in class. The best part about teaching is watching pupils 'get it,' that 'a-ha' instant when the answer to a riddle becomes axiomatic, self-evident."

If the man had revealed a taint of racism, she would have dropped him in a New York second, but it was obvious that Mr. Minnow, Southern gentleman to the core, was on the right side of race relations.

The lights flickered, signaling the end of the affair. At the front door, Beau asked for her phone number.

"Why don't you give me yours?" she said coyly.

"Excellent," he said, scribbling the numbers on the back of a business card. "Look forward to your call." He handed over the card. "Need a ride home?"

No, she replied. She had a car. Before leaving, she skirted back inside and headed to the restroom. Didn't want him seeing her walking toward Coloredtown.

Here she was, nearly six years down the road, still concealing her identity. How sad is that!

Lena opened a can of tuna, separating it into three bowls. Naturally the felines opted for the middle bowl. Let them fight. Her left knee ached. Where to put everything? She positioned the percolator next to the one on the counter. She opened the pantry and cans of vegetables fell onto the floor. No room there. The sliding bedroom closet wasn't an option either, crammed with suits, sport jackets, dungarees, dress shirts, ties, Beau's camouflage hunting cap, along with his boots, shoes, slippers, galoshes, dusty newspapers, textbooks, *Life* and *Look* magazines, *National Geographic*, *Reader's Digest*, *Sports Afield*, *TV Guide*—the piles were impenetrable. She dare not throw anything out. Be like throwing away a piece of her beloved. In the medicine cabinet, there was room for his razors and shaving cream, but not for twelve tubes of toothpaste; nor was there space for the shampoo under the sink. She had no choice but to shove the bag under the bed. Out of sight, out of mind. Anything to avoid a trip to the basement locker. Going up and down those steps made her joints hurt.

She put on Beau's University of Maryland sweatshirt and worked her way through a large bowl of butter pecan ice cream while watching *The Amos 'n' Andy Show* on the tele. Spoon paused in midair, she reflected on those youngsters at the Read's counter enjoying their lunch like anyone else. The world was changing. What about her? She had the same light coffee skin as Lena Horne, light enough to pass. She was the daughter of a piano player, "a love child," something that Naomi, her stepmother, couldn't get past. "From the loins of a white woman, a no-good jazz singer in a vaudeville band."

When the baby was born, Camille, Lena's mother, wanted nothing to do with the bastard. It was all hush hush. The white woman had her career to consider. Lena's father somehow convinced Naomi to raise the child as their own. Seven children followed. Lena had spent a good portion of her childhood taking care of the siblings, didn't leave that two-story slatted house in East Towson till she was well past her fortieth birthday. There was always someone to take care of, including her father, who treated her like a servant after Naomi's death from diabetes.As far back as she could remember, she had a sense of not fitting in, either in the black or white world. She enjoyed being a court reporter because it gave her the opportunity to be an observer, practically invisible. You saw all types passing through.

Beau worshipped the texture and color of her skin, calling her "Creamy." Such a sweetie pie. Four years ago this week they signed the lease for this two-bedroom apartment. She checked the box for race as "white." Between her salary as a court reporter and his as a math teacher at Towson High, they would have enough money to buy a house in three years tops. They started buying furniture, maybe for a farmhouse on a few acres in the Hereford area, some place where you could have a vegetable garden and hear the woops of a farmer calling the cows home. Beau had grown up on a tobacco farm on the Eastern Shore and wanted to live in the country. Worked for her. She'd love to leave Towson. Then Beau had his first stroke...

Returning to the present, she didn't dream of her late husband that night. In the morning she decided against wearing her standard dark attire, choosing to celebrate the season with an amber and black pleated skirt, a yellow blouse, and a brown silk scarf. Tina, the twenty-ish office manager, complimented her change in attire and coif, saying it made her look younger.

"Why, how nice of you," said Lena.

Morning brought nothing out of the ordinary: a few routine hearings and a deposition. During a break, she spent time in the cafeteria with the bailiff, lanky Luke Longley, a childhood chum from East Towson. He always had a story up his sleeve and kept her abreast of the old neighborhood; who's sick, who's moving ahead, who has a new kitchen, who's in trouble. Once she had a crush on him, but that was before he fathered five boys. With Luke, she could be herself. On the darkest of days after Beau's passing, he had a way of making her smile with one of his stupid jokes. Today was no different.

"Lena, hear about the cow jumping over the fence?"

"No, I don't think I have."

"Udder destruction."

The afternoon crept by. Anxious for the workday to end so she could go home to a bubble bath, Lena suppressed a yawn while recording a psychiatrist's testimony. Should the prisoner be released from Patuxent, an institution for the criminally insane? In his orange jumpsuit, the grizzled West Virginian, Sledge Callus, sat ramrod straight at the table, befitting his previous life as a Marine.

"Please, Doctor Faucett," asked the burly prosecutor, "reiterate why this man should not be released into public domain."

"Mr. Callus harbors delusions of grandeur," replied the psychiatrist, "too often expressed in violence..."

Assistant State's Attorney Eckert allowed himself a smug smile. Case sealed, three more years in the pokey for prisoner Callus. He thanked Faucett for his time and turned away.

Callus sprang to life. Howling like a wounded dog, he leaped over the table and rushed the elderly doctor, who was rising from the chair. Callus grabbed him by the lapels and shoved him into the chair. "How could you?" he asked, shaking the psychiatrist. "We had a deal!" Buttons popped from the double-breasted suit. Luke and Jake, the deputy sheriff, were pulling at Callus from behind, but he refused to let go, his bared canines closing in on Faucett's substantial nose. Eckert hit the prisoner in the jaw and it took four men to carry him from the courtroom, who swore that "one day" he'd "get even" with the prosecutor.

"Looks like you saved the day, Rusty," she said. "The nerve of him saying he's going to get you…hear that often?"

The prosecutor straightened his tie. "I get threats," Eckert replied, snapping his briefcase shut. "That's why I carry a .38 in the glove compartment."

"Well, you won't have to worry about that sorry fool for three years. I assume he ruined his chances."

"You think? See you on the homestead, Lena."

Lena was gathering her things when she heard a commotion by the jury box. Luke was sprawled on the floor, being tended to by Jake. "Lena," he cried, "call an ambulance!" She raced into the hallway, dropped a dime into the pay phone, and punched in the numbers. She knew the emergency number for St. Joseph's by heart. When she returned, the fat deputy was pressing on Luke Shiner's chest, using a new technique: CPR. Man might have a heart attack himself, face beet red as he pushed on the chest. Maybe she should take over. Lord, please don't let Luke die. His work here isn't done. Where's that ambulance?

Jake sat back and wiped the sweat on his forearm.

On her knees, Lena checked Luke's wrist for a pulse. "He has a heartbeat!" she exclaimed. His eyes opened and he looked about, disoriented, maybe wondering how he ended up on the courtroom floor. Hearing the siren, she put her hand on his cheek to comfort her friend. "Hang on, sugar."

Luke managed a gap-tooth smile as the medics wheeled him out on the gurney.

God knows no bounds when it comes to cruelty. That evening at Union Memorial Hospital, Luke Longley, first black bailiff in Towson, was pronounced dead of a heart attack at age forty-eight, leaving behind five boys in East Towson. Tina called to give the news. Holding the phone, Lena sat in a state of disbelief at the kitchen table. Preposterous. Luke, dead? Not possible. Orange Lightning leaped on the table. "Not now," she said, tossing the cat.

A wail through the receiver matched her mood. She put the phone back on the kitchen wall. How fragile this life…not an ounce of fat on him. She remembered him ruling the basketball court in East Towson. Sixteen-year-old Lena had a stars in her eyes for Luke, all of eighteen at the time. Nothing came of it, of course. He had already given his heart to someone else.

One never knows. First, you're here, making plans, following your routine, then *poof*, death swoops in to claim another soul. So many afternoons and evenings over coffee, the two of them chewing the fat, waiting for the jury to return. Luke had big plans for his five boys. His eyes bulged with pride as he bragged about grades and science projects. One's going to be a doctor, another a lawyer, a third an engineer, the fourth a general, and the youngest? A funeral director. "So he can make me pretty for the viewing!." She loved his deep laugh…could fill up a room. "Lena, what do you call a pig that does karate?"

"I have no idea."

"A pork chop!"

The day of the funeral dawned chilly and damp. How she wished she could snuggle beneath her stepmother's quilt and sleep till noon. Lena forced herself to rise and put on her Sunday best. She had to see Luke off.

Calvary Methodist was packed when she stepped into the vestibule. She spotted Wide Body in the row behind the family. No surprise there. Lots of votes under this roof. The choir was singing a hymn from her childhood, "...how sweet the Lord. Wash me free of sin." Lena ducked into the back row, hadn't been here in years. Went to Beau's church, Immaculate Conception. Before God took her beloved, she had considered converting.

In the sermon, the chocolate-skinned preacher, who looked about fifteen, declared that Luke had crossed the River Jordan. "Luke's going home!" From the pews, people added their amens and praises to the Lord. The chorus of women, some Lena had known since elementary school, broke into "Swing Low, Sweet Chariot." Their soulful voices lifted the rafters. Tears streaked her makeup; Lina didn't care. She dabbed her hanky around the eyes. She felt like she was washing herself of sin. It was good to be back. Each of Luke's boys, from the youngest to the eldest, read from the Good Book. Luke and his wife Mamie had raised them well. With the six-figure life insurance policy from the county, they would be okay.

Poor Luke...won't get to see his sons fulfill his dreams.

Someone patted the top of her hand, and she looked up at the craggy face of Gregorious Shade, her estranged father. The years had not been kind to him. Lost too much weight, and that Cab Calloway mustache had turned white. At the same time, he still had that "get around look," wearing for this occasion his best suede suit, a big white tie set against black stripes, and a purple felt hat. She leaned over and removed his hat. His bald head reflected the light coming through the stained glass. "You shouldn't wear pimp clothes to a funeral, Daddy."

"These ain't pimp clothes," he whispered. "These show my feelings for Luke. The dude had style."

"He was a peacock."

Lena turned back to the service; her father's hand continued to rest on hers. The two had not exchanged words since their fallout over Beau. She could feel the calluses in his palm, reflecting a half century of hard, physical labor, not the life he would have chosen. For a spell as a young man, he wore a white suit and played the keys alongside Cab Calloway, his hero. Boogie woogie, jazz or gospel, Daddy could make that piano sing, but music gigs were sporadic in Baltimore. You had to go on the road to make real money. Or move to New York. With eight kids and a diabetic wife, he had no choice but to stay in Towson. Instead of a white suit, he donned green overalls for Towson State—good, steady work as a janitor. In the long run, Daddy had no complaints.

The service was coming to an end. "Can we talk?" he asked.

She rose for the final blessing. "What do you want?"

Bitter years had passed since the day she introduced her fiancé to her father on the front porch of their house. Back then, she still craved recognition as his daughter. You'd think he might raise a glass to her happiness. Think again, woman! He was nice enough to Beau, throwing in a "yes, sir" and "no, sir" for effect. Later, she asked what he thought. His reply cut her to the quick: "Always knew you'd turn white! How you think that makes me feel? My own daughter...marrying a good old boy. If he calls me boy, so help me I'll knock his teeth down his throat." Then he told her about Camille, her mother. Said she screwed him on a whim, wanted to know what it felt like "to be fucked by a black man."

Lena was a reminder of the shame he had brought Naomi. After that wonderful revelation, Lena moved out and didn't look back. She avoided East Towson and steeped herself in the white world.

On the steps of the church, she let her father have it: "You didn't even have the decency to come to the funeral. How do you think I felt? Bad enough Beau's parents didn't come; I expected that. But, Daddy? I needed you and you weren't there for me. When I told you about Beau's passing, you snorted…not a word of sympathy came from your mouth. Good riddance for the cracker, right, Daddy?"

Gregorious adjusted his felt hat to a familiar tilt over the right eye, giving him a rakish look, even at this advanced age. "Shouldn't have done that, Lena," he said, kicking at the marble step with his two-tone shoe. "That was small of me."

"Okay, I'll take that as an apology. Why don't you and I grab a bite somewhere? Looks like you could use a meal."

"I know just the place. There's somethin' I must show you."

"What?"

"It's at Hutzler's," he said, "you'll see." He hailed a Yellow Cab, a Chrysler Town Car. Gregorious opened the back door for Lena.

"Thank you. What's at Hutzler's?"

"You'll see."

Traffic crawled along York Road, one light to the next. Gregorious crossed his bandy legs and said they should've walked. The Yellow crept past Finkelstein's, where Beau had bought his suits, slacks, and shirts. She would accompany him. Maybe they'd have lunch afterward at the Penn Hotel, see a movie at the Towson Theatre, and make love that evening, topping off a perfect Saturday. They had their routines as a couple. He wanted her with him at the clothing store because he had no sense of style; he could easily pair blue with purple. No difference to Beau. He was partially color blind.

"Why you have a cane?"

"I had a fall…"

"Sorry to hear that." At the Patriot Triangle, which honored the county's losses in the second world war, he helped Lena from the taxi.

Hutzler's was a Towson landmark. On the top of the five-story building stood a giant cake marking the fiftieth anniversary of the department store. Big display windows were decked out for the season. Bing Crosby crooned "White Christmas" as Gregorious and Lena rode the escalator to the third floor.

Taking her hand, he led Lena into the Valley View Tearoom, past the surprised maître d'. "Sir…Sir!..." Like a beagle on a scent, the prim little man followed the two across the room. Conversations paused in mid-sentence.

"Ah, we're in luck," Gregorious said. A booth was open by the north window. Removing his hat, he made himself comfortable in the booth and gestured for her to sit.

"If you say so," she said, looking about.

"Sir, I must ask you to leave. Please, we don't want to make a ruckus, do we?"

"And this lady?"

"She's free to stay."

"Look, Mr., we don't want no food from your kitchen. I just want to show my daughter this view."

The maître d' gave Lena a second look. "All right, five minutes." The little man retreated.

Near their booth, clusters of women, heavy on the jewelry and perfume, did not look pleased. Gregorious flashed his Louis Armstrong smile. He knew those looks…uppity negroes, my Lord, what's the world coming to?

Lena ignored hostility and stared out the window. "Nice view."

"You can see the whole way to Ridgely plantation." He pointed to the top of the farthest hill. "See the master's mansion?"

"Yeah, I see it."

"I went there recently. Didn't go in the mansion. Wasn't interested in their plunder, those grand paintings, fine silverware, thick furniture, and medieval tapestries. Nope, didn't interest me. Went straight to the slave quarters. Wasn't a soul about…took off my shoes so I could feel the dirt beneath my soles. From cabin to cabin, I studied the furniture they sat on, the bed frames they slept on and the places where they cooked their food, nursed their babies and died. To honor them, I put an iron shackle around my neck. I was in a holy place...so much suffering. Brought tears to my eyes, Lena, and you know I'm not a crying man."

Across the room, the maître d' was pointing to his watch.

"We should go," she said.

"Relax. You know, Lena, freed slaves founded East Towson in 1850. Your roots go way back."

The maître d' returned with a security guard. All eyes in the restaurant were on the couple in the booth. Gregorious knew what they were thinking: What's he doing with that white woman? He reached into his shirt pocket and pulled out a harmonica. Flashing a smile, he played a few bars of Dixie for his audience.

"Sir," said the little man, "while I appreciate your skill with the harmonica—"

"You should hire me to play for the folks."

"I insist that you leave. Your daughter is free to stay."

"Wait a minute," said Lena. "I'm black as the ace of spades. Born and bred in Coloredtown."

"Okay, leave, both of you!"

"You speak as if we're garbage. Suppose I don't leave," said Gregorious.

"Then you'll be arrested."

"What about me?" said Lena.

"Not necessary, ma'am. He's the instigator."

"I insist you arrest me."

"Come on, Lena, let's cut this joint. Don't want to stir up trouble in your life." He handed her the cane.

They left the tearoom to a smattering of sarcastic applause. Gregorious turned to confront these white folks. Lena knew where this was going. If worse came to worse, she'd go to jail too. She tugged at his cuff. "Not worth it, Daddy."

The security guard followed them out the door. On the sidewalk, Lena took his arm, and they walked down the hill to Read's. Lena ordered a tuna salad and tea, and Gregorious a grilled cheese sandwich and coffee. She considered adding a slice of coconut custard pie but changed her mind.

Daddy took his sweet time eating pistachio ice cream, and Lena regretted not ordering pie. Periods of silence crept between them. Neither was good at small talk with one another. So much bitterness. Where would one start?

At the end of the meal, he rolled a cigarette and smoked it to the nub. After paying the bill, he asked if she'd like to join him and her siblings for supper next Sunday. "I'll be making ribs—your favorite, girl."

No one had called her "girl" for a long time. She saw something she hadn't seen—a touch of affection in those tired eyes. He mumbled something about regret...treating her better. "I am a prodigal father."

And now he expected forgiveness. "False analogy, Daddy. The prodigal son was a wastrel. He wasn't cruel. You hurt me bad. I'm still angry."

"I appreciate you taking a stand at Hutzler's. Must be hard to tell people you're black. Can't give it up, can you? You're living a lie."

"I had no choice. What's it to you? Naomi called me the 'Devil's Seed.' You should have said something. You were a coward, afraid of riling the bitch."

"Don't call the love of my life a bitch!"

Lena shook her head. "You forget whom you are talking to."

Maybe reconciliation wasn't possible. Too much bad blood between them. She started to rise. He withered beneath her glare. With pocketbook in tow, she left Read's as quickly as she could.

In the drizzle down the block, she hailed a Checker and heard her father's voice over traffic.

"Wait!" He sprinted toward her, huffing and puffing when he reached her side.

"Lena," he wheezed.

"Yes?"

"Can I call you sometime?"

Traffic was clogging the lane behind the cab…honks from the closest car, a golden Cadillac Eldorado. "Get in, lady!" the cab driver yelled.

"You know my number," she said over the screech of the Number 8 streetcar.

He stood at the curb and watched the cab depart.

Looking over her shoulder, she almost felt sorry for the old piano player.

THE GUNNER

"Dah, dah, dah, dah, dah...dah, dah, dah, dah, dah, fight, fight, fight!" Singing the Baltimore Colt fight song on the stairs to the third floor lightened Eckert's mood. Had to get rid of the stress.

"From that grin, I assume you won," said his trusty secretary.

"Never in doubt, Sally. Thanks for the research. And, by the way, you can't retire."

"Don't plan to."

"Good!"

Before the mirror of his office, he assessed his part in the middle, separating waves of black and gray. Maybe it was time to go with a part on the side, the Clark Gable look.

Eckert removed his suit jacket, flexed his biceps, and shadowboxed his image. That tightness between shoulder blades loosened. He liked to compare himself to Rocky Marciano. The assistant state's attorney had a God-given gift: a photographic memory, the ability to absorb tons of information word for word. When he made his entrance into the courtroom this morning, looking sharp in tailored pinstripes, he pretty much knew the answers he would get regarding the questions he had crafted the night before. All day he was on the mark. Just like the Rock. Slugging Callus topped off a most satisfying day.

He went to the window when he heard the ambulance and watched the medics rush into the courthouse. Who could it be? He waited for their return. In his palm, he rolled a pair of black dice. When he saw Luke Langley on the gurney being rushed to the ambulance, he made the sign of the cross and said a quick prayer. Luke's hands were moving. Good sign. Probably fainted from the exertion.

A familiar itch to gamble gnawed at him. He knew of a bookie joint in the basement apartment across Knollwood Road where one could place a bet on a horse running at Pimlico, an NFL game between the Colts and Redskins, or get a lead on a high-stakes poker game in the Penn Hotel in Towson. Hell, even the cops wandered in, placed the occasional bet with a man who went by the moniker Mo Money.

He loosened his silk tie on his crisp white shirt, removed the gold cufflinks, and rolled up the sleeves. Like Marciano, Rusty Eckert, Sr., was not a tall man. As an elite high-school wrestler, he was called "Stumpy." Couldn't buy suits off the rack. Now he's Wide Body. From the closet, he exchanged his suit jacket for the bombardier jacket, like the one John Wayne wore in *The High and the Mighty.* Assistant State's Attorney Rusty Eckert, Sr., was off duty.

He saluted the stragglers in the office, happy to leave the smoky chamber. Windowless rooms gave him the creeps. He avoided elevators for the same reason. When State's Attorney Frank Usher asked him to join the team, he made one demand: an office with a window. Didn't need an analyst to tell him that a Sherman tank was the source of that mental condition. Had to live with it...had no choice.

Despite the chill, he lowered the top on his '54 Ford, midnight blue with a red and white interior. With Benny Goodman on the radio, he turned up the heat and pulled out of the parking lot. At the crosswalk on Burke, a matronly woman walking a teakettle of a dog waved to him, and he responded with his best grin, the one he used on juries. Eckert liked drawing attention to himself. The assistant state's attorney could see himself on a campaign poster. Time to get with it.

At Whispering Pines, he closed the rag top. As the canvas roof settled over him, he noticed the lights in Mo's apartment across the street. Lots of action going on: college basketball, Friday night fights, Sugar Ray vs. Basilio, thoroughbred racing at Santa Anita…ah, those early morning hours when he came home from poker games, stinking of scotch and cigars. Sometimes he'd wake up Mary Lou and throw a thousand bucks on the bed. They made fine love then, probably leading to a kid or two. Other times, he'd slink beneath the covers, curl up in a ball and pretend the losses didn't exist.

He watched several people come and go from Mo's. One was a judge. What the hell, make a bet. What harm could there be? He was halfway across Knollwood when the voice of his wife inside his head stopped him cold. Eckert had made a solemn promise to Mary Lou to never set foot in Mo's joint or anywhere else like it. Because of gambling, he'd come awfully close to losing his independence to a couple of Little Italy wise guys; they offered to forgive the debt in return for a favor or two down the road. He knew how it went. Bail out some crook. Get some enforcer off. Write a crooked contract. Envelopes of cash in the mailbox. Lots of lawyers did it in the county. Easy money, the Towson way.

When he told Mary Lou about the 20k he had lost in a poker game at the Penn Hotel, God bless her, she didn't throw a fit. "Why couldn't you stop?" she asked calmly. "Rus, you knew you were risking everything we've worked for…."

A war-time romance, he met Mary Lou at a dance hall, a rangy gal an inch or so taller, with fiery red hair, piercing blue eyes, and a great dance step. That night they did them all: the Lindy, Charleston, jitterbug, and waltz. In the shadows of the dance floor, their lips met; like the ballad, their kisses were sweeter than wine. Three weeks later, they eloped to Elkton, Maryland, where they were married in a real estate office. After a three-day honeymoon in Manhattan, he shipped out, leaving her on the pier. Didn't see one another for nearly three years. Upon his return, they made up for lost time, having in quick succession six babies, five girls and a boy.

Mary Lou was the first to suggest selling their Timonium home...sold in two weeks, allowing him to pay off his debt at twenty-percent interest, twenty-four hundred smackers, enough to buy a new Lincoln. From that point on, she controlled the family finances, paying bills out of their joint account and keeping track of the cash flow. They moved into a three-bedroom apartment in Whispering Pines, and she had Dolores, their fourth child, three weeks later.

Eckert turned away from Mo's and headed toward the apartment building on the rise. Management had finished the repairs from Hurricane Flossy. When that oak crashed into the apartment across the hall, he thought they'd been hit by a bomb, practically jumped out of his skin. Thank God 4D was vacant.

At the door of 3C, he heard Mary Lou directing the children to pick up their toys and straighten the living room. "This isn't a pig pen!" The woman ran a tight ship.

"Daddy!" cried Katy, their youngest. The flaxen-haired four-year-old rushed at him, embracing his knees.

"Hello, beautiful," he said, lifting her up. "How was kindergarten?"

"Fun. I was fingerpainting! You want see?"

"Let me say hello to your mother first." Smelling the Friday night special, fish sticks and French fries, he went into the kitchen, where his wife was tearing apart a head of iceberg lettuce to make a salad with tomatoes, avocado and homemade French dressing.

He put his hands on the sides of her buttocks. She shooed him off and gave him a peck on the lips. "And how was your day, Mr. Assistant State's Attorney?" Mary Lou was not what one would call a bathing beauty, but—in his eyes—she was as fine as they came, soft and sweet, with dimpled cheeks and those piercing blue eyes. She favored red: red hair, red lipstick, red fingernails and toenails, and a red polka-dot skirt to go with her white blouse.

"Sweetheart, I had an excellent day." He opened the refrigerator and grabbed a bottle of Natty Boh, popping off the cap with a church key.

"Good to hear. I've something to tell you."

"You pregnant?"

"Not that, those days are over. I'll tell you after dinner." She turned her attention to the children. "Rusty, I thought you were going to set the table. Get with it, young man. Bethany, please take your dolls to where they belong. Dolores, turn off that TV. Pam, you can light the candles. Careful with those matches."

Mary Lou served. Shirl said she did not want any tomatoes in her salad…they made her puke. "Tough," said Mary Lou, doling out a couple of slices. "They're good for you."

"I'm tired of fish sticks," whined six-year-old Bethany.

Mary Lou added a second stick to her plate. "Think of the kids starving in India."

Eckert sat at the head of the table and gave the blessing. As they ate, he asked each child about the day, particularly school. The girls, even the little one, who already knew her letters, showed promise as students at Immaculate Conception. No reason why they couldn't go to college. Because of the war, he never had the chance. Sometimes he felt envious of people who had, particularly those hot shot Ivy Leaguers in the office who never lost an opportunity to mention their Yale or Harvard experience. He had earned his law degree through night classes at the University of Baltimore.

Pam, his precocious, eight-year-old daughter, challenged him over the chance of sending an innocent man to the gas chamber. Wasn't his job to determine who's innocent?

"My job is to present the facts and let the judge or jury decide."

"Couldn't a mistake be made?"

"Good question, Pam." Girl had the makings of a lawyer. "We're only human. If I wasn't sure, I wouldn't ask for capital punishment." For two years as prosecutor, running up a ninety-percent conviction rate, he had managed to skirt the death penalty. Rather hard to raise *habeas corpus* on a stiff. There was, however, a case lurking that may merit consideration, a gruesome murder of a rich society dame beaten to a pulp on the steps of the mansion before being run over by a Rolls Royce and then dumped into a pit of Jones Falls sludge. The cops found the suspect on the edge of the pit with a gun in hand, saying sweet nothings to his wife. This case could put Eckert in the limelight, especially if he did ask for the ultimate penalty.

"Rusty, how was your day at Immaculate Conception?" He worried about his son, who had been held back in the second grade. As the oldest kid in the fourth grade, he struggled to read. He knew that Miller helped Rusty with his homework (the child practically lived here), but Rusty needed that help.

Rusty stared down at his plate.

"Tell him," Mary Lou commanded.

The boy's voice was too low to be heard. Eckert threw down his napkin and leaned forward, resting his cleft chin on his fists. "Speak up, son. Talk like a man."

Rusty's voice cracked, going from low to high, and the girls giggled. Eckert slammed his fist on the table. An uncomfortable silence descended.

Now his boy was shaking. What's to become of him? Needs to be taught a lesson, will be eleven soon. What's going to happen when he's sixteen? Would he become one of those leather-jacket punks who quit school? Half the time they ended up in his courtroom...petty theft, fighting, even rape. The pair he sent to jail this morning had the nerve to chew gum before the judge, as if life were one big joke. Wasn't stupid, was he? Boy could put together a bicycle, take apart a radio, or build a dollhouse for his sisters.

Rusty gained control of his voice. "Miller and I skipped out after recess."

"Got a call from school," said Mary Lou.

"Now why did you and Master Miller decide to skip out?"

"Circus...Barnum and Bailey at Herring Run. Saw the big top rise and a parade of elephants, turds the size of footballs on Hartford Road."

The girls giggled.

Eckert told them they were excused. "Take your plates into the kitchen." Rusty started to rise. "Sit. We're not done yet. Son, do you realize how important school is?"

"Yes, sir."

"I think not. I think you're lazy. I know what I'm going to do. I've been wanting to do this. Please get the scissors, Rusty, the big ones in the bottom drawer."

Mary Lou sent a look that said "You really want to do this?" and he nodded in the affirmative. He had his son sit on a stool in the bathroom. Standing close, he took note of Rusty's long legs. In a year or two, his son would pass him in height. The girls are going to love him. Just needs a haircut. Has to learn there are consequences for his action, good and bad. Eckert clipped off the greasy locks in the back. There goes the ducktail! He looked into Rusty's eyes to assure him that it wasn't the end of the world. He still loved him.

What Eckert saw gave him pause...a glimpse of that angelic face, an Arab boy...about the same age as Rusty...*Clip clip! Clip clip! Clip clip!* He got it down to a manageable length. The electric razor took care of the rest. "There," Eckert declared., brushing the hair off Rusty's shoulders. "You look clean cut with a wiffle." He patted his son on the check. Rusty looked away. "No doubt you're pissed off. I can understand that. Felt that way after a beating. But I'll say this about my old man: he put me on the straight and narrow. I knew better than to cross him."

"One more thing," he said at the door. "If you do something like this again, I'll give you a whipping you won't forget. Understand, boy?

"Yes, sir."

"I hope so! Now sweep up those hairs on the floor."

You'd think that would have been the end of it. Oh no! Cut to two weeks later, a sleepy Friday afternoon at the circuit court. The light outside his office window was beginning to fade. He was sifting through a pile of evidence in the Van Cliffe murder case when a call came through from the Towson Police Station. He recognized the voice of one of his drinking buddies at the Lion's Club. "Hello, Capt'in Armacost, to what do I owe the pleasure of this call?"

"Sorry to tell you this, Rus, but your son was picked up an hour ago at Hutzler's."

"What for?"

"Shoplifting."

Eckert slammed his fist on the desk, knocking over the family portrait. "Damn!"

"Don't worry, no charges will be pressed."

"Be right down…and thanks, Jimmy."

It was a cool day, too cool for the top down. Indian summer was drawing to a close. Leaves were past their peak. Eckert was gripping the steering wheel tightly as he drove down Washington Avenue. If not for his contacts in the police department, Rusty could have been charged. How would that look in *The Jeffersonian News*? Towson was a small town…be all over the courthouse by Monday evening. Do it again and Rusty could end up in reform school. Eckert had dealt with compulsive thieves. Gets in their blood. They like the action. Not much different than his itch to gamble.

Two blocks from the trestle crossing York Road, the Towson Police Station had been built in the 1840s to house runaway slaves and other criminals. It was a fortress, with stone that could withstand a stick of dynamite. On the marble steps, he found his son in his school uniform, slouched and looking small against the cold white stone.

Not a word was said on the drive home. In the parking lot, he put the Ford in park and turned off the engine. Rusty started to open the door. "Not yet!" cried his father. "Let's hear it out here."

"You made me do it," Rusty said under his breath.

"What did you say?

Rusty turned away. "Never mind."

Eckert grabbed him by the arm. "Look at me! What did you steal?"

"A Baltimore Colt wool cap."

"Did Miller have anything to do with this?"

"It was my idea to lift it."

Eckert left the car with a slam of the door and cut off Rusty before he reached the sidewalk. Gripping his son by the collar, he slapped him across the cheek, stinging blows to the right and left. Released from the hold, the boy took off, not toward their apartment in the North Building but up the sidewalk to the West Building. "Come back here!" Eckert roared, "not done talking to you!" Rumbling and grumbling, Eckert knew he had no chance of catching Rusty, who disappeared behind the big green door of 7903 Knollwood. He knew where his son would be. Eckert slowed his pace on the steps. No point in having a heart attack like poor old Luke Langley. Eckert had arranged a scholarship fund for the five boys. Collected ten grand in just two weeks. Didn't hurt to have his own mug on the flyer. Could pick up a lot of votes in East Towson should he run for DA.

At the Nowaki apartment, he gave three sharp knocks, using the metal rattlesnake on the door. The door opened and Alice Nowaki stood there, a good two or three inches taller, holding a roller pin. "Good evening, Alice, I've come for my son."

"You can't have him."

"What do you mean?"

"Just as I said. You can't have him. Go ahead, lose your temper. You're not coming in. My hubby is right behind me, if you need further convincing. Your son is spending the night. You need to calm down."

"And you need to step aside."

"I don't condone what happened, Mr. Eckert, and I'm not entirely against a good spanking, but you went too far. The boy's traumatized. Those bruises on his face—"

"Just a couple of slaps."

"I think he took that hat to get your attention."

"What!"

The door closed, leaving Eckert cursing and confused.

You made me do it...you made me do it...you made me do it.

Mary Lou gave him a tranquilizer so he could sleep. The next day the family went about its business as if nothing had occurred. Rusty turned up and nothing was said. His sisters knew better than to ask.

THE WARRIOR

ROBIN TURNBAUGH, ENGLISH TEACHER at Towson Catholic, was having a bad day. Called into the principal's office at lunch time, he felt like a child being dressed down. Behind the principal's desk, the dark form of Sister Rita Maria loomed, her shrill voice berating him for adding John Steinbeck to the tenth-grade curriculum. "Tell me, Mr. Turnbaugh, how does this story of a dimwit who crushes mice contribute to the spiritual growth of a child?"

What to say to the Franciscan? May he suggest a whack across his knuckles with a yardstick, a little S&M to clear the air? Robin needed this job; he had a knack for opening young minds, exposing them to ideas and possibilities not found in the *Baltimore Catechism*. Sometimes he felt like a spy in the house of God.

With his own money, he purchased nineteen copies of *Of Mice and Men* as a supplement to *The Rise of Silas Lapham*, which he believed should be taught on the college level. William Dean Howells and his realistic description of nineteenth century Boston society had its place, but not in the raging-hormone minds of tenth graders.

"What were you thinking, Mr. Turnbaugh?"

"Huh, oh yes, well, I thought this sad tale would be food for thought, get them thinking about reality."

"You call that reality?"

"Bad things happen, Sister Rita."

"Mr. Turnbaugh, literature is meant to uplift the soul, not to drag it down to the muck and mire of sin. Now, I want you to take the rest of the afternoon off. Think about what I said and come in tomorrow with a fresh attitude. In the meantime, I will confiscate the books. Good day, sir."

Confiscate. Word had a nasty ring to it, like burning books in *Fahrenheit 451.* Not exactly "uplifting," was it? Now don't have a tizzy fit. He was more than happy to leave the building. What to say to the students tomorrow? So emasculating. Have to be careful…a slip of the tongue could find their way back to the Penguin, the students' name for Sister Rita. In the meantime, view this humiliation as an opportunity, a teachable moment. Phrase the right message and the little darlings might read everything Steinbeck wrote.

Had he a favorite student, it would be Milton Hickwolf, a brainy sort with buck teeth and hair parted in the middle whoreminded him of Alfalfa in the *Little Rascals*, a boy likely to be picked on. Robin himself had been one of those boys. Milton loved to read, even enjoyed Howell's novel on his own. What would he think about this confiscation?

A pile of compositions awaited his red pen, but he left them in the desk. Hope the MG starts…darn distributor. He loved the green sports car and how it handled, but the Brits could have done a better job with the engine. He pumped the pedal and pulled out the choke. The engine came to life. He put the MG in gear and drove off.

Robin lived in the East Building of Whispering Pines. He always slowed when passing The West Building, 7903 Knollwood. Thank God for good brakes. He made a left and parked on Garden Street, in front of the East Building entrance. Precious, Mother's beloved cocker spaniel, was pressing her nose against the window. Robin waved and the dog sprang from the davenport., greeting him at the door. Robin spent a minute scratching behind the floppy ears. "Home in the middle of the day?" Mother asked from the bathroom.

Robin leaned against the door.

Before the mirror, Mother stood in her black slip, applying maroon lipstick that matched her nails. Large rollers curled her dyed auburn hair. She glanced at his reflection. "What's up? Anything wrong?" She patted her lips with a tissue.

Since early childhood, Robin had sensed her need to shield him from threats, some imaginary, some real…such as Father. In times of stress, she could break out in hives. Sometimes she still acts as if he were a defenseless child, not a twenty-four-year-old professional in his third year of teaching. That could be annoying. Maybe it was time to move out, be on his own. He could take care of himself; he didn't study karate for nothing. From the beginning, she knew her son was "not like most boys." That's what she told him when they had their first frank discussion about his sexuality at the age of thirteen. Mother became his champion, guiding him through what she called "the difficult years."

Then came what he and Mother would label "The Moment." Father caught him on the bed with another boy. Robin was fifteen at the time. Larry and he were only fooling around, playing grab ass, nothing much. Naturally, Father, an undercover officer on the vice squad, took a far different view of the boys' activity. Down came the billy club. Robin intervened and took the blow across the nose.

That marked the end of the marriage. Mother and he moved into Whispering Pines, among the first tenants in the new development. Now that he was years removed, he longed to put the curdled relationship to rest. No one could say he didn't try to please the SOB. Didn't he step into a boxing ring as a nine-year-old? As Father shouted instructions, Robin was pummeled into tears. Football games in the Pop Warner league on Saturdays? Ridiculous. He'd rather read *The Chronicles of Narnia*. Cub scouts? Forget it. Tying his shoes was a challenge. Camping was absurd, not to mention brown bears. And the scout leader was creepy, telling his ghost stories by the fire. Robin couldn't help it if he was a sissy. After years of psychoanalysis, he had come to accept his biological nature. He had nothing to be ashamed of.

"You gussied up for an appointment?"

"Meeting a client at Campus Hills. I've sold four houses on Goucher."

"I knew you'd be good at real estate. Did you watch *Search for Tomorrow*?"

Over the summer, the two of them became big fans of the soap opera.

"Sure did."

"What happened?"

"Baby Duncan ran out in traffic and died."

"That was mean of the writers."

"I had to turn it off. Excuse me…"

A few minutes later she emerged from the bedroom, maroon pumps clicking on hardwood. She had chosen to wear her blue and white dress, which displayed a hint of cleavage. He viewed the bouffant as the right match for her expressive face. "How do I look?" she asked.

"Fah…bu…lous. You don't look a day over thirty. You could be my sister."

"You should go into advertising. Is there anything you need? Want me to make you a sandwich? Did you eat breakfast? Did school let out early?"

"We'll talk later. Go make a sale."

"I plan to." She patted the dog, grabbed her purse, and went out the door, leaving behind the scent of sage, My Sin.

He checked the *News-American* for movies and settled upon the 5 West on North Avenue; Fellini's *La Strada* was playing in a double feature. He exchanged his coat and tie for the Brando look: motorcycle jacket, black jeans, and engineer boots with heels that added an inch to his five-foot-eight frame. In the full-length mirror on his bedroom door, he admired the well-toned body in black and leather, the Mitch Miller goatee that compensated for his receding hairline, and the mashed nose—a permanent reminder of his estranged father. Robin had made peace with the disfigurement, telling himself that it gave him a rugged look, like a pug who knew his way around the boxing ring. Nothing wrong with projecting an element of danger. He owed a lot to karate. He strove to live as a warrior, not a victim.

In the nearly empty theater, he huddled in the middle of the back row, entranced by the dreamlike, carnival images on the big screen. He could relate to the Italian director's alternate reality. His first experience in this realm occurred in a dental chair. Sniffing the cologne of the dentist, the eight-year-old was flooded with love for the man scraping off the crud, his thick, juicy lips hovering oh so near.

He spent an hour in the Owl Bar in the Belvedere Hotel before heading over to Lautrec's, a French restaurant on Mulberry. Had a craving for the house special: *bouillabaisse*, fish stew made from scratch by the owner. The MG slipped into a small parking spot next to the former speakeasy. The place operated as if it were still illegal. One had to tap on the thick door and wait for the slot to slide open. Once you were checked out, Lautrec let you in. The white-haired restaurateur didn't suffer fools. Or the vice squad. He had a fondness for pretty young men, particularly those gifted in the arts...made them feel welcome. And safe.

Never knew whom you might run into. Any number of musicians could breeze in: Johnny Mathis, Liberace, whoever's playing in town. At 7:40, the place was taking off. Beneath the subdued lighting, a diverse crowd of colors and genders packed the tables. Everybody seemed to be talking at once, gesturing with their cigarettes, totally engaged. On the jukebox, Edith Piaf was singing about no regrets. Taking an open barstool, he ordered a stinger from the bartender, a fat drag queen in a spectacular black velvet gown. "Aunty Helen," as he was known, poured a great drink. Robin was getting a nice buzz when in walked Michael O'Leary, a colleague from Towson Catholic. He taught music in the basement classroom. They had worked together on the student production of *My Fair Lady*, a smashing success. Michael had talent. He was wasting his time at Towson Catholic. He was also one of the most handsome men Robin had ever laid eyes on, with piano fingers, shapely legs, and hair like James Dean. Why, he even walked like Dean, that languid tilt coupled with a street attitude. Nothing seemed to bother the young man, even when the leading actor lost his singing voice on opening night. Michael rescued the budding thespian by singing every song himself, earning two curtain calls.

"Fancy seeing you here," said Michael, taking the stool to the left.

"I'm drinking off Sister Rita's wrath."

"Heard about it, Robin. It's not right."

"Come here often?"

"Now and then."

"Me too..."

Ah, that familiar awkward conversation, the wading about, the probing, guessing at the truth, was he or wasn't he? Only the penis knows. Dangerous to think through one's dick...

Michael and Robin ordered the house special and were not disappointed. Three Peabody students set up at the far end of the bar and started playing chamber music. Michael's foot tapped to the beat. Toward the end of the meal, when they were smoking cigars and contemplating their thoughts over a nightcap, Robin asked Michael if he had any more plans for the evening. "I know a place where there's dancing."

"Dancing?"

"Yes, dancing. You do like to dance."

They exchanged a look of understanding. "Is it far from here?"

"Right down the street, top of a warehouse, big dance hall with black lights. Everyone's incognito. You might even run across a priest from Immaculate."

"Really? Who is he?"

Robin whispered the name in Michael's ear. "Keep it to yourself. For his sake."

"My lips are sealed."

Outside, a biting northwest wind greeted them. Robin's motorcycle jacket and Michael's London Fog trench coat offered little warmth. Hands stuffed in pockets, collars up, they hustled down the street and up the iron grate stairs. Past the metal door, Robin handed the bouncer two bucks and entered what had been a century past a sail maker shop for Baltimore clippers. During the day the space served as a private basketball court; in the evening, it was transformed into a discreet dancehall, dedicated to the American Songbook, known only by word of mouth. A glittering globe spun overhead, casting stars across the floor. Couples swayed to Sinatra's "Wee Small Hours," their faces cast in flickering black light.

"Makes me dizzy," Michael said.

Robin glanced at the sails hanging from the rafters. "You'll get used to it. Care to cut the rug?"

Elvis's croon bounced off the brick walls. "Don't! Don't!"

"Never danced with a man before."

"Do you want to?'

"Yes."

Robin held out his arms and smiled. Michael put his hand in his. His back tightened as Robin slid his arm around Michael's waist. Stiff as a board, Michael did allow himself to be led. The ballad guided their halting steps over the dance floor. Robin wasn't looking for aesthetics, just someone to hold for a while, to have Michael's breath on his neck and the touch of his body. He whispered in Michael's ear to relax, that there was nothing to fear. To Robin's delight, the tension did ease. They started to move as one; they stayed on the dance floor through a succession of hits.

Over cokes Robin asked Michael if he was tired of "living in the shadows."

"Not sure what you mean."

"Wouldn't it be nice if we could be open about who we are?"

"You got me. I'm a communist agent."

"Joke if you want..."

"I resent your assumption. I'm not a homosexual. I have sex with girls."

"Maybe you swing both ways. I have no issue with that."

"That's repulsive."

"Get real, man. Accept who you are. Come on, let's dance..."

The two held their own on the dance floor. The final dance before midnight arrived too soon. The opening horn of "Bolero" lured everyone onto the dance floor. A spotlight shone on the center of the court, where couples strutted their tail feathers, moving in and out of the limelight. Michael and Robin won hearty applause for their tango and did a quick bow Broadway-style before melting back into the crowd for the climatic end, the clash of horns and percussion, dissonance for this broken world.

Floodlights! The crowd was blinded. A dozen uniformed cops swarmed in. The music collapsed, and panic swept across the dance floor. Amidst the cries, Michael and Robin separated. Lording over the venue was Robin's father, Big Jake Turnbaugh, decorated Marine, defender of virtue. His jowly face wore Satan's grin, someone who took pleasure in the pain of others. Maybe Big Jake killed a part of his soul using that flamethrower in Iwo Jima. How does one live with that? He longed to ask Father that question.

"No one's being arrested," Turnbaugh announced through the bullhorn. "Leave in an orderly fashion. This locale is hereby closed for lack of license."

People pushed their way out the door, including Michael. Robin stared at his father, but not in hatred. On the couch, Robin had worked his way through his anger—not healthy for the body and soul to have such venom circulating. He realized that Father had suffered far more than the man let on. His demons had cost him his marriage and the love of his only son.

"Still arresting people for being themselves?" Robin asked.

"Who are you lookin' at?"

"I pity you, sir."

"You pity me? That's a good one."

"With all due respect," Robin said, stepping forward, "you won't admit it, but you're afraid of me. You're afraid that part of me might rub off on you. You're afraid that people will find out about me. I know you want to run for mayor. I've read the newspaper. Don't worry, I won't tell a soul."

"Son, I'm not scared of you. I know you're sick. But I do admire your directness. You speak your mind. That's good."

One of the officers came forward. "Captain, 'bout ready to lock up. This punk bothering you?"

"He and I are having a friendly chat—aren't we, son? Be with you in a minute, Sergeant." He turned back to Robin. Father had aged…skin hung on his face. Big Jake was slowing down.

"I'm surprised you called me son."

"You're the only one I have. How's your mother?"

Robin said she was getting rich from real estate. They were doing karate together. "She's my best friend."

"That's nice."

Was that an undertone of sarcasm? Or jealousy? He said he was thinking about moving to San Francisco. "Maybe I'll take a crack at being a writer."

"San Francisco could be a good place for you. When would you go?"

"Next June, after I finish out the year at Towson Catholic. I'll send you a postcard." He put on his leather cap, slipped into his motorcycle jacket and clomped across the floor. Robin could sense Father's deep-set eyes boring into him. A part of Robin hoped his old man would call out his name. Perhaps they could meet for coffee at the White Coffee Pot on 29th…hash things out, even if it took all night.

He passed the officers draping a chain across the entrance. A phrase popped in his head for a poem: *No dancing aloud.* At the top of the stairs, he hesitated, still hoping Father would summon him. Maybe next time.

Next morning Robin rose at six am. In the quiet of the apartment, he sipped café au lait and calculated a response to the confiscation of books. How would students react to handing over *Of Mice and Men*? A closed mind was a dead mind. If today turned out to be his last at Towson Catholic High, so be it. He'd give his students something to remember him by. The lure of the road called to Robin: point the MG west, toward San Francisco, where else? He fantasized having Michael along for the adventure. Maybe they'd run into Allen Ginsberg at the City Lights bookstore. He had nothing to lose speaking his mind to those tenth graders.

Towson Catholic was a low-slung school, an L-shaped two-story structure next to the elementary school, Immaculate Conception. What attracted him to this coed high school was the size of the classes, from fifteen to nineteen students. While boys dressed in a coat and tie, the girls had to wear a blue blazer, white blouse, and a hideous green skirt that stretched beyond the knees. Nylons were out, white socks were in, along with saddle shoes. Despite the fashion violations, their budding bodies could not be denied. Sister Claire, another nun from the "old country," encouraged the girls in religion class to chew their nails so they would not look like a "tart." She also had them kneel each Monday morning on the floor to ensure the length of the skirt had not been raised over the weekend.

Girls, Robin had found, were easier to teach; they matured faster than boys. Whereas a smart ass like Chad Cicero could be making fart noises in the back row, Helen Klackenbach, a rising star in the drama department, asked questions about Tennessee Williams. He could relate to their repressed sexuality. He saw how students and teachers fawned over the boys who happened to play basketball for the school. They had a special table in the cafeteria; only cool people allowed. Brought back memories of his own exclusion at Loyola.

Since TC was a small school, Robin was positive that word of the confiscation had spread throughout the hive. He parked the MG by the cafeteria and entered the building, saying good morning to students in the hallway, followed by a sprint up the stairs to Room 201. On the desk was a note from Sister Rita, asking him in perfect blue penmanship to stop by the office at lunchtime. He whistled "San Francisco" as he prepared for his first class.

That morning he taught grammar and writing to two rowdy ninth grade classes as well as English lit to a bunch of cynical seniors. By the lunch bell, his headache had subsided. He straightened his tie before entering the principal's office. Be cool, he told himself.

Sister Rita waved him inside, telling him to close the door. "Have a seat, Mr. Turnbaugh."

Settling into the chair, he took a hard look at the hefty woman across the desk, the broken red veins on pasty cheeks, thick sausage fingers, a fleshy face filling the habit. Did her legs ache from carrying that bulk? Learned through the grapevine that she was from Kinsale, Ireland, came to Ellis Island as an orphan, parents killed in the Irish Civil War. Likely entered the nunnery more out of poverty than a love of God, but what did he know? Was he about to be fired?

Sister Rita surprised him by asking cordially about his afternoon. "Fine," he replied. "Went to the movies and had a lovely dinner afterward."

"Have you thought about what you are going to say to your fifth-period students?"

"It crossed my mind..."

What would the poet Ginsberg do?

"I want you to understand, Mr. Turnbaugh, I used to be an English teacher. Though you might think otherwise, I am not some witch hunter out of the Dark Ages who burns books. Monsignor Nellie was none too pleased to receive a complaint from a parent, a parishioner very generous with his contributions. When I asked your students for the books, please know, Robin, I said not a word against you."

First time she'd called him by his first name. Maybe the battle-axe was human.

Just following orders. Sorry, sonny.

Sister Rita said she didn't want to lose him.

"I entered expecting to be fired."

"Are you thinking about quitting?"

Robin had come a long way as a teacher the past two and half years. Any student who walked into Mr. Turnbaugh's English class had better be prepared. One rhetorical question could lead to another; next thing you know students were having an actual intellectual discussion. To keep their interest, he introduced games, stupid sentences, and grammar competitions, which often turned intense. Who wins the Bon Bons? Usually the girls won. Wouldn't be fair to walk out now, would it? "I'll stay if I can make a change in the curriculum."

"What change?"

"I'd like to replace the *House of the Seven Gables* with the *Red Badge of Courage.*"

"But Hawthorne's book is a classic, a mystery with ghosts."

"It doesn't move fast enough to capture the attention of a fifteen-year-old. I'm competing against transistor radios and television."

"Rather bloody, don't you think?

"They're old enough to be exposed to the horrors of war. And it's a quick read."

"I'd add it to the curriculum, but the budget is short."

"I'll pay for it."

"Agreed. Come back for your books at the end of the day. I'll leave them on the long table. Maybe you can trade them for the Crane book."

His fifth period lit class included power forward Louis Richie—"Sweet Lou," as the girls called the slick shooter. He'd saunter in like royalty, raise an eyebrow to the cheerleader Dolores, and choose to sit behind Milton Hickwolf, his target for harassment. Last week Robin overheard Richie asking Milton if he were a homo, much to the amusement of the boys nearby. After class, Robin had "a talk" with Mr. Richie, who nodded in agreement, murmuring "yes, sir" or "no, sir," so contrite and polite. Robin knew it was b-s, but what could he do? If he sent him to the office, the jock would get off with a gentle reprimand.

Aside from Richie, Robin looked forward to teaching the fifth period class. Here was a group of youngsters who read on their own. Maybe they came from homes where mom and dad read the *Saturday Evening Post* and *Reader's Digest* instead of watching those insipid comedies with canned laughter, designed to turn the mind to mush. These pupils were open to good writing. Some kept diaries. That was his suggestion.

He watched them file in. No stragglers today. Even the power forward was on time. Robin came around and settled on the edge of his desk. He crossed his arms and waited for the chatter between Cindy and Anne to cease. After two and one-half years, he understood that silence often was more effective than a demand. "Let's talk about John Steinbeck," he began. "People say he's an atheist…shouldn't be read. But you know what? You can go to the Towson Library or the one in Timonium or the Enoch Pratt downtown. There you'll find plenty of Steinbeck. Couldn't think of a better story than *The Grapes of Wrath*…made me cry as a boy. About a farmer's family during the dust bowl. Lost their land, had no choice but to cross the country in their Model T looking for work. Movie's pretty good, too—with Henry Fonda as Tom Joad. While you're at it, check out *East of Eden*, but warning, there's some shady characters…including a prostitute," he whispered. They laughed. He had them in the palm of his hand. Loved tenth graders, old enough to handle complex ideas, and young enough to not be jaded.

"I saw *East of Eden,*" said Helen Klackenbach. "James Dean was great."

"Movie's good," he agreed. Especially Dean, such a butch. "Book is ten times better. You know why? Because you're inside the character's head. Can't do that so well in a movie. What was Cain thinking when he murdered Abel? The *East of Eden* plot reflects that ancient tale of jealousy and pride. Steinbeck deploys a lot of Biblical symbols in his stories."

He walked around the classroom, telling them "to never surrender their minds," their free thinking. Some countries fear free thinking and do everything to suppress it. In Russia, the communist government decides what people read. "But it's not just in the Soviet Union. Censorship occurs in the USA. There's a trial going on in San Francisco over a poem called "Howl," written by Allen Ginsberg. Do we want others to decide what we read?"

Out of the corner of his eye, Robin spotted Sweet Lou on the verge of flicking Milton Hickwolf's earlobe. "Mr. Richie, do you know what the first amendment in our constitution stands for?"

"The right to own a gun?" he replied, pulling back the finger.

"No, that's the Second Amendment. The first has to do with free speech, our most precious right…" After saying his peace, he opened the floor to a flood of questions. When the bell rang, students applauded his performance.

It was a very good day.

HENRY AND GRACE

On a gray Sunday afternoon in November, a U-Haul truck pulled up in front of the South Building. A young man with mutton chops and a leggy girl with a blonde ponytail appeared; both wore black peg-leg pants, as if their slim bodies were interchangeable. They raised the back panel of the truck and yanked out a mattress. On the sidewalk in front of the brick building, a red-haired kid was tossing a tennis ball against the steps. As they approached with their load, he hopped up the stairs and opened the door.

"Thanks," said Henry.

"Welcome to the quad," said the boy.

Through the drizzle, Miller acted as doorman, watching the parade of furniture and boxes go up the stairs—lots of LP records, two guitars, and no TV. Henry and Grace looked like teenagers, and maybe they were. Last came a threadbare burgundy sofa, which posed a challenge. Miller whistled to Rusty, who was playing catch with his mother, Mrs. Eckert. He dropped his glove and came over. Rusty's hair was growing back; the bruises had faded. At school, Rusty made up a story about falling on his face. At the quad, it was a different story.

"What up?" Rusty asked.

"Meet our new Whispering Pines neighbors, Grace and Henry. They need help with this big-ass sofa."

"Okay," said Rusty, grabbing an end. With Miller directing the ascent, they conquered the staircase without difficulty, placing the sofa in the living room of apartment 4C, a two-bedroom emitting a slight pesticide scent.

"At least there'll be no cockroaches," said Grace in her Midwestern accent.

"Not like that dump on North Avenue," said Henry. He peeled off a dollar for each boy. As one who made his living working with restaurants, Henry believed in tipping well. "How about you, baby?" he asked, closing the door. "You like it?"

"It's swell."

He slid his hand under her sweater. Her warm belly was just beginning to show. "Everything good there?"

"A-OK, love."

The two had come a long way since their high-school days in Minot, North Dakota, site of the Strategic Air Command base, which had nuclear-armed B-52s flying 24-7 over the globe as a counter to a first strike from the Soviet Union. In their senior year, the youngsters became acquainted under their desks during a "duck-and-cover" drill—or, what existentialist Henry labeled the "kiss-your-ass-goodbye" drill. The experience radicalized the seventeen-year-old, who adopted a fatalistic view of life, thanks to his heroes: Camus, Céline, and Sartre. He gave up going to college. He would read the great books on his own. Life was too short. It could end at any time, as in the novel *On the Beach*.

The only thing that made sense after high-school graduation was to say farewell to his sweet Ma, pack a suitcase, and take off before his Pa, Captain Bob Drake, could command the MPs to detain him. His girl Grace, also an Air Force brat, accepted his invitation to see the country. On a warm evening on the Fourth of July, the two snuck out of Minot during the fireworks, climbing aboard a Greyhound bound for San Francisco.

Over the next three years, they made love in all the right places: among the tall grasses in the Marin highlands, beneath the stars at the bottom of the Grand Canyon, on the side of the road in the middle of nowhere in Kansas—the two couldn't get enough of one another. In Las Vegas, they were married in a purple chapel dedicated to the memory of silent-film star Rudolph Valentino. At the suggestion of the minister, who happened to own the tattoo parlor next door, the newlyweds got matching ankle tattoos—nothing showy, just their initials intertwined in the shape of a heart. From New Orleans to Bainbridge Island, from San Diego to Acadia National Park, their thumbs were their magic carpet. Along the way, to build up cash for the next adventure, they would wait tables a month or two wherever tourists flocked: Atlantic City in the summer, Miami Beach in the winter.

Everything changed with Grace's pregnancy. That incessant itch to see what lay around the next corner, town, or state vanished. Time to put down roots...become part of something bigger than their own needs. They chose to live in Baltimore, buying secondhand furniture, record albums, and books for their apartment near the Maryland Art Institute. Tempting to hop on the train at Pennsylvania Station and arrive in D.C. in less than an hour. They were drawn to the protests in front of the White House. If they were bringing a child into the world, they'd better try to make it a safer place.

Within a week, the couple landed waiting jobs at Marconi's, a Baltimore institution known for its lamb chops as well as the writers and artists who frequented those white-tablecloth tables and booths. "Look, Grace," said Henry, pointing at the photo on the wall. "That's H. L. Mencken, a voice of reason in a nutty world."

Their four-night schedule allowed them ample opportunity to travel to Washington and take part in the vigil in front of the White House. He told Grace that maybe they'd be on television and his old man would see him. Wouldn't that be a stitch!

"We're not doing this to be on television."

"I know that."

They joined the few hardy souls holding signs against nuclear weapons. Come rain, snow, or shine, someone would be there on that Pennsylvania Avenue sidewalk, making a stand against the madness. How ironic, thought Henry, that the protest was similar to those B-52 pilots—perpetually on a mission that must not happen.

One Sunday in early November, Grace decided it was time to share what they were about with their neighbors in the quadrangle. Between work and going back and forth to DC on the train, they had little idle time. This would be a way of introducing themselves.

Using scissors, Grace cut out a cardboard square from a box and placed it on the bottom half of the window that faced the quadrangle. It fit. Grace spray-painted the demand in scarlet: NO NUKES! Careful not to smear the message, she taped it to the window.

Didn't take long for a reaction. Henry was studying Marconi's recipes and Grace was arranging bebop LPs in alphabetical order when a tap came to the door. "Now who could that be?" asked Henry. In the hallway stood a stout fellow in a yellow raincoat. He had a Dick Tracy jaw, thick neck, and a probing stare. The man apologized for the intrusion and handed Henry a card. "Rusty Eckert Sr., Assistant State's Attorney, Baltimore County. I live in the opposite building. I believe you met my son, Rusty."

"Nice kid. What can I do for you, Assistant State's Attorney Eckert?" Henry asked, looking at the card.

"It's about the sign."

Henry slid the card into his shirt pocket. "Are you going to arrest me?"

"I put in the sign," Grace said from the couch.

"You can't arrest her. She's with child."

The man grinned, revealing long white teeth. "Boy, I don't arrest people. That's for the police."

"Are they on their way?"

"Of course not. By the way, I didn't get your name."

"Henry. This is my wife, Grace."

"Pleased to meet you both. Look, Henry, let me give you some neighborly advice. First, are you a communist?"

Henry snickered. "Do I look like one?"

"You see, we don't like communists here. I drove a Sherman tank through North Africa and across France…didn't come home to see the country go to the Reds. There are a bunch of vets in Whispering Pines. Some of them might not care for your message…might take offense."

"Is that a threat, counselor?"

"No, no…I would fight to the death for your right to speak out, but I am worried about the reaction of others."

"That's too bad," said Grace, coming to the door. "They might want to consider the future of their children."

"Why'd you two move here? Your accent makes me think of Minnesota."

"Close," said Grace.

"North Dakota," added Henry. "From the town of Minot, where the SAC base is. My father is a B-52 pilot. Grace and I met underneath a desk during a nuclear drill. Are you in favor of nukes, Mr. Eckert?"

"You do your dad a dishonor by having that sign in the window. 'No nukes'—what's that mean? If we didn't have nukes, the Reds could reduce us to cinders. Nukes keep the peace."

"What an oxymoron," said Grace.

"Like military intelligence," added Henry.

Raising his meaty palms, Eckert stepped backward. "Okay, children, I'll leave you be. Just be careful. And congratulations, Mrs.?"

"Drake," she replied. "Thanks for the warning."

Leaving the sign in the window, they made love on the mattress to the music of the Bird, Charlie Parker.

The next evening, as they were listening to the news, a rock crashed through the upper window, spraying Grace with glass.

Grace leaped off the sofa, threw open the other window, and cried, “You piece of shit!”

A woman in curlers poked her head out the first-floor window in the West Building and chastised Grace for cursing. “Think of the children, young lady.”

“I am,” said Grace.

“Take down the sign!” yelled a male voice from the upper playground. Henry bounded down the stairs. Peering into mist, he raced across the quad and up the steps.

Grace called the police, carefully picked the glass fragments from her ponytail, and swept up the living room. When Henry returned, she asked if he had seen anything.

“The guy ran off.”

“Would you recognize him if you saw him?”

“I doubt it.”

“And we thought North Avenue was bad.”

“Cockroaches don’t throw rocks.”

Shivering, Grace clutched her sides. Henry had her sit on his lap with her back to him so he could give her a massage. “Don’t fret, babe,” he said, pressing his thumbs between her shoulder blades. “We’ll make it work…we always do.”

Grace arched her neck. “So far so good.”

“So far so good.”

A knock on the door. “That was quick,” said Grace.

Henry did not find the police outside their door but an unshaven fellow with a medical bag. Said he lived in the apartment below, 1A. “I’m an ER nurse at Union Memorial. I heard what happened. Anyone need attention?”

“We’re fine,” Henry said, slowly closing the door. He slid the chain latch in the slot—something he thought not necessary when they moved in. The guy made him uneasy, especially the way he talked, like a robot. Suppose the rock-thrower turned up at their door. Or a John Bircher who’d rather be dead than red.

On the radio, they half listened to a special report on the Russian invasion of Hungary, hosted by Walter Cronkite. A plump officer in blue arrived. With peach fuzz for a mustache, he might have been a year or two older than Henry, had to be a rookie. The cop approached the crime scene with forced indifference. "Huh!" he said, moving his head from side to side as he inspected the broken glass. The smooth gray sphere, perfect for skipping across a creek, held no clues. Could've come from anywhere. "Any reason someone would throw this?" he asked between pops of Doublemint.

Grace showed him the sign. "No wonder," said the officer.

"What's that supposed to mean?" asked Henry.

"Nothing," he said defensively. All they derived from the call was assurance that the police would keep an eye on the apartment for a time. The next morning Henry called Eckert at his office to let him know what had occurred—if he didn't know already. The secretary said she would pass on his message. Eckert failed to call back.

Randy the plumber, who lived in the apartment below, was called upon to fix the window the following day. As he cleaned out the glass shards and glazed the frame, Henry asked if he had seen anyone throw the rock.

"Can't help you," Randy replied. "I was at the movies."

"What did you see?"

"Why do you ask?"

"Don't mind him," said Grace. "This is what he does when he tells me that the Rockefeller family is running the world, that the Red Scare is just a distraction. He sees conspiracies everywhere."

"Actually, love, it's the Seven Sisters. They've overthrown governments across the globe in the name of fighting communism. I've done research."

"All done," said Randy, happy to leave before sparks flew.

Later, Henry posted flyers in the foyers of the four apartment buildings. Someone must have seen something. The mist wasn't that thick. He walked around the upper quad behind the playground, hoping to hear the baritone voice of the man he had chased. He listened to conversations of men on benches and at the playground. No such luck. He and Grace argued over putting the sign back in the window. He was against it; she insisted on exercising her First Amendment right. After she taped the sign to the window, he slid the sofa to the other wall and spent the afternoon and early evening lurking in the shadows, hoping to catch the culprit in the act. Afterwards, he mulled over the possibility of an inside job. Eckert seemed to have a motive.

Or maybe it was the plumber. After all, he was a Marine. He never did say what movie he saw. And how about that weird guy who talked like a robot? Couldn't be a nurse. Probably a quack.

"Let it go," pleaded Grace.

"Somehow, some way, I shall find him."

With an undertone of sarcasm, Grace wished him luck.

The Wayward Wind

Fresh from a shower, Randy Knight stood nude at the sink, eating Chef Boyardee beef ravioli from a can. After a hard session of lifting weights in the apartment cellar, he needed protein. He also needed peace of mind. It hadn't been easy ending the affair—never was.

The place was mercifully silent of Lonnie's yapper dog Tinkle. What kinda dog has no fur? Gray, pasty skin, mean as cat shit. He'd had to resist stomping the critter. Wasn't Lonnie's fault for the breakup. Same old story: first the flirt, then the wooing, leading to the climax and a stretch of infatuation. Too bad he couldn't stay in that state. The longer he was with a woman, the more he saw flaws. Three times in '56 he'd dumped his chick, first the spring fling with Gilda (too hairy), then the sultry summer with Sandra (snoring that shook the rafters), and now the romantic fall with Lonnie (too much a girly girl, makeup thick as concrete). Randy didn't enjoy making them cry. Face it, Knight, you're a shallow man.

Maybe the next woman would be a match. Maybe she would be the one to love. As a Charles Atlas–bodybuilding plumber who had just turned thirty, he had no lack of chances meeting the opposite sex, sometimes for the wrong reasons. How could he forget that Jane Meadows look-alike who approached him last week while he was fixing a toilet in the basement? Took her blouse right off.

"Like what you see?" she asked.

"Very nice," he mumbled, turning back to the toilet.

"Does this mean I get this for free? What do I have to do?"

No chance he'd touch this dame. Trouble ahead, could be a spying husband or a rape charge down the road. It happens.

"Sorry, lady," he said, putting away the caulking gun. "Forgot I have a pressing job at Whispering Pines…sewer backup."

She trailed him up the stairs, desperation in her voice. "Stay awhile…how about a beer? Or better, a shot of whiskey to brighten the day?"

"Be back for free," Randy assured her, heading out the door. Sure, lady, he'd be back…in his next life.

That afternoon Lonnie and he had a date, supposed to catch a matinee at the Senator. He wanted to see John Wayne in *The Searchers;* she wished to see Charlton Heston in *The Ten Commandments.* Of course, he deferred. When he was with a woman, he was all in, true blue from the first day to the last. One at a time, that's all he could handle. And now, like Gilda and Sandra, his latest had left the scene. Cue the curtain.

He added the can to the stack of dirty dishes, needed to clear his head, get some clarity on the situation. If he didn't, his mind would relive Lonnie's departure, word for word, leaving him gorged with regret over breaking his lover's heart. Maybe he could make it work. Don't do it. Remember the last time, with Gilda? If he won his honey back, he might grow tired of her all over again. How screwy is that?

In the bedroom, he put on an LP of Navajo flute music, a gift from a grateful customer. Randy assumed the lotus position before the Buddha, a boy playing a flute, made in Japan. As a Marine, he'd picked up the philosophy during the occupation. Not bad for a barefoot boy with an eighth-grade education. Closing his eyes, he observed his thoughts passing like clouds…chatter fading into stillness, all is nothing…

The phone jarred him back to the here and now. The manager of Whispering Pines was on the line: bathroom leak in the East Building, Apartment 4D. Time to put on clothes. "I'll be right on it, sir."

Covering sixteen apartments around the quadrangle was, for the most part, a breeze, earning him free rent, saving him ninety bucks monthly, half of which he put aside in case he had a sudden urge to spend, say, a year in India or the south of France. He had no ties.

His combat boots crunched through mid-November snow, first of the season. He always appreciated how snow tidied things up…like those rusting hulks scattered in front of their tin-roof shack back home. He remembered being eight, how the snow transformed the vehicles into dragons. Paddy had good intentions for fixing those cars for a profit but never got around to it. Oh, he'd talk about clearing the yard, planting roses, sprucing it up nice for Ma and Sis, but young Randy knew it was just the moonshine talking.

As the lungs deteriorated, Paddy dedicated himself to teaching his only son how to feed the family. They spent time in the woods and on Pigeon Creek, his father teaching him the ways of animals and fish. "Don't want to depend on charity," Paddy said. "That's not the Knight way, we take care of our own."

The end came quickly. On a hot afternoon in August, he took to the hammock. "Good a place to die as any," he wheezed. "You take care of Ma and Sis, hear me, son?"

"You're not dying yet."

"I'm like an old dog. Time to go…do life right." Those words would become Randy's motto. When Paddy passed the next day to coal-miner heaven, he left in peace because he knew his eldest had become a crack shot; the icebox had plenty of meat.

Randy brushed the flakes off his jacket and entered the East Building. Coming up the stairs, he heard the TV in Apartment 4D, had to knock twice. A roundish woman in a colorful woven dress opened the door. Barefoot, with Caribbean-green toenails, she had to be less than five feet. As he passed near, his keen nostrils, at times an impediment for a plumber, picked up her exotic aroma, couldn't place it. The apartment was warm, too close for comfort. In the living room, a little boy in shorts and a coonskin cap was jumping up and down on the sofa. Elvis was singing "Don't Be Cruel" on *The Ed Sullivan Show.*

"*¡Detener esa tontería!*" yelled the mother. The child leaped off the sofa. She led Randy to the bathroom, telling him the leak had occurred when her son took his bath. "He fills it up…—to float."

He ran the water, opened the access panel, and checked the pipes. Dry as a tomb. As he did some caulking along the tub and around the faucet, he became aware of two black eyes peering through the crack by the door.

"Howdy," Randy said. "What's your name?"

The boy in shorts stepped into the light. He was wearing a Mickey Mouse T-shirt and had a six-gun on each hip.

"Are you the marshal?" Randy asked.

"I am. I'm here to arrest you for robbing a bank in Tombstone."

"Aren't you Wyatt Earp?"

"My name's Sean."

"My name's Randy, pleased to make your acquaintance."

"What's that mean?"

"I'm happy to meet you." From his knees, Randy extended his hand.

The boy said he was not supposed to touch people. "Solo mi mamá." He removed his coonskin cap and exposed his bare head. "The boys on the quad call me baldy."

"How old are you, Sean?"

"Siete. Seven and a half."

"Well, I'm thirty and bald too." He removed his Baltimore Orioles cap and showed his dome, speckled from ear to ear. "Lost most of my hair before I was twenty-two." That blow to his vanity drove him to become a bodybuilder.

"What's that?" Sean said, pointing to the blue letters tattooed on the hairy forearm.

"United States Marine Corps," he said proudly. "Served in the Big One."

"Shoot any Nazis?"

"Not a chance...joined in '44, the day I turned seventeen. My ma signed the papers. I wanted to be a sharpshooter, but they found I had plumbing experience...saw every latrine from Parris Island to Guam."

He eased away from the tub and pulled a pack of Camels from his flannel shirt. He verged on lighting a mule but realized that might not be copacetic, with the boy and all. Sometimes, Randy admitted, he was blind to the needs of others.

As he moved on to the overflow, Sean peppered him with questions. Did he make a lot of money? Enough. Why'd he become a plumber? "Well, I was a Depression kid. We had no latrine."

"What's a latrine?"

"Toilet."

"Did you have to go to the bathroom outside?"

"Until I put in a toilet and septic tank. Got tired of going to the rising half-moon, the outhouse, in the middle of the night. Might run into a bear."

"A bear?"

"We had bears around."

He replaced the gasket in the overflow. "That should do it, Sean. Careful not to splash too much when you're taking a bath, okay? And don't let the boys in the quad bother you." Easy for him to say.

He scribbled out his phone number, tore the page off the notepad, and handed it to Sean's mother in the kitchen. If there's a problem, call him. He usually wasn't in the habit of giving tenants his number (rather, they went through the manager). But lines on her face showed fatigue. No evidence of a man around.

"You want some tea?" she asked.

Like the boy, she had almond eyes and cocoa skin. Not bad to look at—but not his type. He was a fool for showy women, the

Marilyn Monroe type—the buxom babe who looked good on his muscular arm when he turned up at a ballgame or the Dixie Ballroom. "Please," he said, putting down his toolbox.

Now he wished he'd showered after lifting weights…felt grimy sitting at the kitchen table with this woman. She did have beautiful skin, so smooth. Randy glanced over his shoulder. The boy was playing chess against himself in front of the TV. "What's with your son?" Randy whispered. "Don't mean to pry."

"No, thank you for asking. Do you know what a blast cell is, Mr.—"

"Knight."

"Pleased to meet you, Mr. Knight. Call me Sacniete…means White Flower."

"Aztec?"

"Maya. My late husband worked for the United Fruit Company. I met him at Guatemala University. I was his Spanish teacher."

Inky black hair with a trace of gray tumbled to her shoulders. He guessed her around thirty-five.

"You don't have much of an accent."

"Spanish is my second language. Let me return to the question. My son has leukemia—cancer of the blood. Basically, the bone marrow is not functioning. The blood cells it produces don't reach maturity. Instead of becoming white blood cells that fight infection, they turn into blast cells and feed off the red blood cells. Think of them as thugs in the bloodstream. I hate them." A knock on the door. "That must be Miller, here to play chess with Sean. Abre la puerta, Sean."

"Hi, Mrs. Clover," Miller said.

"Hi, poopyhead," Sean said.

"Sean, be nice," said Sacniete.

"That's okay, Mrs. Clover, he can call me anything."

"Okay, poopyhead!"

"Sean! You want a time-out? *Ve a jugar al ajedrez.*"

Randy watched the boys settle in front of the television. A juggler was now onstage, spinning plates on poles. Aside from an occasional glance, the boys kept their eyes on the board.

He could have gone for a second cup of tea, but that might be intrusive. He thanked White Flower for the hospitality.

"Are you depressed, Mr. Knight?"

"Very perceptive, Mrs. Clover…I did break up with my girl today. It'll pass. Remember, call me if you need me."

An inch of snow had fallen when he stepped from the building. He loved the stillness and clarity. That night he did not dream of Lonnie; instead, he dreamed of Sean, the child floating on water, speaking some ancient language. *Caw!*

He awoke to the newspaper slapping the doorstep. Still dark outside, might as well rise and shine. Quite a dream, magical. Loved being a crow. Was that some sort of sign? What language was he speaking?

He smoked a Camel at the card table. The black-and-white photo on the front page of the Sun reminded him of the date: December 6, 1941. There it was, the USS West Virginia in flames. Randy lost Uncle Jack there; tough one. After Paddy's death, he had leaned on his uncle for assistance, such as fixing a leaky roof, putting in the septic tank. The man was there for him. Hard to believe fifteen years had passed since Pearl Harbor. The world had moved on. Now humans could blow themselves off the planet.

He unlocked his metal case and pulled out the Colt .45 pistol, the M1911 he had worn on guard duty in Japan. The gun fit nicely in his palm, as if it belonged there. He pointed it at the window, then his temple. Click. No one would mourn his passing. Sis died in an automobile accident six months past; his ma and pa were gone, and he had lost contact with his cousins in West Virginia, scattered to the wind. What did he have to live for?

At 7:20, the phone rang. He put down the gun. Please let it not be the manager. Wasn't in the mood for work, not yet. Needed a second cup of coffee to ease into the day. He wanted to peruse the sports section…see how this rookie quarterback for the Colts was doing. Unitas had potential.

With great reluctance, he picked up the black receiver. "Hope I didn't wake you, Mr. Knight," a woman said.

He didn't recognize the voice. "Who's this?"

"Sacniete."

"Oh, yes, White Flower…call me Randy, please. What can I do for you? Is it leaking again?"

"That's not why I called. I decided to take you up on your offer to help. Be honest with me, Randy. I won't think worse of you if you were referring to plumbing. I would apologize for the misunderstanding."

"No, I mean, yes…yes, of course, Sacniete. I can help you. What do you need?"

"Would you go with me to Johns Hopkins this afternoon? My son is scheduled for a spinal tap. It would help if you could drive. These procedures can be nerve-wracking."

"Long as you don't mind riding in my pickup. It's a little dirty."

"Sean would love riding in your pickup. He's crazy about trucks."

"He can help shift gears."

"As long as you don't let him steer. By the way, that was sweet of you when you showed your bald head."

"My pleasure…"

He locked the gun in the case. Not today.

The morning dawned clear; sunlight sparkled off snow. In an alley, he cleaned out the pickup, throwing into the dumpster cigarette butts, cans, bottles, spare parts, wood, newspapers, menus, and a small pile of chicken bones. Then he drove to a car wash, vacuumed out the cabin, and opted for the deluxe wash. Save for a few dents, the neon-blue Chevy shone like new when he parked in front of their building. Sacniete and Sean stepped from the foyer. The boy looked fragile coming down the icy steps, holding his mother's hand.

"Climb in," said Randy. Sean scooted to the middle, and Randy wrapped him in a USMC blanket and turned up the heat.

THE OFFICE PARTY

A FEW DAYS BEFORE Christmas, Harold Snodgrass, manager of the Pimlico racetrack, walked into Sandy Goldberg Advertising on Pennsylvania Avenue in Towson. At the reception desk, next to the Christmas tree, sat a pretty young woman in a green chiffon dress, Mrs. LuAnn Chowder, girl Friday for the agency, which specialized in local retail, sports, and politics. As was the inclination for some Towson men, Snodgrass's rheumy eyes scanned her front, from the French roll to the cleavage. "Mr. Snodgrass," she drawled in a mock Southern drawl. The old codger did bring in a six-figure account. "How good to see youu!" Like my tits? Can't have them!"

"Happy holidays, LuAnn…to you and your family."

"Likewise to you, sir. Please go on in. Party's just warming up."

Back to work. Had to straighten out this mess before she could join the festivities. A quarter-page print ad for the *News-American* had a wrong number in the phone listing. The proofreader had missed it, along with the designer, copywriter, and account exec. Usually LuAnn checked all ads before they went out the door, calling every number listed. This one must have slipped by during her lunch hour. Call and you wouldn't reach Sleepy Joe's Furniture, but Spring Grove State Mental Hospital. Mr. Goldberg would be pissed, not to mention the client.

She stopped the ad before the second edition of the newspaper went to press. The new version would be there in ten minutes. Another save by Super Chowder, her nickname at the agency. In six months, she had made herself indispensable. Not only could she type 150 words per minute, she knew how to spell and focus on detail, making her a natural proofreader. She also kept track of what was coming in and going out the agency door, where and when and what was needed. The busier she became, the more she felt valued. She wanted to be recognized as a professional. Up till now, that had been a problem in other venues.

After earning her associate degree in business, she worked as a secretary at Baldwin Real Estate. Paid well, but the male agents were a pain in the ass, couldn't take their eyes off her, couldn't stop talking about her, snickering and smirking like schoolboys. Felt like she was back in high school. Even the women were catty. In the next job, three married guys were like flies at a picnic, wouldn't leave her alone, kept taking turns asking her out. At first she thought it was a joke, but it persisted. Maybe they had a bet on who could snake her. On to the next job.

Along the way, LuAnn gained a reputation in certain Towson circles for being "a social snob." Could she help it if she bore a resemblance to Brigitte Bardot? Were she more like Olive Oyl, might it be easier? Then again, Mr. Goldberg might not want Olive Oyl as the face of Sandy Goldberg Advertising.

Twisting a strand of light brown hair, she glanced at the street. Snow flurries. People huddled in overcoats, waiting for the streetcar. She wanted to go home, throw on some loose clothes, play with the boys. Couldn't wait to see their faces Christmas morning. Yawning, she covered her mouth. She and her husband were up till one putting together the bikes in the basement.

Out of the corner of her eye, she espied Sandy Goldberg, the silken, silver-haired owner, gliding across the floor with a drink in each hand. Here comes trouble. Since his divorce went final, Goldberg would linger by her desk under the auspices of sharing his knowledge of retail. He praised her work. "You have potential in this business." She'd heard this move before, this "taking her under the wing," a ploy used by the boss to get her on the couch. She couldn't quit fast enough. Men could be such pigs…glad she nabbed a good one.

She did appreciate Goldberg's knowledge in the art of persuasion. "The principles of Aristotle's Rhetoric still apply," he said, with the flourish of a manicured hand, festooned with a gold disk on the pinkie, how quaint. She could see why he had been successful in building a multimillion-dollar shop from scratch. His enthusiasm for ideas was infectious, and he treated his employees well, calling them "his talent." At times, Goldberg hinted at trying her as a copywriter. Said he could tell she had "imagination." She would love the chance to show what she could do, but she kept her distance, refusing more than once his offer of a drink at the Penn Hotel, so they could continue "their chat." Sorry, had kids to pick up, but thank you.

"Hey, LuAnn, I'm a two-fisted drinker. I order you to take one of these Mai Tais. Help me out here…"

"If you insist, Mr. Goldberg."

"I insist."

She accepted the Mai Tai and took a sip. Wasn't much of a drinker, but this rum concoction she could get used to. The boss took her by the elbow and guided her into the presentation room. Amidst the jabber of conversation, she helped herself to the raw bar, slurping a dozen oysters with cocktail sauce. Delicious! The combo played jazz, and life was good with an open bar, premium drinks, and a spread of Maryland seafood and prime rib. She settled in with a plate of Russian caviar on toast. The drink went down easy, maybe a little too easy. Goldberg handed her a second Mai Tai.

The crowd lit up when the band switched to rock and roll. How could anyone not move to "Rock Around the Clock"?

"Care to jitterbug?" Sandy yelled.

"Sure!" she cried. He draped his coat over a chair. She slipped out of her green pumps, and he took her hands. Off they flew to the hard-driving beat. Moving in and out of his arms, LuAnn kicked her legs high like the cheerleader she had been in high school. Sandy moved like a gymnast, leading her around the room; the crowd clapped and cheered on boss and girl Friday. Sandy finished with a flourish, flipping LuAnn over his back. Landing, LuAnn lurched toward the oyster table and banged her arm on the edge. A hand broke her fall. It was the artist, Diego, who worked in design. She suspected him as a homosexual, but his fingers sampling the merchandise indicated otherwise.

"Crazy," she said, wobbling away.

She grabbed Goldberg's arm and whispered in his ear: "Think I'm going to be sick."

"Hang on…" They edged their way through the crowd and entered his corner office.

"I can take it from here," she said, closing the bathroom door, just in time. The thick stream of vomit hit the intended target. Nice job, Chowder, wiping off the toilet seat. News of her drunken behavior would soon be all over Towson. Super Chowder, Queen of the Hop, blahhh! All business, she washed out her mouth, added a fresh coat of lipstick, and adjusted her French roll. Splashing water on her face, she felt sober enough to consider taking the Number 8. Or she could walk…clear the head. Don't want to enter the apartment tipsy.

Sandy was waiting.

"I'm so sorry, Mr. Goldberg."

"Hon, don't you mind one bit. I should drive you home. You're in no shape for the streetcar. Where do you live?"

"Whispering Pines. What about your party?"

"They'll get along without me. Come on, LuAnn. Let me drive you home…and please call me Sandy."

Behind the bravado, the good cheer, LuAnn sensed the loneliness in Goldberg. Could be rough spending the holidays as a divorced man. "Okay, Sandy, you can take me home."

Sleet stung her eyes as they made their way to the parking garage. He opened the door for her. The Cadillac Eldorado, a golden beauty capped with pointed fins, still had that new-car smell. Her dress crinkled as she slid across the leather. As the daughter of an Essex steelworker, she had never been in such a luxurious vehicle. She and Chuck shared a six-year-old Nash Rambler wagon, which suited their growing family just fine.

"Let's drive to Florida," he joked on York Road.

"Where?" she said with a yawn.

"Miami Beach. We'll drive straight through…tomorrow night, we could be watching Jackie Gleason on stage."

"You sound almost serious."

"Why not? The agency is closed for ten days."

"Don't think Gill and Tracy would appreciate Mom missing Christmas."

"I envy you. You have family. I lost mine."

"What happened?"

"Work got in the way. Too many weekends in the office. Too many evenings entertaining clients. Laura found someone else to spend time with. Can't say I blame her."

In the parking lot, she thanked him for the ride. He asked if he could have a Christmas hug. "Okay," she said. What could be the harm?—a short-arm hug, the kind reserved for a distant uncle. Before she could retreat, however, he grabbed her arms, and his mouth closed in for a blubbery kiss that stank of Limburger. *Euu!* Her teeth chomped on the tongue as if it were a Coney Island hot dog. Blood splattered the upholstery.

"Bitch!" he said through the monogrammed hanky. A red spot bloomed in the linen.

She tried to open the door; the lock clicked shut.

"Let me out!"

"I could sue you for this," he said, checking the wound in the mirror.

"Do you see that man at the window in the lower apartment? My husband is waiting for me to come home. Isn't that sweet?

He happens to be a member of the Baltimore Police Department. If you don't let me out of here…well, you get the picture."

"I know for a fact he's been suspended."

"How do you know that?"

"Word gets around." He unlocked the doors.

LuAnn stomped off, wondering how much Chuck had seen. Now she'd have to find another job. If only women ran the world. Why not start her own business, a typing service? Towson lawyers needed typists. Charge a quarter a page, maybe more. Four bucks an hour—real money. And more time at home. Be nice to greet the boys when they came home from school. She'd make it work.

Arms folded, Chuck peered through the window, watching her trudge up the slushy steps. Be hard to see through the sleet. The Eldorado was too far away, wasn't it? Be great to shed the pumps…spiked heels, murder on the toes. What sadist thought them up? Had to be a man, like Louis XIV inventing ballet. If she did typing from home, Keds would be her work shoe.

Nine-year-old Gill and seven-year-old Tracy barely acknowledged her arrival. No surprise there, eyes glued to the TV, watching Cheyenne, "the roving cowboy." A half-eaten baked chicken sat on the kitchen counter. No homework tonight. No need to help Gill with fractions or Tracy with reading. "Hello," she said, giving each a hug. Soon they'd be too old for cuddling.

"Fancy car," said Chuck from behind.

"And hello to you," said LuAnn, putting her wool coat on the closet hook.

"Your lipstick is smudged."

"Mistletoe, you know how it is."

"No, I don't…"

The little lie stung…not her nature to hide the truth.

Since his suspension from the Baltimore police, he wasn't the same man, not like the fellow she met a decade ago at Fort Meade, where he was stationed as an MP. She had a thing for men in uniform, especially someone who bore a resemblance to Montgomery Clift. As a waitress at the Silver Leaf Diner on Ritchie Highway, she worked six eight-hour shifts a week while taking a full load of business courses at Goucher. She had no time for dating.

But Chucky (that's what she called him then) was a different cat. Maybe his isolation attracted her, like the kind you might find in an Edward Hopper painting. As a girl, she'd been drawn to strays—stray cats, dogs, stray kids on the playground, the ones others shunned, the geeks and nerds. In high school, they were far more interesting than jocks, who just wanted to get into your pants. Wham, bam, thank you, ma'am! Not for her. She had plans.

Several mornings a week, Chucky would wander in. He'd settle in at her station and stutter what he wanted: black coffee and a slice of apple pie. He had a memorable face, moody and sensitive. Did she know him from somewhere? Sure looked familiar. When asked how he was doing, he garbled a response. LuAnn touched the top of his hand with the tip of her fingernail, letting him know that she understood.

"Who kissed you?"

"What?"

He took a step forward. "Who smuh-smudged your lipstick?"

"What's this, the third degree?"

"You have a bruise on the arm."

She looked down at her forearm. "I slipped while dancing."

"Who were you dancing with?"

"Who cares!"

"You...you don't have to yell, LuAnn. You seem awfully d-defensive."

"For once, stop being a cop."

"I'm not a cop. I'm a security guard..."

How could she forget? When he worked on the force, he wanted her to stay home with the kids. They could live on his salary.

She had no problem with that when Gill and Tracy were little (she cherished that part of her life), but once they were in school, she went back to work, first part-time, and then full-time. She loved being a mother and a wife, but she also appreciated having a separate identity.

"Look, I'm done in…can we talk about this in the morning? I'm going to take a shower." She had to wash off any residue of Sandy's cologne.

In the shower, she decided not to give Chuck the news of her unemployment until after Christmas. It would only make things between them worse. Good thing she had in her purse a bonus check for a hundred dollars. Better cash it soon, lest Goldberg put a stop on it. Be tight for a while. Why'd Chuck have to break that negro's jaw—and in front of a dozen witnesses? She knew why. The drug dealer had mocked his stutter, a curse as well as a gift. Childhood taunts had led him to the boxing ring at the YMCA.

As his waitress, eventually she did figure out who this moody MP was, once she got past the mustache. She found his picture in the yearbook. She'd had a crush on him at Essex High. Three years ahead, he never noticed the fawning ninth grader when they passed in the hallway. No one messed with Chucky Chowder; even the greasers, those wannabe gangsters, steered clear of his fists. He fought in the Golden Gloves. She and her girlfriends saw him fight at the Baltimore Coliseum, screaming for their Chucky when the ref raised his hand. They even coaxed a smile out of the fighter. After high school, she lost track of him…heard he joined the Navy and spent his tour boxing his way through the South Pacific, fighting on aircraft carriers and in hangars. So serendipity that her "heartthrob" walked into the Silver Leaf Diner. Like it was meant to be.

Being a cop in his hometown had been his dream job. He wanted to help people and protect the vulnerable. He wanted to put bad people in jail. Officer Chowder was well respected in the ranks for being "a straight shooter." Then came his assault on the drug dealer, which made the local news. The chief had no choice but to fire him, despite his distinguished seven-year record as a crime fighter.

Her Chucky had lost his way, and she feared for their marriage. She toweled off and put on sweatpants and an Ocean City sweatshirt. Now she could relax. She found Chuck in the easy chair, flipping through a Motor Trend magazine. A Cadillac was on the cover—Car of the Year. "Let's not fight, sweetie," she said, looping her arms around his neck. "It's Christmas."

He tossed the magazine aside and opened *Popular Mechanics.* LuAnn gave up. She went into the kitchen and poured herself a tall glass of Coca-Cola.

The Caretaker

Along the south side of Whispering Pines stretched Garden Drive, four blocks downhill, great for sledding and the contraption Rusty intended to build. "It's simple," he said to Miller: a few bolts and screws to secure the steel wheels, lifted from roller skates, and a slab of strong wood, cut to size to form two carriages. "Put it all together and off we go, sailing like a seagull."

"Let's do it," said Miller.

In a scrap heap next to the railroad tracks, they found an eight-foot plank, ten inches wide. With Miller leading the way, the boys carried it a half mile up the side of the street, keeping their distance from traffic on the two-lane road. In the basement of Rusty's building, they went to work. Using his father's saw, Rusty cut the plank to the dimensions they had calculated, rounding off both ends. Next came the wheels, positioned front and back. Miller's mom contributed a couple of brushes and tubes of black, orange, green, and red. Rusty painted a raven on his skateboard, Miller a variation of the Oriole bird.

"Not bad, boys," said Alice. "Not bad at all."

The next morning, the mercury did not climb above freezing. The brilliant, crystal light illuminated Miller's smoky breath. His glasses fogged. The ground of the quadrangle was frozen like a rock. He felt thick, padded with a woolen cap, ski gloves, two sweatshirts, a heavy coat, and a scarf. Rusty appeared in a T-shirt and denim jacket, rubbing his black leather gloves, ready to go. They tried a few short rides on the sidewalk. Rusty took to the board; Miller, not so fast.

Wearing a paint-splattered apron, Alice stepped outside in shirtsleeves to observe the shaky progress of her son. "Come here," she said after he bailed on the grass.

"I'll get it, Mom," he said.

"I know that." She wagged a finger beneath his freckled cheeks. "No riding in the road, you hear?"

"I won't."

"Now you look like a duck. Quack, quack."

"Don't, Mom."

"Hear me?"

"Hear you."

Her steelworker fingers freed his cheeks. "That's a promise. You too, Rusty. No riding in traffic. Where you goin'?"

"Towson High," Rusty said.

"Excellent…won't be a soul on campus. Be careful crossing streets. And don't run over people. Look where you're going. No fooling around, you hear?"

"Promise," Miller said.

He knew better than to ignore his mother's plea. Whenever he crossed Knollwood, Mr. Turnbaugh's MG was foremost in his mind…still had bad dreams about it.

On the plaza of Towson High, they bore their bruises and scrapes with little complaint as they tried different moves across the span. Miller shed his coat, scarf, and one sweatshirt. It was one of the greatest days of his life. Like flying in a dream.

The following day Mom insisted that Miller put on Grandpop's leather football helmet. Miller complained, saying he preferred his Baltimore Colt cap. "I look like a dork."

"A tough man wore that helmet. Keep it on."

Rusty laughed when he saw his friend coming across the quadrangle. "Where'd you get that helmet?"

"My grandfather…played football at Johns Hopkins. I look like Alfred E. Neuman."

"Only if you knock out a front tooth."

An icy breeze whistled across the plaza at Towson High. Rusty tossed his jacket aside, declaring he had "a need for speed." He jumped on the board. His left leg lashed the concrete pavement. The board shot across the plaza. Arms spread, knees bent, Rusty skated toward the steps.

"Turn!" Miller yelled.

An instant before the board flew down the staircase, Rusty threw himself into the trimmed boxwood that separated the plaza from the parking lot. Without so much as a scratch, he extracted himself from the shrub. "What a gas!"

"Don't do that again."

"You sound like your mother."

"Thanks for the compliment."

During that frozen week, Rusty soared while Miller took a more tentative approach toward mastering their invention. He analyzed the nuances of the skates and angles of the body. Rusty showed him how to lean into a turn. Already Rusty had mastered "stopping on a dime," shifting his weight to the rear and flipping up the board. Worked like a charm. Miller was impressed...wouldn't dare try it himself. He knew his limits.

As the new year approached, the chill blue days held: no snow, no ice. By the end of the week, Rusty could do curbs and small steps; Miller preferred swerving back and forth on the macadam that sloped gradually to the football field. When they both reached the field, Rusty declared Miller "ready for Garden."

"You may be. I'm not so sure."

"Just do a swerve or two, so you can say you did it. I'll take care of the rest. Meet you at the bottom."

When you're half blind, one tends to be cautious. But he went along. They had come too far to stop now. Maybe he'd do a swerve or two. Mom would never know.

♦♦♦

Another double shift in the Union Memorial ER for Niles Blackwater, RN, called to duty on his day off because of the flu. His colleagues were dropping like flies. From eleven p.m. to three in the afternoon, he treated this passage of humanity, be it a groaning old man with an impacted bowel, a four-year-old having a seizure, a junkie in cardiac arrest, or the teenage girl whose face had been ripped open in a crash. All the same to him. During any crisis, no one was better in the ER than "Cool Niles."

He knew he was strange. Been that way all his life. His alcoholic mother described him as a "loner." Couldn't disagree. In high school, he had few friends, save a couple of guys who shared his passion for making cartoons. Gym class was a pain. He was a gangly boy with big feet and hands, an easy target. Didn't much mind the words. Who gives a fuck if these losers didn't like him? Long as they left him alone, he'd be fine.

Then came the day when he had to make his stand. Eddie Jenkins, senior point guard and Prom King, called out the sophomore during lunch break. A dozen or so boys and girls were having a smoke by the church. They surrounded Niles and wouldn't let him pass.

"Hey, freak," said Jenkins. "What makes you tick? You a homo? Want to suck my dick?"

Staring at Jenkins, Niles maintained his stillness, inside and out. Then came the punch. Blackwater shifted, the fist grazing his cheek. The crowd cheered and gave the fighters space. Stepping back, Niles raised his hands. He knew this moment would come. Pop had predicted it.

Circling his prey, Niles remembered the words of his late father, a disabled Army Ranger: Stay centered, warrior.

Yeah, Pop. I got you.

Ducking a wild swing, Niles sprang at his off-kilter foe, hitting the bridge of the nose with a chop that cracked cartilage.

Game over. Jenkins's knees gave way. Hands caught him before he hit the pavement.

Without a word, Niles walked past the group. No one in school ever put a hand on him again.

Bone-tired from sixteen hours on his feet, Niles chose to parallel park in front of his apartment building. With inches to spare, he surmised that the sedan could fit between the MG and the Hudson. Soon he would be drawing the curtains, plugging his ears, and lowering a black mask over his eyes. Had he his druthers, he'd live in a place with no windows.

After two attempts, the Packard backed into the parking place. He was about to open the door when a sound froze him: *whoosh!* A black-haired boy flew by on a board with steel wheels. Had he opened the door an instant before, he would've pancaked the daredevil. Take a gander, see if there's another fool coming.

The heavy black door of the Packard, the Ranger's old car, creaked open. The driver's seat bore the imprint of Pop's wide torso. Niles had enlisted in the Army, hoping to follow in his footsteps as a Ranger. Instead, he ended up being trained as a medic, based on the psychological tests they had given him.

He owed his vocation to Phillip Flowers, a black private from Birmingham, Alabama. The nineteen-year-old arrived at the Fort Houston Burn Center as the sole survivor of a Huey helicopter crash in the desert. Only the soles of his feet were spared from scorching. The stink of burnt hair and flesh sickened the orderlies. The flames had consumed the flesh on his legs down to the bones. It was hell finding a vein for the IV; Spec 4 Blackwater pumped him full of morphine. Through the long night, he sat with Private Flowers. During that span, Niles made peace with his condition; he knew he wasn't capable of feeling empathy for the victim, but his father's wisdom had left him with a moral compass. He was not repulsed by the odor or the gruesome flesh.

"I'm freezing," Private Flowers whispered.

Spec 4 Blackwater swaddled him in a special sheet for burn victims. He held the soldier's hand through his last breath.

Niles stepped from the car into the damp air. Head down, hand on the banister, he took the three steps like someone twice his age. His lower back ached.

Maybe it happened because of fatigue. Whatever the reason, he didn't hear the approach of skates on the sidewalk. The boy yelled, but it was too late. Niles's leg caught the board, and the kid tumbled toward disaster, a hard scrape on the sidewalk, face down. Niles rushed to the fallen figure. Blood trickled down the sidewalk. But the kid was crying…good sign.

"Let me look at you," he said softly. "I'm a nurse."

He carefully turned Miller over. Folding his scarf, he placed it under the boy's head.

"Better?" Niles asked.

"Better."

At first glance, one might think the boy was seriously injured. His face was covered with cuts, but not too deep, except for that forehead wound. The leather helmet might have averted serious damage.

"Be right back," said Niles. "Don't move."

Had to get that towel from the YMCA bag, stop the bleeding. No longer fatigued, he took the steps in a single leap.

"What happened?" asked Rusty.

"Should've taken the road…stupid!"

"I'll get your mom."

Back up the stairs, Niles crouched and removed the broken glasses, split in the middle. He pressed the white towel lightly against the gash.

"Any dizziness? Nausea?"

"Mom's going to kill me."

"Mmm."

"Because of the glasses."

"I can fix them with black tape."

"Thanks, but I'll be dead by then."

"Any nausea? Headache? Feel dizzy?"

"Can I get up? I'd rather face my mom standing up."

"If you feel up to it."

Niles removed the bloody towel to inspect the wound. The flow of blood had slowed. He helped the slight boy to his feet.

"Any sharp pain?"

"Not yet."

Miller hated seeing Mom so upset. Her gait was like the charge of a lioness. Hives flecked her neck. Once again, he had made her miserable…couldn't win. As was her way, Mom opened with a question.

"Wadda I gotta do, Miller? Put you in a padded cell? What the hell happened? I told you not to ride in the street."

"I didn't. I was riding on the sidewalk."

"My fault," said Niles. "Wasn't watching…tripped him."

"You live in the South Building, right?"

"Yes."

"Sorry to meet you under these circumstances, Mr.—"

"Blackwater."

"I'll take it from here, Mr. Blackwater. St. Joe's will patch him up."

"I can do it. I'm an ER nurse at Union Memorial. Here's my identification."

He opened his jacket and showed the ID hanging over his blue scrubs.

"I don't know…" Alice wasn't sure about this one. Sure had an odd way of talking, as if he were speaking from a distance…no inflection whatsoever.

"My apartment's here on the first floor. Your boy needs stitches. Everything's in my medical bag."

"I'd rather have a doctor at Saint Joe's—"

"You might have to wait. You could be sitting around people with the flu."

How could she resist? She told him she would accept his kindness and offered to help, should he need assistance.

Niles lived in apartment 1A at 302 Garden Drive. He didn't have visitors, preferring solitude as he devoted himself to his pet project.

"Sparse," Alice said, looking over the tidy space.

Niles didn't respond. His mind was locked on the impending procedure. He settled the boy in the easy chair and tilted it back, giving him a good angle on the wound. He turned on the reading lamp, carefully removed the helmet, and handed it to his mother.

"Good thing you wore this," said Alice.

"Good thing," said Miller.

After scrubbing his hands, Niles sterilized the Donald Duck TV table with bleach, washing and wiping the tin twice.

"Anything I can do?" Alice asked.

His focus did not waver from putting on the gloves, a step-by-step process to avoid contamination. Must not touch anything outside the sterile field. On the TV table, he placed his instruments and supplies in the order they would be needed.

Using an alcohol pad with saline, he cleaned around the jagged gash. Then he squirted sterile water into the wound.

"Be still," he told Miller.

The stitching began. Holding his mother's hand, Miller held firm; only the dimple on his chin trembled as the needle poked through the skin flap. From one side to the other, he sewed the stitches. Like knitting, thought Alice. The skin came together with fine precision.

Niles cut a long piece of gauze and wrapped it around the boy's head.

"Will I get a scar?" Miller asked.

Blackwater demurred, but Miller persisted.

"Will I?"

"Possibly a small one."

"Yay, I'll look like a pirate! Better than Alfred E. Neuman."

"He's obsessed with Mad magazine."

He had Miller stand and checked the eyes with a pin light.

"How do you feel? Headache? Nausea?"

"I'm fine...sore."

"That's to be expected."

He told Alice that the stitches should come out in a week. And to keep an eye out for swelling.

"What's over here?" Miller pointed to what looked like a model boat. It sat on a worktable, the sole items in the room.

"My project," Niles said, peeling off the gloves.

He put the instruments in hot water and disposed of the gloves. Then he turned his attention to the glasses, nothing that electric tape couldn't fix.

Miller and Alice checked out the ocean liner that covered the length of the worktable.

"Neat!" said Miller.

Niles needed an art project to give his life order. Been that way since high school. Spent most of his senior year in the art room. In the spring, Mr. Ghisson, his portly art teacher, convinced the quiet student to paint the background for the play Our Town. Niles painted a rotating collage of faces that related to each soliloquy... big hit opening night. Mr. Ghisson called for him to take a bow, but he was already long gone, having ducked out the back exit while Rebecca was expounding on the vastness of the universe.

It was all about making art, nothing more. One could call his current motif "precision," fitting all the parts together, down to the smallest detail. Nothing less than perfection would do. And after he finished a project, he destroyed it, usually by fire, more ceremonial than throwing it in the trash. The gesture befit his Cherokee blood.

"Matchsticks," said Alice. "Amazing."

From stem to stern, she marveled over the creation, the smokestacks, bridge, three decks, the lines and anchor, everything in exact order. "How many?"

Her question went unanswered. His bedroom door was now closed. The taped glasses hung on the doorknob of the front door. She took her son by the hand and left apartment 1A.

NEW YEAR'S EVE

SHADES DRAWN ABOUT THE apartment, he spent the waning hours of '56 focused on his project, the ocean liner. He conjured an image of himself on the bridge, steering the vessel. Captain Niles Blackwater, explorer of the fourth dimension.

"Boom!" A cherry bomb shook the back window. A hammerhead followed. "Boom!" Niles raised the shade and threw open the window, searching through the smoke for the source of the explosions. Laughter from a dark corner—sounded like chipmunks—had to be Miller and his sidekick. From the first-floor window of the West Building, Alice's voice cut through the quadrangle: "Whatcha doin'? Wanna lose a finger?"

Niles checked his watch: ten minutes to go. Doors in the apartment building were opening and closing...footsteps on the stairs. The people of Whispering Pines spilled out into the quadrangle. Four Eckert girls were twirling sparklers around Miller and Rusty. Niles poured two fingers of Rémy Martin in a tumbler and pulled a chair up to the window. Swirling the cognac in the glass, he recognized some of the voices in the gathering, people he saw coming and going...: a tall blonde with a short Irish guy in 2B...think her name was Monica...his upstairs neighbors, Henry and Grace, the protesters, passing back and forth a bottle of champagne. Recently changed their sign to "Give Peace a Chance."

A boy in cowboy boots rode the broad shoulders of Whispering Pines's plumber. Beside them walked the mother, about half his size. She was wearing a colorful wrap, looked Indian. The boy yanked off the man's camouflage cap and exposed the dome. He rubbed the plumber's head and returned the cap to its proper place. The big man laughed and said something to the child. From this perch, Niles had observed Sean this past year, first running about with a head full of black hair and now bald as a cue ball. Chemo was such a crude tool. Had he not been a nurse, he would have gone into medical research.

"Two minutes!" proclaimed a fellow he vaguely knew, a long face with turned-down lips. Lived across the quad. Drove a Studebaker. Didn't he also drive a white Cadillac Coupe de Ville? Saw it in the parking lot during the hurricane. Had an Italian wife, hadn't seen her in a while.

"One minute!"

The countdown began: 59, 58, 57…

Ten seconds before the new year, a two-foot-wide plastic crab began its descent from the Eckert apartment. Across the crab shell, 1957 lit up at midnight. Sean shot his cap pistol at the sky. Firecrackers sparked in the center of the quadrangle. Miller's father set off a small rocket. It flew above the apartments and burst into a bouquet of colors. People hugged and raised toasts. Sipping the cognac, Niles caught a glimpse of two men kissing before they disappeared around the corner.

Alice, hanging on the arm of her husband, Ralph, stood before his window. She was puffing on a Tiparillo. "Hey, handsome, whatcha doin' in there?"

"How's the stitches?"

"No swelling whatsoever. They come out on Monday. Why doncha come out and join us? Let's get drunk!"

"You already are, my dear," Ralph said.

"So are you. Love getting drunk with my honey. Give me a smooch."

Looking up at the window after the kiss, Alice found it shut and the shade drawn. She called out to Miller: "Show's over. Time to go home. Good night, Rusty."

"Good night, Mrs. Nowaki."

Arms intertwined, Alice, Miller, and Ralph walked back to 7903. Big Brother Glenn was spending the night elsewhere. Yay, Miller had the room to himself. He stepped over the chalk line and invaded Glenn's territory. Fingering through his 45s, Miller searched for something that matched his mood. He found what he was looking for, put the record on the spindle, and turned on the player. He watched the needle rise and land. After a crackling pause, Elvis's voice filled the room. "There will be peace in the valley for me..."

One final old-year task: with scissors, he sliced across the front page of the newspaper, removing December 31, 1956, from the masthead. He added it to the collection covering the wall,

Sixty-two days since his brush with the Grim Reaper...

AN UGLY GASH

To keep the peace, LuAnn delayed telling about the loss of her job at Goldberg Agency. She wanted to enjoy the holidays, spend time with Gill and Tracy. During this lull, she had business cards printed...not only for typing services, why not editorial and proofreading too? She intended to solicit every lawyer's office in the county seat. She also planned to pitch folks in real estate. *Have typewriter, will travel.*

On the morning after New Year's, the boys were getting themselves together to catch the bus to Towson Elementary. LuAnn was in the kitchen making peanut butter and jelly sandwiches when Chuck entered the apartment in his night watchman uniform. He didn't find LuAnn dressed for work but in dungarees and a faded orange top, a remnant of her cheerleader days.

"Why the casual look?" he asked. "Not going to work?"

"No need to." She slathered Skippy across Wonder bread, added Welch's grape jelly, and included the boys' favorite: Utz potato chips in wax paper bags. She filled the lunch boxes—Superman for Tracy, Davy Crockett for Gill. Last, she added a red apple in each box and snapped them shut.

"You ill?" he said, placing his hand on her forehead. "Flu's going around."

"Feel fine," she said, brushing away his palm. She handed him a business card.

"What's this?"

"TYPE Communications, the name of my company. Typing, proofreading, editing. And I'm the principal. Like the ruby logo?"

"You quit your job for this?"

Oh that skeptical tone, that "Baltimoron" whine! She'd heard it from her parents. If it's sunny out, that means rain'll be here soon. If it's spring, winter's right around the corner. Friends on the force called Officer Chowder "Black Cloud." As a cop on the beat, anticipating the worst helped him become an excellent law enforcement officer. But you don't need to carry that attitude to every aspect of life. He was particularly hard on the boys, pointing out their flaws all too often.

"There has to be more to this," he said, handing the card back to her. "You don't just up and quit your job without running it by me. We're a team, remember?"

She told him about Sandy Goldberg, how he tried to kiss her.

"And you quit your job because of that? Maybe he was drunk. It happens."

"Can't believe you're defending him. He's a pig. I bit his tongue."

"Let me get this straight, LuAnn. May I assume you weren't under the mistletoe?"

"I was in his car."

"The Eldorado I saw."

"Correct. I had too much to drink at the Christmas party. He drove me home."

"Ah, *now* we have the truth," he said in his bad cop voice. "You were French kissing."

"You don't under—"

"I do understand. I understand you think I'm a loser. Maybe you're checking what's out there, be quite a step up to nab a rich Jew—"

She smacked him across the cheek.

"You dirty—" He pushed her away and she lost her balance, landing on the floor with a thud.

In rushed Gill and Tracy. "What happened?" Gill asked.

"Mom-Mommy tripped," said Chuck.

"That's right, Mommy tripped," LuAnn said, rising from the linoleum. Gill offered his hand and she accepted. "Thank you, Sir Lancelot, for coming to rescue me. Here's your lunch. Quick like a bunny. Bus'll be here in five minutes. Love you!"

They listened to the boys bounding down the steps.

Chuck uttered an apology.

"Get a grip," she replied.

His state of mind was having a bad effect on the boys. When was the last time he did anything with them? She knew it was hard, him working at night, but he had to make the effort.

And when was the last time they made love? She kept that question to herself. She missed the romance and intimacy they shared, back when he called her "Kitten." He was putting on weight and losing his boxer physique. She didn't want to live with a brooding, fat roommate. Without complaint, Chuck did his rounds as a security officer at Black & Decker, working nights and sleeping a few hours during the day. He paid the bills and took care of business, driving the boys here and there, but he had a weariness, a heaviness, about him. Her Chucky had lost that bounce in his step. He was gravitating to a neighborhood bar in Roland Park, Alonso's, where cops hung out, swapping tales and dirty jokes between bites of twenty-two-ounce bacon cheeseburgers. She pictured him at the circular bar, downing National Premiums beneath that upside-down Christmas tree over the cash register. Every time the swinging door opened, Chuck would look over, hoping to see one of his old buddies. All his close friends were cops. Must be tough losing that fellowship, that common purpose. Something had to give.

♦♦♦

Upon reflection of his firing from the Baltimore Police force, Officer Chowder realized that what did him in was the racism of his fellow cops. As a youth, he had little contact with the colored in Dundalk. The schools were mostly white and the janitors were black. His four years in the Navy had cured him of any sense of racial superiority. He had worked with all sorts: black, yellow, red. Skin color meant nothing to him. He had grown to judge people by their character. That approach served him well as a cop. During his seven years on the beat in some of the toughest neighborhoods in the city, he did not harden toward the communities he served, unlike other Blues.

Yes, he despised the drug dealers, not those selling weed—he mostly ignored the petty stuff—but the heroin pushers. Some cops shook them down, robbing them of their stash and cash…nothing said about it, see no evil, hear no evil. He wanted no part of the thuggery, yet how could he do his job? He felt the hate on the streets. In his last year, he didn't even walk the beat. Now, he and his partner cruised in an Impala, like they were part of an occupying army.

He could understand why a man might turn to drugs to make a living. The negro veterans who came home to Baltimore City really got screwed. The Feds barred them from taking advantage of the GI bill, and they weren't eligible for FHA loans if they wanted to move to a better neighborhood. Redlining was a common practice. Once a black family moved into a block, realtors would scare white people into selling at a low price. Then they flip the houses to negroes at double the price. Adding to the injustice, many black veterans were squeezed out of jobs in manufacturing and along the waterfront. Most of the unions wanted no part of these colored men, who fought and bled for their country. Thinking about it pissed him off.

As a cop, he did everything he could to protect upper Pennsylvania Avenue, where the cream of black culture flourished. Folks dressed to the nines patronized jazz clubs to see Miles, the Duke, or Cab Calloway, who grew up in the neighborhood. Officer Chowder made a point of befriending the "players" on that strip.

He knew there was smoke going on, as well as the world's oldest profession. Just keep the hard stuff out or he'd bust their butts.

His stutter rendered him sensitive to others getting a raw deal in life. For five years, he had been a volunteer at the Max Lewis boxing gym. Teaching a boy to box was secondary to teaching self-discipline and respect. Then he lost his temper on North Avenue and was barred from the gym. That hurt as much as losing his job.

He decided to have a chat with this Sandy Goldberg. That golden Eldorado shouldn't be hard to find. The more he chewed on the thought of that slick ad man coming on to his wife, the more preposterous the possibility became that LuAnn would fall for such glitter. He had let his own feelings get in the way. Give the gal credit. She's as true as they come. He had to get a grip.

On a bitter afternoon, he found the Caddy on the second floor of the jury parking garage. He checked the Timex, 4:45. Could be here any minute. Be a shame to damage such a sharp vehicle, but the crime calls for retribution. The Whispering Pines key, a thick Yale key, should do. From the door to the fins, it dug into the gold, leaving an ugly gash. Satisfied with his work, he walked to the other side and leaned on the Rambler hood, giving him a wide berth for Goldberg's approach. Had no problem waiting…like being a cop again. He unfurled a stick of Wrigley's spearmint and began to chew ever so slowly.

His man came up the stairs at 5:17. Chuck watched his approach. Goldberg had the keys in his hand when he saw the gash. The sight jolted him, as if he had been hit with a cattle prod. "What the?"

"Terrible thing, isn't it?" said Chuck, strolling toward him. "Ruining such a fine paint job, a sacrilege, if you ask me. Car's a piece of art."

"You know who did this?"

His big left hand, his knockout hand, shot out, grabbing the silk tie and starched striped collar. He slammed him against the car.

There was whiskey on Goldberg's breath, probably from a brand that a security guard could not afford. "Know who I am? Take a guess."

"Never seen you," Sandy gurgled.

"Well, I saw you…I'm that fellow at that window in Whispering Pines."

Sandy's eyes looked as though they would pop from the sockets.

Chuck's hand fell away; he let the bad news sink in. The man was less robust than he had envisioned, not more than five feet four. Goldberg tangled with the wrong polecat when he took on LuAnn. Good for her, biting the prick's tongue.

"What do you want from me?"

So satisfying to see the scumbag shaking in his slick Italian shoes. "How about a heart attack? That would even things."

"You need some dough?" Goldberg asked, reaching for his wallet. On reflex, Chuck grabbed Goldberg's hand. Never know… could have a derringer.

He released the hand. "No-not here for mon-money. Nor am I going to beat you up. Wouldn't be a fair fight. I made my statement. Call the cops if you like. I won't deny it. But I'll also tell them you assaulted my wife. Assistant State's Attorney Eckert is a friend of mine."

He crossed the lane and opened the door of the station wagon. Goldberg glowered as Chuck drove off, whistling to "Little Darling" on WCAO AM 60, where the hits live.

Heartbreak Hotel

Couldn't say if heaven had heard L. Wayne Sheer's rant in the empty apartment, but it sure seemed like it. It didn't get any easier in the weeks ahead. Perhaps God was "piling it on." Word of the travesty hit the front page of the community section in the *Baltimore Sun*: "Towson Man Nearly Drowns in Cockeysville Tunnel." He would have some explaining to do at work. Before he had a chance to defend himself, his supervisor called, told Wayne he need not come in for his shift; his job had been terminated.

"Don't I get an appeal?"

"There's no appeal in cases of criminal conduct."

Wayne slammed down the receiver. Seven years of impeccable service down the drain.

Assistant State's Attorney Eckert went easy on his neighbor: no jail time. The defendant lost his driver's license and had to go to AA meetings for six months. Wayne cashed in his pension to pay the fine. Because of negligence, the insurance company rejected the claim. He paid to have the impounded Cadillac towed to the dealer, who bought it back for eight hundred bucks; of that, six hundred went to the lawyer and another fifty to the towing company.

Then came the divorce notice. There were no disputes; she could have it all, even the family heirlooms she'd taken. He signed the papers, costing him his last hundred bucks, putting him on the verge of losing the apartment.

Without purpose, he walked slowly to the playground. At the far end, a mother played with her infant daughter. A pink bow crowned the baby's head. *If only*...the saddest words in the

English language. On the swing, he curled forward, arms crossed at the waist, as if in pain. *If only.* A drop of drool fell to the sandy soil. Hadn't slept much lately. Lyrics from a country song twanged in his head: Next time I won't get married, I'll give her a house…

Somewhere near, among the white pines, came a hoot. Mating season. Wayne cupped his ear and listened for the reply. He spotted the horned owl among the branches, staring at him with those cold, black eyes. Handsome specimen, broad and powerful, talons that could sever a man's finger. Hadn't seen such a predator since he was a teenager hunting deer with a bow and arrow. Another hoot. A flock of sparrows flooded a bush. The baby squealed in wonder.

Time for a drink: a healthy shot of V.O., strictly medicinal, nothing more. Margo had been kind enough to leave the bottle behind. Hadn't touched it since the accident. Along the way, Wayne changed his mind about that snort. One would lead to a second, a third…yes, booze might dull the pain, but to what end? He took the bottle out of the cabinet, unscrewed the cap, and sniffed the tangy aroma. "Gonna miss you," he said, pouring the whiskey down the sink.

That evening he went to his first AA meeting in the smoke-filled basement of the Towson YMCA; a week later he testified that he was an alcoholic. He was the last to raise his hand that evening. The shared stories of heartbreak gave him the courage to speak openly about his time as an ambulance driver in Korea. "I still get panic attacks. A backfire from a truck can set me off." Coming from a religious family that did not share feelings, he had borne this trauma in silence, stiff upper lip and all that jazz. Given a second chance, Wayne planned to make the most of it, one day at a time.

After that meeting, he sat in the booth at Read's drugstore with his sponsors, Steph and Will, a shrunken couple, dry for a decade.

"Three thousand, six hundred, fifty-seven days," said Steph.

"And counting," added Will, blowing smoke out his nose.

The fingers of Steph and Will were yellow with nicotine—Lucky Strikes, LSMFT. He'd seen the two on the streetcar several times, taking the Number 8 to Oriole games. They praised him for being so open about his past, said they were proud of him. Their encouragement failed to lift his spirits. He ordered a vanilla milkshake and a cheeseburger. He had a five-dollar bill in his pocket, all the money in the world.

In the back, the white owner and black cook were exchanging insults. The cook, a teen with a baby face, tossed his apron across the counter and left the drugstore. Steph, Will, and Wayne exchanged looks.

"Now I need a short-order cook," the manager muttered in his East European accent. Wayne knew Constantine Kaseris, a short, squat man with a terrible comb-over who migrated from Greece after the war. Worked a lot of hours. Had a ton of kids he complained about, said they'd put him in an early grave. He was always here, manning the post whenever Wayne came in for a milkshake.

"I can cook," Wayne said.

"I thought you were a streetcar man."

"Was, till recently. Had a mishap," he said, grinning, as if to dismiss it as something small, nothing to worry about.

Kaseris tossed him the apron. "Let's see how you cook that cheeseburger, Mr. Streetcar Man. And make some fries for your friends. On the house."

He started the next day: the two-to-ten shift, six days a week, two bucks an hour. He didn't mind the hours, not at all. The gig had similarities to the streetcar...serving people coming and going. Most of the time, he got along with the kids from Immaculate and Towson Catholic who would drop in before taking the Number 8 downtown.

"What are you doing here?" they would ask.

"New job," he'd say from the window. "How do you want that burger?"

Slowly he dug his way out of the financial and emotional hole. He made rent, ate most of his meals at Read's, and bought a futon at Hutzler's and a couch and table from Goodwill. He found a reading lamp in the trash and rewired it. Add a few odds and ends (a television would be nice) and he'd have what he needed.

On Sundays, he went on long walks around the area, sometimes along the railroad tracks, crossing the trestle at Black & Decker or through the woods on the edge of Towson. One snowy morning he put on his pea coat, slipped on his galoshes and gloves, and hitched a ride in a snowplow out to Pine Ridge. Following the tracks of a cross-country skier across the golf course, he savored the silence, the lack of machinery. His senses sharpened in the cold blue air. The shriek of a red-tailed hawk pierced his ears, followed by the conversation of crows and a glimpse of wild turkeys among the underbrush; last trotted a fox with a beautiful orange tail. At the seventeenth hole, overlooking Loch Raven, Wayne found a golf ball embedded in the frozen green. Prying it loose with his Swiss Army knife, he flung the ball high over the ice. It bounced and bounced toward the center of the reservoir.

With the day waning, he returned to Towson, sloshing several miles to an AA meeting. In the warm basement, the pipes clanged, the radiator hissed, and the stories droned on. He tried to listen but drifted off in the folding chair, head tilted back, mouth open—quite a sight, no doubt.

"You drinkin'?" Will asked over coffee.

"Not a drop."

"You never have it whipped."

He nodded his head in agreement. At the same time, he had no desire to be what was called a "dry drunk," counting off the days of sobriety. That's no way to live, not for him.

So he lived the days, tracking the ebb of winter, the first crocus and snowdrops, buds on trees, songbirds, robins from Florida, the sun intensifying by the day. He spent many a morning before his shift rummaging through secondhand shops and flea markets in quest of something interesting to hang on the wall: a scatter-brained Jackson Pollock print, an Aubrey Bodine photo of a skip-jack, or a broken cuckoo clock bought for a buck. The apartment was becoming a reflection of himself, his better self.

♦♦♦

Margo wasn't the sort to have regrets. Soon as the divorce was final, she changed her name back to Catalano. The Cadillac had been the last straw. Wasn't Wayne's fault…wasn't anybody's fault they couldn't have babies. After the third loss, she couldn't take it anymore. Had to pull away. Was cruel how she did it. Be glad the fool didn't drown in that tunnel. That would've sent her straight to hell. Instead of hitting her, her husband bought a Cadillac—how thoughtful. Parts of that awful, stormy afternoon were starting to fit together. When Wayne saw her in the car with Stan, he must have assumed they were lovers. She did touch Stan on the shoulder, meant nothing, but Wayne didn't know that. Yet, he still tried to win her back. And she told him off before running after the umbrella. Her meanness put him over the edge. Big sin.

Don't get her wrong: she wouldn't go back. When you lose your baby thrice, then your ovaries, game's over, like Jolting Joe and Marilyn. Hope Wayne finds someone who can give him what he needs. She couldn't take Wayne's hound-dog eyes reminding her every second of what they'd lost. Margo clung to her new life. She shared a delightful second-floor flat in West Towson with Lanny, her old college roommate, together again for mischief and fun. Margo felt like she was back in college. She lost herself in crowds.

Slowly she began to heal. She discovered gardening. Not exactly good for the nails, but it gave her a sense of peace. She also devoted herself to the children. Little buggers helped fill that hole in her heart. If she couldn't have kids, why not love the ones she had during the day? Margo could live with that.

Recently she resumed dating, dipping her toe in the water with a long-haired Maryland Art Institute professor whom she had stalked among the marigolds in Radebaugh Florist. The man had a distinguished look...nicely trimmed beard, flecked with gray, in tweed like an Englishman, broad shoulders, no ring on his finger. She passed him twice before returning, sparking a discussion about marigolds, which she knew nothing about. She found that he used marigolds as inspiration for his art—also to keep rabbits away. Clever.

"Are you married?" she blurted.

"No."

"Got a regular girlfriend?"

"Not that I know of."

"You seem to be a gentleman. Here's my phone number. Call me sometime." Her boldness shocked her. Maybe she was ready.

He called the next day and invited her to the Lyric. The American Ballet Theatre was performing Giselle. Such an evening of magic, from champagne to the final bow. After a nightcap at Kent's, he walked her to the front steps of her apartment and leaned forward to kiss her forehead. At the last instant, she pulled away from his touch...wasn't ready, not even for a kiss on the brow. Too much scar tissue.

The following day Tom called her. "Just checking in," he said.

"Thank you for the wonderful evening, Tom. Giselle was amazing."

"I'd like to see you again."

"I'm not sure...been through a lot."

"Let me tell you who I am."

"A Russian spy?"

"Let's say I prefer the company of men. Does that bother you?"

"Not at all, Tom," she said, relieved by the revelation.

"I think we're going to be good friends."

"I agree. You can invite me to the ballet any time."

Tom introduced her to the world of art, music, and dance, yet there were times when she needed solitude, maybe to work in the garden or paint a bird by numbers. She came to the realization that she still had unfinished business. She went to confession to rid herself of the stain, but the priest's forgiveness and the Body of Christ brought little relief.

She had to see Wayne.

On a midafternoon in May, Margo sailed past the glass door and took a center stool at Read's counter. Further down at the grill, Wayne flipped a burger and watched her settle in. Beneath a blue pillbox hat, her raven hair was coiffed with flips that slid along her oval face—the "Annette Funicello" look, his favorite. God, she looked good.

"Aren't you going to say hello?" she said, lighting a Tareyton.

He looked down at the grill. "Let me finish this cheeseburger."

She had picked a good time to come. The lunch crush had ebbed. Constantine was in the back room, going over the books. After Wayne gave the black girl the cheeseburger, he took a stool beside his ex-wife.

"Why are you here, Margo?"

"Thought I'd drop in and sample one of Read's famous hot fudge sundaes. I've had a craving for chocolate all day."

"I'll make it." He started to jump up.

She placed a hand on his arm. "Forget that…I wanted to see you. How are you, Wayne?"

"Big of you to ask."

"You look like you've lost weight."

"Stopped drinking. Lost my beer belly…" Staring at her emerald-green eyes, he thought of the early days of their separation, how he would fantasize on sleepless nights about what he would say if chance brought them together on the streets of Towson. At first, his words were full of anger, resentment, and jealousy. As the weeks passed and the bile in his gut faded, what he wanted to say evolved. He settled on this: "You were hurting, and I wasn't there for you."

"Well, this is a change from the Gary Cooper routine."

"I'm working on it."

"I appreciate the honesty. Don't beat yourself up. I wasn't exactly the best wife."

"The food could have been better."

They both laughed, and something between them eased. He checked out her shapely finger. The chip of a diamond ring he had given her at graduation was gone, along with the wedding band. Tempted to ask if she was with someone, he avoided the question for fear of what he might hear. He tried to enjoy the moment, how she smiled, showing her pearly white teeth, perfectly straight thanks to braces in high school. He had loved her since the tenth grade. She was his girl, the one and only. Even in Korea, he carried a torch for her.

Can't go back. She knew it too. Behind that makeup and eyeliner, Wayne detected melancholy, perhaps regret. They had some good years together. He told her he was sorry they couldn't have a child. "Things may have been different for us."

Margo crushed the Tareyton into the silver ashtray, lit another cigarette, and blew smoke at the ceiling. Now or never, girl. "Wayne…have something to tell you…I'm sorry for what I said to you in the parking lot. It was mean. I drove you crazy."

"You're the reason I lived."

"I read the story in the Sun. What were you thinking?"

"I wasn't." He described the water streaming into the car and his acceptance of fate—until he thought of her.

"Please...stop." She lowered her head in shame.

"Had to find a way out so I could see you again."

Margo tugged at the bottom of her tight skirt. Couldn't get comfortable. Maybe this wasn't such a good idea. "Almost killed you," she said, looking at the floor.

"What?"

"Almost killed you."

"Don't blame yourself, Margo."

"Got to go!" She grabbed her purse and escaped.

What else is new. Wayne returned to the grill. He took orders from the hungry scholars lining the seats. This was his favorite time of day. He enjoyed bantering with the students. A few still called him Streetcar Man.

At six he removed his apron and headed out the door with dinner in a brown bag: a burger and fries, perfect food for the Oriole game on TV. Connie Johnson was pitching.

He nearly dropped the bag when he spotted Margo in the shadows of the building. She was smoking a cigarette...made him think of Lauren Bacall. But he sure wasn't Bogart.

"What gives?" he asked. "You ran like you'd seen a ghost."

"I lied."

"Lied about what?"

"Having an affair."

"I don't understand...what are you talking about?"

She lowered her voice. "Remember when I told you I was unfaithful?"

"In so many words, yeah."

"I made that up so you wouldn't love me anymore."

Wayne shook his head. Her presence made weeks of self-improvement seem a ruse. He didn't need to hear this. All the pain came rushing back. *Jesus!*

"I felt trapped by our grief. I wanted you to go away. I hope someday you can forgive me."

"Stop it, please." He realized he had to go to an AA meeting. Forget the Orioles.

She patted his forearm. "Good for you."

Huh? Adjusting her hat in the reflection, she bade him goodbye and wished him luck. Then she walked out of his life a third time.

He allowed himself one last glance as she crossed York Road...poetry in motion.

NEW DAY COMING

Lena Minnow's encounter with her father at Luke's funeral spurred memories, some she wished not to relive, such as being mocked on the playground: "What's up, High Yellow? You black o' white today?" *Poor baby.* Always deferring, deflecting insults, never confronting, most of all at home when she tried to win Daddy's approval through a drawing, dance, or poem. He'd give her the onceover and move on. Didn't want to rile up Naomi, her stepmom.

From an early age, she cared for her younger siblings: Matthew, Mark, Luke, and John as well as Mary, Elizabeth, and that lovable runt, Toby, who had Down syndrome. Even as the brothers and sisters moved out, she stayed put in that slatted house in East Towson. She stayed because Toby needed her. Naomi shied away from the child, blaming herself for his state. "One too many…too old to have 'im."

So it fell to the stepdaughter to take the boy to the doctor, dentist, and special school. Lena gave him baths when he was little, showed him how to tie his shoes, and made sure there was a present for Toby under the Christmas tree. She didn't complain. The two had a connection. Besides, she had the attic to herself, free to fill the closet with clothes and shoes, stacks of Hollywood magazines, a hundred sticks of lipstick, boxes of hairspray, a pile of makeup, and enough hair straightener for two lives. Eventually, everything sort of spilled across the attic. Daddy called her "a chump" for straightening her hair, for trying to pass. As the years slid by, Lena accumulated so much stuff that Gregorious had difficulty opening her door. He threatened to set the place on fire, to get rid of the shit. "Be easier to build another house." When Toby went to his heavenly reward at fifteen, only then did she anticipate moving out.

Meeting that Towson High math teacher six years ago at the Lion's Club shuffled the cards in the deck of life. Suppose she hadn't accepted Eckert's invitation to attend the social? Would she still be in that slate house, under the thumb of Daddy? God forbid. Maybe fate brought them together.

She remembered holding off calling Beau until the next afternoon—didn't want to appear too anxious. He answered the phone in a groggy voice.

"Sorry disturbing you..." In the background she heard violins. "Let me turn down the radio...now I can hear you. So nice of you to call, Lena."

"Hope I didn't wake you."

"Not at all, I was listening to *Don Giovanni*. It's my favorite activity on Saturday afternoon, lying on the couch and being transported into another world. Helps recharge the batteries. You like opera?"

"Don't know much about it."

"You doing anything this evening?"

Nothing she could think of. Could darn her socks, do some laundry—she was a busy woman.

"I'm busy, too...almost finished the *New York Times* crossword puzzle. I'm a font of extraneous knowledge. Want to see a movie tonight? The *King and I* is showing at the Senator. How about the six-thirty show?"

"Works for me...meet you there at six fifteen."

"Don't you want me to pick you up?

"I'll be running around. See you there."

After she hung up—she had a private line so Daddy wouldn't listen in—Lena was thrown into action. What to wear? Hair a mess. Which nail polish? Skirt or slacks? So many choices. She went through scores of outfits crammed in the closet, some with sales tags. Deliberating in the shower, she chose a pleated leather skirt short of the knee, a Caribbean-blue silk blouse, dark nylons, and faux suede boots. She painted her nails a light shade of brown to match the leather, took a chance with an off-white lipstick, and, using the iron, straightened her shoulder-length hair. It was black with a tinge of her mother's auburn. In the mirror, Lena scrutinized the image. Too often she fixated on the booty. Not this time. *Damn, woman, you a knockout!* She added a spritz of perfume as a last touch.

She snuck out the back door to avoid Daddy "foot propping" with his rum and coke on the front porch. She refused to give him the chance to comment on her appearance, destination, or purpose.

Gregorious Shade blew a mean harp, taking it down to the bone; bluesy riffs trailed his daughter for a block. She took the Number 8 down York to Northern Parkway, a block from the Senator. He was waiting in front of the art deco theater. As she approached, Beau was a sight to behold: green bow tie, stiff white shirt, and high-waist khaki pants. Add the round specs, and he became the proverbial math nerd, complete with Einstein hair and a high, lined forehead that gave him a perpetual look of wonder. She liked what she saw.

Halfway through the movie, he took her hand. His touch made it difficult to focus on the big screen romance between an English woman and a Siam royal. The Rodgers and Hammerstein songs didn't move her; she preferred Daddy's boogie woogie on the piano. You couldn't sit still. Beau, however, was enthralled, his right hand swishing to the beats of the orchestra. Deborah Kerr and Yul Brynner skipped around the royal court. "*Shall we dance! Shall we dance! Shall we dance!*" For Lena, the Brit was too deferential to the stuck-up king. Should've told him to shove it.

In the lobby after the movie, he asked if she had driven here.

"To tell the truth," she replied, "I don't have a car."

He opened the door for her. "Then why did you tell me yesterday you had a car?"

At nearly the same height, 5'6", they faced one another on the sidewalk, not sure what came next. She considered telling Beau she did drive a car yesterday, Daddy's Desoto, but why add another fib to the mix? The heck with it. She told him she would "tell all" over a drink. Swallow at the Hollow was down at the corner. She could catch the Number 8 there. A couple of pops at the bar should suffice.

"I made reservations at Southern Comfort."

The high-end segregated restaurant gave her pause. "Isn't that formal?" she said. "We're not dressed for the occasion."

"Oh, that's the main dining room of the hotel. We're going to the Guadalajara Villa, their roof garden on the twelfth floor."

"The roof garden…"

"Is that a problem? We can go somewhere else."

"No, of course not, let's go to Southern Comfort. Be my first time."

"You're in for a treat."

"I'm sure."

Across the parking lot, Beau's car was tucked away in the corner, away from the other vehicles. The last rays of the sun shone on the sparkling black hood of the '55 Thunderbird. Daddy would love this original car. The white seats seemed to glow.

"Your chariot, madam. Hope you don't mind the top down."

"You kidding? I have enough spray on this helmet to stop a hurricane."

Beau didn't drive like a math teacher. He drove more like Sterling Moss, zipping through the gears, chirping over the wind about "his baby," recently purchased at an auction on North Avenue for a third of the original price. Only had 10k, didn't think he could afford such a vehicle…

Half listening, Lena enjoyed the speed and hum of the engine, the sense of freedom she felt with this man. It was an adventure.

"You have to steer the mass," Beau said, handing the key to the valet.

How true, thought Lena.

They rode the glass elevator. The blinking lights of Baltimore Street shone below. Beau commented on the barkers, the vaudeville at the Gayety, the action.

"You go there often to see strippers?"

"No, but my seniors do. They tell me all about it."

"So," Lena said playfully, "might you be a voyeur?"

"The very opposite. You're looking at someone who's hopelessly romantic."

The doors opened and a garden of palms, orchids, and ferns beckoned. A man in a white tuxedo led them to a table by a fake banana tree. Below, lights of the working harbor flickered on the docks. Excursion boats were crossing Patapsco. Tugboats tooted and the bells of Peabody rang in the nine o'clock hour.

Lena scanned the diners, not a brown skin in sight. Could hear Daddy now, calling her a hypocrite. She sipped her margarita, hoping to make the best of the situation.

"Well," said Beau, "please tell me why you fibbed. Did you walk home?"

"Yes…I didn't want you to see where I live."

"And where is that?"

"Please, don't use that tone like I'm one of your students."

"Sorry…"

"I live in East Towson…Coloredtown. And, by the way, James Baldwin is my favorite writer, not Hemingway. And my Daddy is a janitor. Sometimes he cleans the music department."

"O…kay."

"It's complicated." Lena looked out at the harbor, wishing she were on that yacht heading for wider waters. Did she lie because she felt ashamed? Maybe, deep down, she longed to be white. Be so much easier. A feeling of loss flooded her heart. Why did she have to choose one race over the other? She suggested a second margarita and he readily agreed.

Beneath the canvas awning, a mariachi band took the stage. Each man wore tight black pants, a vest lined with silver, and cowboy boots. They broke into song, scattering the sea gulls. She shouted over the blare of trumpets: "Let me explain!" She never knew her white mother, Camille, the vaudeville singer. Daddy raised her, along with Naomi, his wife—

"You have exquisite cheekbones."

The compliment struck her as contrived, too quick on the draw, for she hardly knew the man. Turning toward the stage, she pretended to take an interest in the band. She had no wish to be viewed as an object of curiosity, something exotic, as had occurred on past dates when she revealed her identity.

A sip of a fresh drink gave her face a warm glow. Might as well try to enjoy this rare evening out. Perfect weather, soft breeze… could be worse.

Stilting their conversation were the guitars, trumpets, and the lyrics, a lament about *una amante,* a lover left behind in Guatemala. During the second course—grilled rockfish stuffed with crab, washed down with chenin blanc—the show, mercifully, ended. Bowing in sequence to the polite applause, the mustached men left the stage. The bells and toots on the harbor returned.

"Please go on about your stepmother. I'm so sorry I interrupted you."

Lena took a deep breath. "Sometimes she called me 'the Devil's seed.' "

He raised a single, bushy eyebrow. "You don't look like Beelzebub to me."

"Don't make fun of me. It's a touchy subject."

"Ah, the chocolate mousse—"

"Not sure I should continue."

"Please," he said, taking her hand.

"Your right eye is off."

"You noticed." He removed his round specs and pointed to his eye. "I was born cross-eyed. Then they botched the operation. Boys on the playground designated me as One-Eyed Jack because I wore a patch. I know what it's like not to fit in. I'm a bachelor at fifty. Will you please tell me about your stepmother?"

Over strong Mexican coffee, Lena shared her story in a matter-of-fact way. Painful as it was to talk about Naomi and her father, she didn't want her audience to see her as a victim. She was talking about Toby when a more immediate concern arose...lot going on down there. Wasn't used to this much drinking. Had to compose herself in the restroom, splash some water on the face, add a fresh coat of white on the lips. That's better. Now, if she could return to the table without stumbling, concentrate on each step...

Beneath the string of colored lights, Beau was gazing at the moon. As she eased herself into the chair, he broke into song, "Blue Moon...you saw me standing alone...without a dream in my heart...without a love of my own."

Lena's fork tinged the water glass in appreciation. "Didn't know you could sing."

"I'm a closet lounge lizard."

"Thank you for the lovely dinner." *Hic!*

"You're welcome."

"There's one problem," she said with a slight slur. "I'm tipsy. You can't take me home like this. Don't want Daddy seeing me."

"Oh, your Daddy, I see. How about coming to my place? Sober up with some green tea and then I'll take you home."

"As long as you go easy on the gears."

On the way to his apartment, Beau started jabbering about the car, and the world started to spin. Please, she told him, please be quiet. Silent for the rest of the drive, he smoothly shifted the Thunderbird, and Lena made it to their destination without drama. Beau lived in a fourth-floor walk-up on upper Calvert, a block from Johns Hopkins University. His arm steadied her as they took the steps. Passing apartment C, they heard a television blaring a commercial for Ice Blue Secret, "…for superior wetness and odor protection!" On the third floor, the door to apartment F was open, and they came upon a smoke-filled party, hosted by JHU students. People were jitterbugging to Chuck Berry's "Maybelline."

"Time I get to the top, I'll be sober," joked Lena.

She hadn't intended to spend the night. Only wanted to rest a spell, so tired…

Next thing she knew she woke up on the bed, beneath a sheet. Still had her clothes on, save for the shoes. Her mouth tasted like the Sahara. She vaguely remembered asking for a bucket. There it was, by the bed, unused.

With a throbbing headache, she rose and tested her balance. Squinting, she shuffled into the living room; Beau was on the sofa, snoring up a storm. The sunlight streaming through the big windows was almost too much to bear. A spider web hung from the molding. Place must have been a grand at one time; even had pocket doors.

Beau's eyes opened, and he gave her an upside-down smile. Never dated a blue-eyed man. Without glasses, he appeared younger, more vulnerable. His skin was fair, verging on albino. Bet he stayed out of the sun. "Want some orange juice?" he asked, throwing off the blanket. Dressed in Baltimore Oriole PJs, he padded into the kitchen. On a silver tray, he brought back two crystal glasses along with a pitcher of orange juice, made from frozen concentrate.

"Like your pajamas," she said, gulping down the juice. She placed the glass on the tray.

"Birthday present from Mama."

What Mother would give her middle-aged son PJs? Lena explored the space, combing the antique desk, the pile of math tests between inkwells, the paintings of horses, the family photos lining the shelf, going back generations.

"What's this?" she asked, scrutinizing an oil painting.

"Our farmhouse. Mother painted it. She also painted the horses. That's her specialty, equestrian painting."

"She's very good."

"I'll tell her next time I see her."

"And where in the South would that be?"

"We're Marylanders, born and bred, one of the original families on the Eastern Shore. Our plantation isn't far from Crisfield, where you can get the best seafood on the East Coast."

Plantation? She poured herself a second glass of orange juice. Never had any wish to visit the Eastern Shore, not exactly the best place for black folk. Back in '33, the last lynching in Maryland occurred on the other side of the Chesapeake. Wasn't that long ago. Bet things haven't changed a bit. Lena emptied the glass, ready to go home.

Gregorious was waiting for her on the porch, playing a version of that old "Rugged Cross" on his harmonica. He lowered the harp; his eyes narrowed as he watched Beau open the door of the Thunderbird, holding Lena's hand as she rose from the bucket seat.

"Hope you're feeling better, sugar," he said.

"Hangovers don't last forever. Thank you for a most interesting evening, Mr. Minnow." She shook his hand. Lingering at her fingertips, he asked her to call him sometime.

"I'm not sure. You and I come from different worlds."

The bells of Calvary Methodist rang down the street. A septuagenarian couple in their Sunday best slowed their walk on the opposite sidewalk. Had to look at that straw-haired man. Who was he? Didn't know Lena had a boyfriend.

"Give us a try, Lena. What do you have to lose?"

Beau waved and pulled slowly away from the curb, not wishing to disturb the peace of this Sunday morning. That had been Lena's last request, not to rile Daddy with a rip of the tires. Pocketbook in hand, she walked toward the house. Daddy was giving her the third degree before she reached the steps. She didn't appreciate his snooping, not today.

"By the way," he added, "you look awful."

"Thanks for the compliment. Had a little too much fun last night."

"That's what you get for hangin' around that cracker."

"How do you know he's a cracker?"

"From the way he spoke, sweet and polite. Got the master's blood running through his veins."

"Who I see and what I do is my own business."

"Not while you live under this roof!"

Two days later, she called Beau, more out of spite than anything. He asked if she'd like to see *The Ten Commandments* at the Timonium Drive-in.

"What time?"

"Eight thirty."

"Pick me up at Read's."

"Whatever you say, Lena."

On a moonless night, the T-bird rolled into the Timonium Drive-in. During the previews, Lena asked Beau if he knew what he was getting himself into.

"I'd like to find out," he answered.

Strategically parked in the last row, Beau made his move while Charlton Heston came upon the burning bush. As God spoke to Moses, Lena accepted Beau's touch. Big surprise—great kisser, soft on the lips, no rush to the promised land. She kissed him till her tongue got tired. At the end of the date, she gave him the number of her private phone.

Next date they went on a picnic at Federal Hill, spreading the checkered tablecloth on the crest of a knoll, among the cannons that protected the harbor from the Confederates. He had made crab cakes, his mother's recipe; egg potato salad, also her recipe; and a beet salad, yes, inspired by his mama. Didn't really care for the red vegetable, but she tried it anyway and found it delicious. Not only could this man sing, he could also cook.

A white policeman approached on the sidewalk that ringed the park. He was flipping his billy club out and snatching the black wood on its return, a playful motion, but, for her, it hinted of violence. Suppose her skin tone was like Daddy's? Would the cop tip his hat like now? Would he leave us be? Or would he prod us to move on, as if we were trash.

They watched the sunset and finished the last of the Riesling. She agreed to go to his apartment for "a spot of tea." They were in the bedroom before the teapot was whistling. She requested he light a candle…and turn down that grim photo of his mother. Putting Mama in the drawer, he removed his boxers and slid under the sheets. What was she getting into? Looked like a whole lot of loving. She dropped her slip and joined him. Been a long stretch since a man held her with such reverence, if ever.

Beau 's Thunderbird became a familiar sight in East Towson. Lena Shade and Beau Minnow, math teacher at Towson High, became the talk of the neighborhood. The spinster was dating a white man with a black sports car. Gregorious, not pleased by this budding romance, knew he could push his daughter only so far. He let her be, hoping the fling would run its natural course. He had no problem being solicitous to the white man, exchanging pleasantries about the weather and the baseball team—been doing that all his life. *You go along to get along.*

Through the summer and into the fall, Beau and Lena became inseparable on weekends, going to Colt and Oriole games at Memorial Stadium, movies at the Senator, an opera at the Lyric.

Not only were they lovers, they had become best friends, sharing many common interests. The only time they didn't spend the weekend together occurred when he paid his parents a visit to the plantation. The word simmered in her mind...she knew for a fact that in Maryland, a biracial couple could be thrown in the pokey if they marry. In the eyes of the law, Lena Shade was a negro through and through.

On an Indian summer evening, Beau proposed to her on the fire escape outside the window of his apartment. They were watching the sunset when he popped the question. What did he mean, marry? What about his Mama and the plantation? Lena had a hundred reasons to say no. But, looking at the emerald ring in his hand, she said yes, surprising herself. Usually had the hardest time making decisions. At forty-six, she was still living at home, for God's sake!

Beau said the ring once belonged to his great grandmother, meant a lot to him. If she didn't care for the antique, he could find something else.

"Don't you dare," she said. He slipped it on her finger. The blue stone had a brilliant sheen. To her dying day, she would wear this ring.

She dreaded meeting the folks. Joseph and Mary Minnow lived on a 250-acre tobacco plantation outside of Crisfield. It had been handed down from one generation to the next. Only thing Lena knew about Crisfield, aside from the seafood, was the James Reed lynching in 1907. She read about it in the Brown Section of the Sunday Sun. A mob strung up the negro for supposedly killing the police chief.

Beau said his father asked that they wear work clothes. "Why?" Lena asked.

"Maybe he wants us to muck out the stall...show what we're made of."

"You're kidding."

"I am."

Going over the Chesapeake Bay Bridge that chilly November Sunday didn't stop Beau from riding with the top down. With the windows up and the heat on high, it was tolerable. On the Eastern Shore, she felt as though they were entering another country—saw more Confederate flags hanging from houses, shops, and car antennas than the Stars and Stripes. At the Esso station, Lena could hear Daddy's voice in her head when she used the white bathroom.

Down the road, she asked that they stop at a stand for homemade ice cream; a scoop of vanilla might settle her stomach. Then Lena eyed the sign. "We have the right to refuse service." She sat at the counter and ordered nothing.

"Thought you wanted ice cream."

"Lost my appetite."

Back on the road, Beau insisted they be open about her heritage. There shouldn't be secrets in the family. She asked if his parents were racists. Cultural racists, he admitted, not mean people but God fearing and honest as the day was long.

"Cultural racists. Never heard such a term."

"They treat the help well and equally, no matter their skin color."

"Will they view me as the help?"

"My ass, they will. I won't have you disrespected."

"I hope this works out, Beau, for your sake. My daddy, I'm afraid, doesn't want anything to do with you. Would be nice to become part of your family—if they can get past their culture."

"Is your Daddy a racist?"

"Pull off the road."

"Why?"

"Do it!" The car ground to a halt on gravel, next to a fallow corn field. He turned off the engine. It pinged as he stared at the flat land, waiting for her to speak. A semi rolled past, shaking the Thunderbird. "Look at me, Beau." He turned to face her. "You have no idea of what Daddy's been through…" Back in the early twenties, while visiting relatives in Carolina, he hid in a hayloft and watched his cousin Zeke be tortured for spitting on a white woman in a dispute over unpaid wages. Sheriff arrested him for assault and put him in a cell. Then the sheriff decided to teach this young buck a lesson in manners. At sundown, he marched the prisoner to the edge of town, ripped off his shirt, and tied him to a tree: started bull-whipping the back, slow at first, nips at the skin. Between slashes, he'd say something to the boy. It became a spectacle, with half the town showing up, including the KKK. Sheriff handed over the whip. They took turns, seeing who could make the negro scream the most. "Can you imagine? No, you can't. Neither can I…because I have spent most of my adult life passing as white."

"What happened to Zeke?"

"They let him crawl home. Weeks later he hung himself in the barn…don't want to talk about it anymore. It's too much. Maybe, Beau, we should call off the engagement. Might be best for everyone."

"Not for you and not for me, the hell with everyone else!"

"You needn't shout."

Lowering his voice, he said he didn't live for the approval of others, did she? "We love each other, that you cannot deny. Why shouldn't we be together?"

"It's not that sim—"

He leaned over, took her face in his hands, and kissed her lips. Cars swished by blowing their horns. "You win," Lena said, coming up for air. "Let's go see Joseph and Mary."

Beau started the engine and spun out of the gravel.

By the time they reached the Minnow farm, Lena had prepared herself for whatever was to come. If Beau's folks were polite on the surface, she would give them space to accept her. Might take a while getting used to having a biracial female in the family.

Seeing the sculpture of the black lawn jockey by the driveway didn't help.

Mr. and Mrs. Minnow lived in a nineteenth-century brick farmhouse that Lena could grow used to, particularly the wrap-around porch and view of the pond. She could see herself at sunset on the swing, iced tea in hand, watching the blue heron fish.

Mary met them at the door. She was a bent woman in a faded yellow dress. Her knuckles were swollen with arthritis. Beau hugged his Mama as if she were glass, about to shatter at any point. Mrs. Minnow shook Lena's hand; the firmness of the grip surprised her.

In overalls and a checkered flannel shirt, Joseph grimaced, rising from the rocking chair. He turned off the football game. He was a weathered man with defined features, prominent cheek-bones, spotted hands, and veiny forearms. Hard of hearing, he greeted Beau with a shout: "There you are!"

Lena glanced at the oil painting of Jesus above the fireplace. Impossible to miss. Surrounded by a halo, He was stepping from the tomb. "Like it?" Mr. Minnow asked. "Mother painted it."

Lena didn't quite know what to say. The Savior was practically buck naked, his wounds elongated. "Striking," she replied.

"I was inspired by the Lord," said Mary. "By the way, what religion are you?"

"I was raised Methodist."

"As long as you believe in Christ, you'll be saved. We'll pray for you—won't we, Joseph?"

"Huh? Oh, yes, prayer is good. Welcome to our house, Lena. Glad you took my advice and wore down-home clothes. Ready to go on the water?"

One thought dominated as Joseph drove them to the dock in his pickup: Sitting between the two men, she wondered when Beau would raise the reality of their impending union. She wasn't about to. That had always been her way, to go passive and avoid confrontations; there was no other way dealing with Naomi, her late stepmother.

Beau could say something to his father on the crab boat as they peacefully chugged along the bluish gray waters of the Little Annemessex. Upriver lay Mr. Minnow's oyster bed, seeded six months earlier with spats.

"Would you call yourself a waterman?" Lena asked, watching him pull in a crab pot.

"Goodness sake, no," he said, shaking a few crabs into the cooler. He replaced the bait and tossed the cage back into the water. "I do this for fun. My daily bread comes from tobacco, next on the tour. But first, the oysters. You do like oysters, don't you, Lena?"

"Raw, fried, breaded, baked, bring them on."

"Music to my ears." Joseph pointed out the osprey nests and bald eagles along the shore. She couldn't help but like the tobacco farmer. Using long tongs, he scraped the oysters into the metal basket. "Now you do it," he said to Lena.

"Can't."

"Why not?" said Beau. "You can't be part of the family until you go oystering with Dad."

"Use 'em like scissors," said Joseph.

Lena was pleased to haul in a few oysters, add them to the pile. Joseph picked through the oysters, throwing back in the river the ones with spats on their shells. There was no mention of race on the return to the dock…nor in the tobacco barn with its gables, frame construction and ventilation for air-cured tobacco. Standing beneath the leaves, taking in the scent, Lena had a burning desire for a cigarette.

When Beau and his dad fell into a deep discussion about the tobacco business, Mrs. Minnow showed her the home, warmed by fireplaces and a pot belly stove in the kitchen, making it the most comfortable room in the drafty house. Lena scanned the tin ceiling, iron oven, deep sink, and sturdy oak table that Joseph built early in their marriage. Most of the Shaker-style furniture, she learned, had been crafted by his own hand.

Later, she, Joseph, and Mary sat at that table slurping chilled oysters as fast as Beau could shuck them. For an early dinner, Mary served baked crab imperial, smoked sea bass, and squash from the garden.

Lena helped with the dishes, doing the washing while Mary dried and stacked them on the shelves. Maybe Beau was postponing the revelation. Fine with her. She was enjoying the visit. Up the spiral staircase, Mrs. Minnow showed Lena the bedrooms that once held their children, now scattered around the country. In the fading light, she took Lena to see the family cemetery, situated in the eastern corner of the property. The setting sun illuminated the worn markers, mournful angels, and crosses. "Resting in the arms of Jesus," words dating back to 1846, the year of the master's death. Wonder if any of Edgar Minnow's slaves were buried here, resting in the arms of the Savior....

Back at the house, Joseph said the land had been in the Minnow family for 120 years, meant the world to him. Now it was a question whether it would be passed on or sold to a developer. The other children had no interest in farm life. Couldn't wait to move to the big city. He and Mary had pinned their hopes on Beau, the youngest. Maybe he would study agriculture at the University of Maryland and take over the place. Instead, he decided to become a teacher, which turned out to be a good choice. He was no farmer. "You must be special, Lena. I thought my son was the eternal bachelor."

By the time they got to the rhubarb pie and coffee in the living room, Lena assumed that Beau had put off spilling the beans. Could be wise, get to know one another first. On the hi-fi, Perry Como was singing about some enchanted evening. Mary was humming along. Joseph threw a big log on the fire and sparks shot up the chimney. He puffed on his pipe between sips of brandy. The crystal glass bore the family initials. Lena viewed him as the picture of contentment, a man at peace, so different from Daddy.

"What a nice time," Lena said, thanking them for the hospitality. "I have a new appreciation for watermen...and oysters."

"You're welcome, Lena," said Mary. "We loved having you and Beau. Have you made plans for the wedding? Can't wait to meet your family."

"There's something you need to know," said Beau. "Lena's father is a negro."

The plate slipped from Mary's hand, clattering on hardwood. "Oh dear...oh dear!" Mary retreated into the kitchen. The fire roared and Joseph clenched his jaw. Hell, even the beagle howled after gobbling up the cake.

It was the oddest thing. Joseph spoke as if she were invisible. "Son," he said, turning his back toward her, "should you marry this negress, you could end up in jail. Don't you know the law?"

"What law?" asked Beau.

"That a white person is forbidden to marry a negro, American Indian, or Asian. The white race shouldn't be diluted. People should stay with their own kind."

"Bullshit, I have every right to marry Lena."

"Not what the law says. At least you won't be having children."

"So disown me!"

"Maybe I will..."

As the argument escalated, Lena withdrew into herself. On the way here, they passed a big billboard showing young Martin Luther King in a classroom. The bold red headline accused King of being a communist. Scanning the AM radio dial last week, she came across some authority saying that J. Edgar Hoover, the FBI director, had proof that King was a Russian stooge, trained to tear the country apart. The capper came in Kent's, a local watering hole where she and Beau liked to meet on Fridays after work. Sitting at the bar, she overheard Judge Grayson, a man she respected, discussing civil rights and the push for voter registration in the South. "They're not ready," Grayson concluded.

They're not ready.

Lena rose and headed toward the bathroom in the hall. She washed her hands and looked at herself in the mirror. What was she doing here? In the hallway, she took her coat from the closet and discreetly opened and closed the front door, stepping into the chill. Felt good to move, to get away. Reaching Stonewall Road, she turned left and headed toward Crisfield, leaving the tobacco field behind. Surely there would be a Greyhound bound for Baltimore this Sunday evening. If not, she'd spend the night in a cheap hotel, using her white skin as a passport.

Night was closing in. She could see her breath as she walked along the edge of the road. The smell of fish from packing plants permeated the air. Through the window of a tar roof shack, a black family of six sat around the dinner table, hands folded, heads bowed in prayer. Made her heart ache with envy. Naomi had poisoned her relationship with her younger stepbrothers and sisters. Lena was looked upon not as a true-blue Shade, but someone tainted with sin.

Ahead, an ebony man in a white mink coat sat in an idling Lincoln Continental. The electric window came down as she approached. In a voice that conjured Harry Belafonte, he called her "sister," asking with a Cheshire smile if she be in need of "a taste." Felt as though Old Scratch himself had been waiting for her to come traipsing down this dark passage. Tempting to join him in the warm front seat. Maybe he could give her a ride to Baltimore.

Shivering, Lena shook her head and passed on. Approaching the lights of Main Street, she resisted looking back…might be following in that big white car. The smell of fish intensified…no bus station in sight. Not a whole lot going on. Watermen rose early in Crisfield.

The T-bird came to a screeching halt. Beau leaned over and threw open the door. "Lena," he pleaded, "please get in.

"What happened to your eye?"

"Joseph poked me."

"You fought your father over me?"

"Aren't you worth it?"

After a glance up the slope—the Lincoln had vanished—she climbed into the car. "Let's go home, Beau." She was asleep on his shoulder before they reached the Bay Bridge.

The next day Lena looked up the miscegenation law in the courthouse library. Yep, still on the books in Maryland. Been there since 1692. Three weeks later, Beau and Lena were married in Elkton, an intimate affair without family.

"Here's to my partner in crime," said Beau, toasting his wife on their wedding night.

Looking back, she wouldn't change a thing. The story of their first date, Lena with her bucket, became a running joke in their four-year marriage. Not only was he a terrific lover, he became an intimate friend, someone she could confide in, someone always there for her. After his death, she caught herself for months wandering from room to room in the apartment, talking to him as if he were still alive instead of buried in the family plot on the Eastern Shore.

At Beau's funeral at Immaculate Conception, no one from either side of the family attended. Dozens of his former students and colleagues at Towson High did turn out. Hadn't realized how beloved Beau was as a teacher. When she told Mrs. Minnow on the phone about Beau's passing, Mary alluded to Lena that she might have been the cause of the strokes. Thanks for nothing. When the Minnows requested Beau's body, Lena had a mind to turn them down, but what would be the point? After the funeral, she drove Beau's T-bird behind the Hearse until it turned down the dirt road leading to the plantation.

Something was different now. That incident in Hutzler's tearoom had galvanized her. When Daddy told the story of walking through the slave quarters, she began to see her father in a different light. He never did call her—proud fool, probably waiting for her to make the first move. How forlorn he looked in the rain, watching her cab depart. didn't want that to be her last memory.

The phone rang several times, and she was on the verge of hanging up when she heard his voice rasp a hello. "I thought you were going to call me," she said.

"Been busy," Daddy said.

"Get out…what've you been doing?"

"Why should you care? Ain't I the one to blame for your misery?"

"Let's not go down that road. I called because there's something I must say to you."

"Say it then."

"I forgive you…"

Dead silence on the other end. Was that a sob?

He hung up. She called him back. He answered on the first ring. Before he could say a word one way or the other, she said it again. Then she asked if he would care to come to her Whispering Pines apartment for Sunday supper, "Apartment 3C, 7903 Knollwood." Give them a chance to become reacquainted. And if any of the brothers or sisters were around, invite them too.

"You sure? Might blow your cover if people found out your immediate family was colored."

"I don't care. Five o'clock work for you?"

"I'll bring a bottle of burgundy."

"Good…see you then."

Lena looked around her apartment. Recently, she had reclaimed this space. So freeing to let go of Beau's shoes, suits, shirts, pants, and ties, along with his books, magazines, including much of the furniture they had bought for the house they intended to buy. She also had pared down her own stuff. How many pairs of shoes or cans of hair spray did she need? Now she could have people over without being embarrassed by the state of her home. So what if tenants grumbled about negroes on the property. Get used to it.

That afternoon she decided to pay a visit to the Whispering Pines white-haired manager, Murray Sherwood. His office was across Knollwood. Tapping the cane, she made her way down the sidewalk, crossed the street, and took care going down the cement steps to the basement office. Opening the door, she was pleased to find Murray at his desk. He swung his chair around. "How can I help you, Mrs. Minnow?"

Leaning on her cane, Lena caught her breath. "Murray, I have a strange request. Could you please find my application from '49? I need to change something."

"Not sure I can find it." He removed his rimless glasses and blew on the lens. "Why do you need this document?"

"I marked the box that I was white. Should've checked black. I'm a biracial person."

Murray methodically cleaned the glasses. A sly grin appeared at the corner of his mouth. Did he find this amusing? You never know with white people. He said it was no longer an issue.

"What about the covenant? No black people. Aren't you going to make me move?" She was half-hoping to make a spectacle of being thrown out of her apartment, maybe chain herself to the banister or something. Get on the evening news.

He placed the glasses back on the bridge of his nose. "Times are changing, Mrs. Minnow."

"Not fast enough."

Outside the office, she looked at the breaking clouds and speculated on her next move. Maryland needed changing, and she wanted to be part of that change. She knew about Route 40: negro couldn't get a cup of coffee in any number of establishments. There were separate restrooms and entrances across the state, north and south, east and west. If arrested at a sit-in, would she lose her job as court reporter? She had been in the courtroom when those brave defendants entered, freedom riders, arrested for trespassing and disorderly conduct. They were bruised and bandaged. Wonder how they got those wounds? They were sentenced to thirty days in the Towson jail, a stone fortress that once held runaway slaves. Was she willing to take that risk?

Might be shameful of them putting a widow with a cane into a paddy wagon. Yes, there would be risks. Could get violent. Could end up in jail. But she had no choice. Lena had to be true to herself. It's a new day coming.

ANGER LESSONS

ASSISTANT STATE'S ATTORNEY RANDY Eckert, Sr., was in his office, glaring at the mirror. He was angry that he was angry. His face was beet red. Laughter and chatter in the hallway. No wonder. Look what you did yesterday at Pine Ridge, during a spur-of-the-moment match on a rare warm day in late February. The ground was mushy, causing him to chunk his shots over and over, till he lost it on the fifteenth, helicoptering a nine iron and nearly beheading a goose. This morning his boss, State's Attorney Frank Usher, spread the rumor that Rusty had maimed a duck at Pine Ridge. Ha, ha, ha, very funny, Frank, who pocketed Eckert's twenty-dollar bill at the end of the round.

Then there was Shirl, who flinched when he touched her hair in the kitchen last night. Afraid of her own father? That wasn't good.

And don't forget the fine job you did with Rusty. For weeks now he and Rusty had been ships passing in the night.

He threw himself into the Van Cliffe case. He had no qualms asking for the gas chamber. Some in the courthouse might accuse the assistant state's attorney of being a publicity hound...didn't hurt seeing his name in the *Jeffersonian* paper or being quoted on WBAL radio. Come on, the man had beaten his wife to a pulp; then, just to ensure that Mrs. Van Cliffe was deader than roadkill, he pulverized her bones with his Rolls before dumping her into the Jones Falls sludge. The police found him next to the pit in his station wagon, a .38 in his hand. He was talking to his beloved Mildred as if she were sitting next to him, hanging on every word. The cops convinced him to surrender the gun.

Van Cliffe pled temporary insanity. Bullshit, Eckert told the DA. Usher had considered trying the case himself for political reasons (like flies to pies, high-society crime attracts media), but he deferred to his burly assistant because both men knew Eckert was the better man for a case like this. He was a shark in cross-examination. And he could connect with juries.

Eckert drew pleasure from exposing liars, especially the pros on the circuit. Not every expert witness was crooked, but for those who were, he loved nothing more than tearing apart their arguments, getting them to contradict their own testimony. He had parried twice with the psychiatrist scheduled to testify on Van Cliffe's behalf, one Doctor Lee Curtis, who had an irritating, tinny voice and a haughty attitude that came from a lifetime of self-praise. Eckert had lost both cases because of that intellectual snob. He looked forward to a third bout.

He spent his evenings, amidst the swirl of six children, studying the medical books he checked out of the Enoch Pratt Library. He wanted to know everything about this term "temporary insanity." Was it really a medical condition? How does that excuse this murderous behavior? He also had Miss Peters, his intern, investigate similar cases in the law library. Based on rulings that narrowed the interpretation, temporary insanity was a shaky defense, not often used.

The defense, the best money could buy, chose not to put Van Cliffe on the stand; wise move, thought Eckert. Would have loved the chance to cut that snooty bastard a new one. Through the testimony of cops, doctors, and the coroner, Eckert painted a picture of the crime, from the initial blows in the kitchen to the Rolls rolling over her body. "Imagine the snapping of bones…" The photos were gruesome, and he knew he had drawn blood when he saw the revulsion on the faces of a couple of jurors. He had to convince them of the man's malicious and calculated intent beyond a reasonable doubt.

Mrs. Peggy Grove, a Roland Park socialite who hosted the party the Van Cliffes attended, was the last witness before Doctor Curtis. He asked if she had seen any tension or anger between Mr. and Mrs. Van Cliffe.

"Oh no," she said. "They spent most of the evening holding hands."

"Didn't Mrs. Van Cliffe make fun of her husband's height?"

"I was in the kitchen. Not sure what happened…." Something was amiss. He had made that up. Stepping down from the witness stand, she glanced at Van Cliffe. Eckert read her sympathy for the defendant.

No matter. He had plenty of evidence. Everything was riding on his cross-examination of Dr. Curtis, who testified that Mr. Van Cliffe, because of his "episodic disease," was not responsible for the murder of his wife.

Now it was his turn. Flexing his deltoids, Eckert rose from his seat.

"Dr. Curtis," he said in a leisurely tone, "help me out here. You claim this episode of mental illness was a temporary condition. Is that correct?"

"That is correct."

"How long would this condition last?"

"Until the anger recedes…"

"So, was he insane when he beat his wife to death?"

"Yes."

"Was he insane when he ran his Rolls-Royce over her body?"

"Yes."

"When he wrapped her corpse in a blanket and stuffed it into his station wagon, was he insane then?"

"Yes."

"Okay, so then he drove approximately eleven miles down Falls Road. If he's traveling at the thirty-mile-per-hour speed limit—don't imagine he'd want to attract attention by driving fast—and we take in the chance of red lights along the way, thirty minutes or more would pass before he reached the pit. Now, let me ask you this, Doctor Curtis: was he insane when he dumped his wife into the sludge?"

Dr. Curtis hesitated. "Possibly."

"Possibly..."

In his closing argument, he read the letter the police found on Van Cliffe after the arrest. "Good-bye, darling, wherever you are. Please believe I am desolate at losing you and heartbroken that I made it so. If only you had eased off...." Scanning the jury, he repeated the statement, letting the words sink in. "Ladies and gentlemen, does that sound like someone insane?"

He pointed to the defendant, who was impeccably dressed in a double-breasted gray suit, giving him an aristocratic bearing, with roots back to the Calverts. Eckert pointed out the defendant's wealth, his standing in high society. "Might he not feel exempt from the constraints of ordinary life—that he could do what he wished, even murder his wife?"

After eight hours of deliberation that stretched over two days, the jury returned to the courtroom. Squeezing his lucky dice in his palm, he read their faces. Right away he knew that the verdict would be less than first-degree murder, hopefully second-degree, good for twenty years, long enough that there would be good odds Leland Van Cliffe would die behind bars.

But manslaughter? He couldn't believe his ears when the foreman announced the verdict. Meant no more than ten years in the state pen, depending on the mood of Judge Turnbull at sentencing. With good behavior and influence, this wife-killer could be sprung in less than four years. Peachy.

The verdict took something out of him. "Tough one," Lena whispered, snapping the recorder shut. The assistant state's attorney gave his neighbor a tired shrug and left the courtroom.

Today was Ash Wednesday, a good day for penance. Hands in pockets, he made his way up the slope to Immaculate Conception, taking time to notice the crocus and daffodils, lined up like soldiers. Good to be in fresh air, free from that fluorescent lighting and monotonous buzz. Snowdrops dotted the graveyard near the big stone church where he had served as an altar boy. Kneeling in the back pew, he absorbed the silence, the candles, the Cross. He prayed for the soul of Mrs. Margaret Van Cliffe, dead at fifty-two. May she be at peace.

Walking up the aisle to receive ashes, he recognized a man returning to the pew. He had seen him at Whispering Pines with his wife, a dispatcher at Blue Valley Cab; until now, he hadn't made the connection with his South Building neighbor. The short legs gave him away. Hadn't they served together as altar boys? Eckert was in the Army when he heard that the kid had joined a seminary. Couldn't recall his name. They were a few years apart. Guess he didn't become a priest.

When he returned to the pew, the man had left. The ashes on Eckert's forehead put the disappointment of the day in perspective. On the way to Whispering Pines, he vowed to give up chocolate for Lent. Be hard to forgo those hot fudge sundaes at Read's after Communion. Starting to look like Jackie Gleason. He also decided to give up anger. Nip it in the bud. Good luck with that one.

He climbed the steps to Apartment 4C; the screeches of his daughters put a smile on his face. In the background he heard Mary Lou trying to end the bedlam. God love her. If that oak… don't give it a thought. He opened the door and put down his suitcase.

"Daddy!" He took Katey by the hands and spun her around the living room, knocking over the ashtray stand.

"Uh-oh!"

"Hey!" Mary cried.

"My error." He opened the closet, took out the broom, and swept up the remains of the cigar he had puffed the night before.

Mary Lou had outdone herself for this Friday night dinner. No fish sticks tonight. Hadn't eaten a smidgeon since breakfast. He wolfed down fried oysters, mashed potatoes, and candied carrots. Two Natty Bohs and a slice of blueberry pie completed the feast. He hugged Mary Lou, his ballast, so nice to squeeze.

"How'd you do today, Mr. Assistant State's Attorney?"

His smile vanished. "Manslaughter."

"I'm so sorry, Rus."

"So am I."

Eckert washed the dishes while Shirl dried. He was careful to maintain his distance and asked about her day at school. In return he received monosyllables. "Good."

"How are the ballet lessons?"

"Good."

He approached Rusty's bedroom, which he shared with little Kate. The two bunk beds in the master bedroom took care of Pam, Bethany, Dolores, and Shirl, while he and Mary Lou squeezed into the smallest bedroom. It had worked out up to this point, but something had to be done soon. They were bursting at the seams. Rusty deserved his own room. Eckert tapped on the door.

"Enter!"

"How's it going?"

His son sat at his desk, arms over the textbook. "Test tomorrow," he mumbled. His Elvis hair shone beneath the hundred-watt bulb.

"What's it on?" Eckert asked, sniffing the Vitalis.

"The Revolutionary War."

"Washington saved this country. Otherwise we'd be saluting Queen Elizabeth."

Rusty's eyes were glued to the textbook. "Don't read so good," he mumbled. "Might flunk fourth grade."

Today hadn't gone well for the eleven-year-old. It began with cranky Sister Florella calling upon him to read. He had slouched next to Miller, avoiding eye contact. No such luck. "Your turn, Randall." Why this ancient nun continued to call him by the wrong name was beyond him. More than once he had corrected Sister Florella. Was she deaf? The boy started to read. "Can't hear you! Speak up, Randall!" Halting here and there in a voice that started high and ended low, he negotiated the paragraph as he would an icy path. Miller's whispering pronunciation helped him avoid getting stuck, and he reached the last sentence without a significant mishap. Then his tongue betrayed him in the worst possible way: "Con-shit-tushun." Laughter rained down. Rusty stood rigid, not knowing what to do. With the yardstick, Sister Florella slapped the knuckles of the nearest target, Blake Spear, a big kid making fart noises on his forearm. Spear never lost an opportunity to mock Rusty's intelligence. On the playground, of course, Spear was the first to insult him: "Dummy Eckert, duh, anybody home?" Worse was a fifth grader who had been his classmate in the second grade. "Hello, retard," said Michael. "Hear you can't read." Once they had been friends. Not anymore. Miller wanted Rusty to knock his block off, but it wasn't Rusty's nature to fight. If a bully attacked Miller, sure, he'd come to his rescue, like he did on the trestle. But for himself? Nah! He felt like Ferdinand the Bull. He wanted to graze in a sunny meadow, sniffing the buttercups.

"Hey," his father said, clapping his hands, "you're good at math. You're good with tools. Look at those skateboards you made. Practically led to the death of Miller, but it did show your skill. Maybe you're not the best reader, so you won't be a lawyer. Doesn't mean you don't have talent. Why, you could be an engineer—someone who builds things, such as bridges or ballparks."

Rusty continued to stare at the textbook. "I see words different from what Miller sees. Letters look different…sideways or something."

"How long has this been going on?"

"Since the second grade."

"Could be dyslexia. I'll have your mother make an appointment with the eye doctor. In the meantime, do your best. Want me to read to you? That way, you can be ready for the test."

The boy nodded his assent.

February drifted into March, and Eckert kept his Lenten vow despite the temptation of Mary Lou's warm chocolate chip cookies, Hershey's kisses in the office, and Read's hot fudge sundaes after Mass. Regarding his vow to give up anger, there was progress. He was becoming aware of how often its ugly head reared up in a single day. Could be someone cutting him off on the road ("Go have an accident!"), a package he couldn't open ("Rip it to shreds, that'll fix it!"), or losing his favorite pen ("You dickhead!"). Ridiculous. He knew he couldn't banish anger, but he could stop those temper tantrums. Try deep breathing and counting to ten. Maybe that would work.

Playing catch in the quadrangle on a Sunday afternoon, he asked Rusty if he was going to play Little League this year.

"Planning on it. Coach wants me to try pitching."

Eckert could see his son on the mound, those scarecrow arms and legs in a windup. And here comes the speedball. It smacked the pocket of his old glove, stinging his palm. Had to make more games this year…too often other priorities: drinks at the Penn Hotel, preparing for a case, or sheer laziness. After a tense day in the courtroom, fueled by black coffee and adrenaline, he could feel like a used rubber afterward, not good for anything but sitting like a blob in front of the TV.

One rainy afternoon, in the basement of Taylor Avenue Duckpins in Stoneleigh, he and Rusty were having post-bowling cokes and greasy French fries at the table behind the alley. They had split four games.

A colored boy at the end of alley six was setting pins, looked about Miller's size, only younger, seven or eight at best. At the other end, some drunk greaser in a wife-beater T-shirt flung the ball before the pins were in place. The boy set the last pin and pulled away as the ball arrived, picking off the corner pin.

"Almost got 'im!" bragged the slob.

Eckert wanted to tell the goon to lay off and started to rise, then changed his mind—wasn't the time or place.

"Asshole," he muttered.

He reached into his top pocket for the black dice, tossing them on the linoleum table, coming in at five and three, a good number for craps. He scooped up the dice and rolled them around in his hand.

"Let me tell you something about these dice, Rusty. They belonged to a Tunisian boy not much older than you, my first kill as lead gunner in a Sherman tank. The medic could do nothing. I said a prayer over the child. In his palm, I found these black bones." Eckert paused to gather himself. "Carried them through the invasion of Sicily, across the French countryside, and over the Rhine. Maybe they brought me luck. I killed a lot of people and stayed alive. When I cut your hair, that beautiful brown face appeared, just for a nanosecond, the face of an innocent. For every breath I take, that boy is a part of me. I pray you never have to go to war."

"What's it like?" Rusty asked through a mouthful of fries.

"What do you mean?"

"Being in a tank."

"Depends. In the desert, the temperature in the can could top a hundred twenty-five. Crowded, too. With a bow gunner, commander, loader, and driver—you can't imagine the stink. It's also noisy, especially the rat-a-tat of the .30-caliber machine gun. In a firefight we had to wear headphones to communicate. Wasn't like a John Wayne movie. Creeping along, three, four miles per hour, in a standoff with a Panzer. The cannons on the tanks were similar. The trick was getting off shots quicker than the Jerrys. We had a breech loader; the soldiers in the Panzer had to eject the shells with a hand crank. Big advantage for the good guys."

The killing numbed him. He remembered standing among the dead soldiers, picking through their letters, wallets, photos of girlfriends and mothers. Hadn't thought of the Nazis as human beings.

"Were you scared?"

"I was too busy to be scared."

Searing memories flooded back: buddies he had lost, too many to remember. Was that where the anger started? He told Rusty about sleeping under the tank in the desert, shooting down church steeples to eliminate snipers, and negotiating Normandy hedgerows packed with trees and bushes. Behind them could be Germans with bazookas. As soon as the tanks busted through, the enemy would retreat to another hedgerow. Certain he would meet his Maker in one of those fields, he wrote Mary Lou a dark letter telling her she might be better off with another man. He kept that detail to himself.

"You should write a book," said Rusty.

"It's good to talk about it."

He placed the dice in Rusty's hand. "Now I have a question. Be honest now. Did you really blame me for shoplifting?"

Rusty fell silent, didn't know what to say.

His father saw the reticence and switched the subject. "Know what I gave up for Lent?"

"Chocolate?"

"Well, that too. I gave up anger. How am I doing?"

"Good," said Rusty.

Eckert smiled. Of course, Rusty would say that. Don't want to rile the old man up. It would take time to set things right. He had work to do.

Watching the pinsetter, father and son sat in silence, for once at ease with one another. Eckert did not miss a baseball game that spring. He was there for every pitch, cheering on Rusty in his new glasses.

FORGIVEN

WALTER MCGRADY WAS LYING on the sofa, head resting in Monica's lap. "I'm too comfortable," said the former priest.

"What do you mean by that?" Monica replied, toying with his curly hair.

"I'm only happy when I'm miserable."

"Biggest b-s I've ever heard."

"I need to do something. Lena's been arrested…made the front page of *The African American*. She's doing something."

"Do you want to lead a crusade, Father McGrady?"

"Those youngsters putting a sign in the window: NO NUKES. Even after the window was shattered, they put the sign back. What am I doing? I get up in the morning, go to work, record the business of the day, and come home to my lovely wife."

"Isn't that enough? Being a bookkeeper for Hutzler's beats driving a cab."

"I'm too comfortable."

"Would you like a drink?"

"Yes, a martini would be lovely."

"Please lift your big Irish head, and I'll make you one."

It was as if God were prodding him. *Thought we were done, Big Guy*. He had forsaken the divine in Korea.

McGrady's relationship with God had been adverse from the get-go. "God is watching you," said Sister Mary Francis. Nice message for an overly sensitive eight-year-old. In his tender mind, the child had equated God with Santa Claus. Better watch out, better not cry…

Yeah, but Santa doesn't send you to hell.

His initial confession, what a nightmare. Waiting in line for the light to turn green, told "to examine his conscience," whatever that meant. Had to make up sins—couldn't think of any other than pissing on the toilet seat. Entering the dark box, he panicked and tapped on the wall. Where was He? No one home. Master Walter left before the priest pulled back the screen.

The full impact of his sin hit him on the day of his First Communion. Everything was a lie: the white suit, the photos, Granny fussing over him, all lies. When time arrived to file up to the communion rail with his classmates, Master Walter was terrified. The dream was haunting. On his knees at the communion rail, he shivered watching Father Andrew approach. Something bad was going to happen. Squeezing his eyes shut, he stuck out his tongue. But the Body of Christ did not turn to flames. It did not burn through his tongue. Chewing the host, Master Walter returned to the pew puzzled. What happened? Surely the milk bottle that represented his soul was full of darkness. You can't be forgiven if everything is a lie.

Sadomasochistic? Gee. Wonder where that came from…

Growing up, he did everything he could to avoid damnation. Kneeling by the bed, the boy did not miss a night saying his prayers, with the intent of acquiring what he called a "get-out-of-purgatory" card. Each Hail Mary or Our Father lopped off so many days of torture. At Granny's urging, Walter became an altar boy. Around the age of thirteen, he developed what could be called a vocation. Granny hailed him as "the Chosen One." He had to accept the role. God is watching. Please…was God watching in Korea?

"Here's your drink, dear."

"Aren't you having one?"

"I'm bushed…going to turn in early. Had a rough day in the steel ballet."

"Love you."

"Love you back..."

As he sipped his drink, McGrady understood that he had to make peace with the past. On Ash Wednesday, the following afternoon, he stepped into the church of his youth, Immaculate Conception...hadn't darkened a sacristy since handing Monsignor Gonzalez his letter of resignation.

He sat in a pew and contemplated the memories—the statues, the Stations of the Cross, the scent of incense—could almost hear the rustle of rosary beads on Sister Mary Francis as she patrolled the pews. He glanced at the confessional where the blasphemy took place and saw Master Walter stepping into the stained-glass light, hands folded in prayer. He had to forgive himself...for the soldiers who died in his arms, for the soldiers who invaded his dreams, for the boy who looked for God and couldn't find Him.

He rose from the pew. Before the communion rail stood a young priest, dispensing ashes from a goblet. His thumb formed the cross in the center of Walter's forehead. The press of flesh on "the third eye" had a surreal touch.

He basked in the crisp sunlight on the walk home. Winter was waning. What did he miss most about being a priest? Wasn't the celebration of the Eucharist, the big show at Christmas, or the weddings and funerals. At Mission Dolores after Korea, he knew his Latin by heart and had a decent voice for singing the High Mass... didn't mean it was sincere. His sermons often dwelled on the theme of suffering. Instead of Aquinas or Augustine, he quoted Camus from The Plague, how the protagonist, Doctor Rieux, couldn't accept a child's innocent suffering. Even Jesus on the cross questioned the order of the universe. "Why did God allow the Holocaust?" That was his question of the day. He stood frozen at the pulpit, staring at the back of the church, searching for an answer.

The congregation grew restless. What's he doing? Did he have a stroke? From the front pew a Hispanic matriarch spoke up: "Father McGrady, are you all right?"

"No, I'm not, Señora Zupata." He apologized for stopping the Mass and descended. In the sacristy, he removed the green vestments of Ordinary Time and left the Church.

No, he did not miss the rituals. What he missed was the confessional. Before going off to war, he was intimidated by his role. What did he know of life? Upon his return to the States, he had a different perspective. The sacrament had nothing to do with him. How humbling—hearing these strangers share their most intimate secrets! Thoreau was right: most people did lead lives of quiet desperation, particularly the veterans home from the war. Some carried a heavy load. Though he never saw their faces, he thought of each man as a brother, and he did his best to lighten the load.

"God has already forgiven you. He sees your sorrow. Now you must forgive yourself. For your penance, I want you to spend the week being kind—not only kind to others, but kind to yourself. You are still a child of God."

By the time he reached Whispering Pines, McGrady had charted a new path. What would Monica think? A month back she'd traded places with the day dispatcher so they could spend their evenings together. Monica had a wonderful imagination and loved playing the role of the French maid, the innocent one he could ravish, night after night. He hardened walking down Knollwood. Down, boy!

Monica was at the kitchen table, engrossed in the sports page of the newspaper. He noticed that the tobacco smell in the apartment had faded.

"You quit smoking?"

"I did," she said, turning the page.

He positioned himself behind her and began massaging her shoulders and neck, a daily routine. "Had an interesting conversation with Wayne Sheer the other day."

"Who's Wayne Sheer?"

"He lives in the North Building. Used to be a streetcar conductor and now works at Read's. I stopped in for a hot fudge sundae. We got to talking. Turned out he was in Korea at the same time as I."

"Is he the idiot who drove his car into the tunnel during the hurricane?"

"That's the guy. Been through a rough patch. Wife left him."

"Well, yeah?"

"Be nice. He's gotten his bearings straight in AA. We had a great conversation about healing, got me thinking."

"About what?"

"What I'm going to do."

"Do what?...Don't stop…yeah, right there…"

"Now that you've quit smoking, from whom should I bum cigarettes?"

"Tough luck, padre."

"I have something to tell you."

"Oh yeah?" She turned toward him, saw the ashes, and chuckled. "I knew you'd go back to the fold. That's okay. Just don't ask me to go to Mass with you. Sunday's my day to sleep in."

"I've decided to leave Hutzler's."

"You're not going back to the Church?"

"Not this week."

"What's wrong with Hutzler's? Boss on your ass?"

"I can do better, Monica. I have an M.A. in psychology. No reason I couldn't raise a shingle as a psychotherapist. With all these lawyers in the county seat, there's a need for a good listener."

"You'll be a shrink."

"No, that's another area."

"Will your patients lie on a couch and talk about how their mama didn't like 'em?"

"That's analysis. I'm a Freudian."

"You lost me."

"Not important," he murmured, kissing her neck.

"Well, that's great," she said, rising toward him. "I imagine you'd make more money on your own than at Hutzler's." She took his hand and placed hers on his shoulder. She stood over him by a good six inches…didn't matter. They waltzed without music around the apartment, each in tune with the other. Leading, Walter said he'd die of boredom if he stayed.

"The money will come. I'm very excited."

"You should be," she said, licking his ear. "I'm pregnant."

"Oh my God!"

WHITE FLOWER

FOR THE PLUMBER, RANDY resolved to help Sean and his mother any way he could. At the same time, he didn't want to intervene and get in the way. Those long days at Hopkins drained Sacniete. She needed time to herself. Randy wasn't a member of the family, but, sure as gun's iron, he was a man she could count on. As winter slipped into spring, he was there for every appointment at the oncology center. Sean became quite adept at shifting the gears of the pickup.

The child was a trooper, enduring a crash of red blood cells, dehydration, diarrhea...lost track of the complications. Trips to the ER became routine as the patient endured twenty-four chemo sessions. Randy couldn't get behind the rationale of these drug cocktails designed to kill malignant cells but at a terrible price. His neighbor in the South Building, Niles Blackwater, RN, had looked after Sean twice in the Union Memorial ER. During these crises, Blackwater's flat tone calmed the child, who accepted the probes and needles with hardly a whimper.

"Chemotherapy is the worst of healing choices," Nurse Blackwater explained one bleary, fluorescent midnight, "but it's the only choice we have." He'd like to see more investigation of natural cures. There had to be something out there, something that could boost the immune system.

During those interminable times with Sacniete in antiseptic waiting rooms, he tried to fill space with words, babbling about his disasters with past girlfriends, growing up poor in West Virginia, seeing Kyoto for the first time, how Buddhism changed his life. Sacniete seemed to enjoy his tales, admittedly stretched a bit. He asked if he was talking too much. "Say the word and I'll shut my big trap." She told him no…it helped pass the time. She said he had lived an interesting life. Not really, he thought. Too many aimless days. Now he had a purpose.

Sacniete shared little about herself, preferring to keep the focus on her son. Whenever conversation veered toward her homeland, she would change the topic. He did learn that her husband, Victor, had perished the previous year on the Baltimore-Washington Parkway, rolling his Imperial across the median.

"Did he work for the Feds?"

"Yes and no. He was a company man."

"What company?"

"United Fruit."

"Don't they sell bananas?"

"I prefer not to talk about Victor."

"Sorry to pry."

One cherry-blossom afternoon in early April, he took Sacniete and Sean to the Baltimore Zoo. From the elephants to the big cats, from the snake house to the polar bears, the boy walked on his own, wanting to see every animal, big and small. The doctors were guardedly optimistic.

Randy treasured those rare, intimate evenings after the dishes were done and Sean was tucked into bed. By the light of a black candle—"a truth-telling candle"—Sacniete sipped herbal tea in the shadows, ready to talk, ready to listen. He had never known a woman like her. Early on, she perceived "his hungry ghost," always on the move, looking for something different from the here and now. "What can I say?" he said. "I'm a lousy Buddhist." His eighteen-month stay at Whispering Pines had been his longest stint in one place since leaving the Marine Corps in '49.

"What you are searching for will not be found out there, whatever 'out there' means to you. Look for your treasure here." She pointed to her heart. He couldn't disagree. Wherever you go, there you are.

On the first of May, Sean had his final treatment, which, aside from a short bout of nausea, didn't sicken him. The weather warmed; through the open windows floated the voices of children in the quadrangle, luring Sean to the outside. There was chess to be played, balls to be kicked, and swings taking him to the moon. Color was returning to his cheeks; he regained his appetite with a craving for Kraft mac and cheese. He had it for a snack every afternoon before returning to the quadrangle.

"Take it easy," Sacniete said, wiping the sweat off his forehead.

"I will."

"Don't get overheated."

"I won't."

Toward the end of the month came bloodwork and more tests. The conclusion? The leukemia had disappeared. Sean was in remission for the second time. Pray to God this one holds. The three of them celebrated at the Valley View in Hutzler's. Sacniete even ordered a cocktail.

"Didn't think you drank."

"Victor introduced me to the Manhattan."

"What was he like?"

"Can't talk now," she said, nodding to Sean, who was slurping his cream of crab soup.

Must be hard on the boy, losing his father. Never heard Sean mention him. Maybe too painful.

After dinner that evening, Sacniete and Randy settled with their tea by the living room window so they could keep an eye on the quadrangle. The Good Humor man was ringing his bells in the parking lot. Mr. Softee had come and gone. Darkness was settling in. Sacniete lit the truth candle. Children were playing hide-and-go-seek. Sean was out there somewhere, counting to sixty. Randy stared at Sacniete's face. In the candlelight, those almond eyes, hooked nose, and full lips looked ancient; her face could be on a mosaic.

"How interesting," he said, "that I've revealed so much to you about my past loves...usually not that open about my love life."

Sacniete chuckled. "I coaxed it out of you."

"You're easy to talk to, White Flower. Yet I know so little about you, other than you are the widow of a man who had something to do with the United Fruit Company."

"In my village, Paha called it *Compañía del Diablo*—the Devil's company."

"Wait a minute. This doesn't add up. From what I know, can't see you hitching up with a guy working for the Devil. Guess Papa wasn't too happy."

"He had already been murdered."

"Whoa..." Randy sat back and crossed his arms, ready to listen.

"Let me tell what it was like when I was a teenager in the western highlands, a girl dreaming of going to the university in Guatemala City. My people had another name for the United Fruit Company, "*pulpo*," octopus. Behind the government, military, and Church were the tentacles of *el pulpo*. Under dictator Jorge Ubico, the United Fruit Company paid no taxes. Imports from the States paid no tariffs. *El pulpo* owned nearly half the land in my country, as well as the telephone company and railroad. It was all about bananas—cheap bananas in the US market."

The story poured out of her. "Paha was a landless farmer, indebted to the company. Most of the highland farmers were in this position. To keep bananas cheap, *la Compañía del Diablo* paid the lowest wages possible, barely above starvation wages. Act up by trying to start a union, and the police would arrest you as a Communist agitator. You could disappear."

In her poor village, *el pulpo* tried to wipe out Quiché, the language of her people. The company, working with the military, made it a crime to teach Quiché in schools. This war on culture began with the conquistadores and the padres, who enslaved her people in the name of God.

Sacniete glanced at the clock on the wall and called her son's name out the window. Alice's voice cut through the darkness. "He's with us, Mrs. Clover...your son's tuckered out." Across the dewy grass, Sacniete and Randy found Sean curled on the blanket, sleeping next to Miller, who was staring at the constellations. Randy carried the boy back to the apartment. Sean's mother tucked him in and returned to her story, lighting another black candle.

"You asked me about Victor. I let you assume that he was Sean's father."

"Who's the father?"

"Babajide was tall for a Maya...had the most beautiful eyelashes. We met on campus in the spring of '44. Revolution was in the air. Dictator Jorge Ubico had to go. *¡El dictador tiene irse!* That was our chant in the streets. I was twenty-two years old and in love with this fellow highlander from the West. We were fighting the good fight. Then, a miracle: Ubico did flee with his bags of cash. The cucarachas in his administration fled too. I was so proud of my people. I hugged a hundred compatriots that glorious day in Plaza Central. '*¡La gente ganó!*' Randy, you can't imagine what it was like to vote in a free election for the first time. The people's choice, Doctor Juan José Arévalo, was elected president. We modeled our new constitution after los Estados Unidos: all men are created equal. *¡Qué tiempo!*"

"What happened then?"

"Babajide and I, true to our roots, had a Maya marriage ceremony in a highland church, calling upon Maria, goddess of maize, to bless our union. Instead of wine for Mass, we drank pulque, drink of the ancients. Both villages attended. The fiesta lasted three days."

In Guatemala City, they settled into a tiled apartment off the plaza, which they filled with plants, native art, and two cats. Both taught at the university. For her PhD, Sacniete investigated indigenous languages. She felt protective of the twenty-two Mayan dialects, only recently allowed back into the light of day.

On the side, she mastered English, speaking without an accent. Tutoring Spanish brought home good dinero, more than what she made teaching four classes. Some of her clients worked for the United Fruit Company. It helped to speak their language. She wanted to know more about these men, what made them tick. For the most part, they treated her with respect. She had to watch her words. No taunting el Diablo…must not shine attention on her family's involvement in the *Partido Guatemalteco de Trabajo*. She didn't dare bring up the topic of land reform. Could be dangerous, no matter how polite they were on the surface.

She met Victor the Texan around this time. He had a gap-toothed grin and a bow-legged waver, as if he had just gotten off a horse. Mr. Clover was vague about his employer. He said he was a consultant. His job was to provide information. "To whom?" she asked.

"The United Fruit Company, who else? Aren't we supposed to be speaking Spanish?"

He dressed like a lot of men who had spent time in the military. The former Marines providing security for UFCO had those buzz cuts. The CIA guys preferred flattops. Victor sported a blond flattop and had acne-scarred cheeks. His restless blue eyes scanned the plaza when they spoke Spanish in the Abraham Lincoln Café, a known hangout for communists. She had a feeling that the Texan's Spanish was better than it seemed, that he might be playing her. The money was too good to pass up: a crisp five-dollar bill at the end of each hour.

Meanwhile, Babajide was teaching botany. His passion was land; the United Fruit Company had too much of it. Babajide joined an on-campus organization to press the new president to tilt the scales of justice toward the people and end this Yankee domination.

Those years were good for Sacniete and Babajide. Sean came along in '49. In 1951 there was a peaceful transition of power when Colonel Jacobo Árbenz, who ran on a platform of land reform, was elected. He allowed the Communists in Guatemala to participate in the government. Babajide and Paha served on a land-reform panel.

The president's Decree 900 would distribute undeveloped lands to landless farmers. This would be no land grab. The government would give property owners fair restitution based on assessments kept low. The owners paid little in taxes. Now the United Fruit Company demanded true market value. Can't have it both ways. The Supreme Court supported the president. Never in all her days did Sacniete think this dream would come true. Now Paha could work his own land and not be forced to give half his harvest to the Company.

Sean was now a precocious four-year-old. "My little man wasn't himself," she said, wiping away a tear. "He had no energy… bruises up and down his legs." Sacniete and Babajide took him to the doctor at the public clinic, who ran some tests. The result? Leukemia, cancer of the blood. That afternoon Sacniete met Victor and broke down in tears during the lesson. He insisted on knowing what was wrong. Perhaps he could help. She told him about Sean's disease. "*¿Qué hospital? ¿Tenemos suficiente dinero para el mejor doctor?*"

Victor answered in English. He proposed the American Hospital as a solution. They had the best doctors and the latest treatments, a direct line from Hopkins.

"Aren't they reserved for *Americanos*?"

"Sean will have no problem being accepted, Mrs. Canul. I have connections. Maybe someday I'll have the pleasure of meeting your son, after he's beaten this lousy cancer. Allow me to help you out."

Sacniete did not trust Victor. What's he going to want in return? Information? After talking it over with Babajide, she knew they had no other choice but to accept the spook's proposal.

For the rest of the year and into '54, Sean endured chemotherapy. He didn't lose his hair and went into remission a month before *el golpe*—the coup. During that time, she and Victor met thrice weekly to speak Spanish in the Abraham Lincoln Café.

Babajide and she knew the coup was coming. The propaganda mill filled the airwaves with tirades against communists, about how they would set up death camps if given the chance. Try to refute the charges on another station, and the Company would jam the signal. It was a total con job, a show brought to the Guatemalan people courtesy of the CIA. Over the airwaves roared an invasion of military might. A couple of fighter jets strafed the president's palace. Truth be told, there was no force of US Marines storming the shore, only a ragtag army of 150 men, led by "the liberator," Colonel Carlos Castillo Armas, a wiry man with a Hitler mustache. When President Árbenz resigned, it was like a death in the family.

"What happened then?"

"I should back up here. I'll put on a fresh pot…"

The purge began soon after Colonel Armas took power. The military was unleashed against the indigenous, who were viewed as terrorists supported by the Soviet Union. Their villages were burned to the ground. If Red, better off dead. That was the Company's motto. Victor sincerely believed he was making the world safe for democracy.

Paha and Babajide made plans to flee the capital. At dawn, she saw the men off at the bus station, wondering if she would ever see them again. She had no idea where they were going. It was better that way. The next day she met Victor at the Abraham Lincoln. Maybe he could put in a word for Babajide and Paha.

Victor arrived early, wearing a Panama hat, gray linen pants, and a flaming-red Hawaiian shirt: the tourist look. No smile today. He began with his standard opening: "*¿Cómo está Sean?*"

"*Muy bien, gracias.*" She asked if he could intervene on behalf of "*mi padre y marido, Babajide.*" What's to become of them? They were peaceful men, not *terroristas.*

Victor lowered his voice. Amidst the movement of military vehicles around the plaza, she had to strain to hear him. *"Lo siento, Señora Canul. Ambos se han ido."*

"¿Dónde?"

"Ellos están muertos."

How could this be? She had kissed Babajide just yesterday, as if he were going away for a short holiday, back before she knew it. Her voice seemed detached from her body. "How?" she asked in English. "Were they shot? Who did it?"

"This wasn't what I signed up for…I was told they were set upon by a crowd of patriots."

"That does not make sense. They were beloved by their people."

"I'm only as good as my information."

"Your information is a lie, like this new government."

"Watch what you say. You're in danger."

"Me? I'm a mother and teacher."

"President Armas tolerates no opposition. He's wiping out entire families. You're on the list…you and your son. You know I helped you before."

"I shall always be grateful for what you did for my son."

"Let me help you again."

He reached for her hand, but she withdrew it. "Not until you show me the bodies. I'm like Saint Thomas. I have to see the wounds."

It took every ounce of fortitude to hold herself together as they rode in a tuk-tuk to the morgue. Along the boulevard, where President Árbenz had walked among the people after his inauguration, soldiers with bayonets stood on every corner. She wanted to scream in mourning for her country, her people, Babajide and Paha, drowning in a sea of violence, another chapter to add to centuries of oppression.

On one level, she knew Victor Clover was telling the truth, but she denied it anyway. Upon reaching the morgue, she said she had changed her mind. She would not go in. Should she see their mutilated bodies, she might lose her mind. She did not want the morgue to be her last memory of them. She must think about Sean, what was best for him. She would grieve when they were safe.

Sacniete yawned and stretched her arms. "Randy, I'm too tired to talk."

"I'll let myself out. Good night."

"*Buenas noches, amigo.*" Had to turn in. End of a perfect day… Sean in remission at last. She blew out the truth candle.

Spy in the House of God

English teacher Robin Turnbaugh considered his oration to the class the day after the Steinbeck books were confiscated his finest moment in the classroom. It's not often you receive such applause. Much as he enjoyed the students, as the year progressed he could feel himself counting the months, then the weeks, and then the days until the school year would end. Every day he wrote a poem in his journal. He wrote sonnets to Michael in iambic pentameter, calling him "Apollo," celebrating the man's body, mind, and soul. Robin longed to live in a place where they could celebrate their union in the open. He wanted to live in North Beach, among the Beats, and eat, drink, and sleep writing. He wanted to meet Allen Ginsberg.

The cool thing about all this was that he managed to convince Michael to come with him and pursue his own dream. He too was a writer, wanted to compose symphonies, serious music. Their passion for art matched their passion for one another.

And Father? He should call him, let him know of his plans, but he kept putting it off through spring. Why not today? He could call him from the phone booth at Kent's. Be easier to talk to Big Jake after a couple of Manhattans. He wanted to tell Father he'd found love in his life. Leave on a clean slate, no secrets.

How sweet to have no more papers to grade, no more classes to prepare, no more bells marking the hours. Robin ambled around the classroom, removing pictures of Poe, Lawrence, and Wolfe, framed quotes from writers, and Van Gogh prints—sunflowers, golden fields, and stars—anything to stimulate the teenage brain. He wiped the dust from the corner of an Oscar Wilde quote: "Be yourself. Everybody else is taken."

Surprised he'd made it to the finish line. Quite an experience, filling young minds with illicit thoughts that skirted the League of Decency, such as "taking a peek" at J. D. Salinger's *Catcher in the Rye.* He read a few passages to give them "a sample" of writing they could relate to.

Church bells chiming the four o'clock hour drew him back to the present...supposed to meet Michael at Kent's to celebrate the beginning of their life together.

"Mr. Turnbaugh? Can I talk to you for a second?"

Milton Hickwolf lingered at the classroom door. The boy had grown a couple of inches in nine months. His Alfalfa hair was now a Pat Boone cut. Robin approved. Put the kid on a college campus in a couple of years, and he could be hot with the girls as the Arthur Miller type. All he had to do was survive Louis Richie, the basketball player.

"What's up?" Robin asked, shoving a few more paperbacks into the cardboard box.

"I want to thank you."

"For what?" Not all the books would fit. "Hey, want a copy of *Call of the Wild*?"

"Sure."

He flipped him the book. "It's about a dog, blood and guts on the Klondike. You'll love Jack London."

Milton flicked through the pages. "Thank you for introducing me to books. There are no books in my house. My parents are Hungarian refugees."

"Young man, that's the nicest compliment I've had as a teacher." He shook the boy's hand. "Let me give you some final advice, Mr. Hickwolf. Don't sell yourself short. You have great potential as a human being."

The boy's face lit up. Why, he nearly floated out the door!

Robin made three trips to the MG, carting briefcases stuffed with lesson plans, two cardboard boxes filled with books, and a pair of rubber plants that refused to fit in the sports car. He left them on the curb and sprinted up the stairs to take one last look around the class, making sure he hadn't overlooked something.

"So this is it," Sister Rita said, entering the classroom. "You're leaving us. Anything I can do to convince you to stay?"

"I've already burned my bridge. I gave my fifth-period students their copy of the Steinbeck book…a parting gift."

Sister Rita cackled. "Those teen angels will read everything the man has written."

"Baltimore has excellent libraries."

"If you change your mind…"

"I won't."

"God be with you, then. I hope you stay in teaching. You have a gift for opening young minds."

At Kent's Bar and Grill, Michael had taken the booth at the far end, in the shadows away from the patrons. Good choice. Might steal a kiss or two during lulls in the action. They toasted their good fortune. San Francisco, here they come. After two Manhattans, Robin excused himself. "There's someone I must call."

The phone booth cut off the bar noise. He dropped two nickels in the slot, dialed Father's private number, and listened to the ring, half hoping he would not pick up. Father had a way of ruining one's day. But that was then. This is now. Just be straight, like a warrior. The truth shall set you free.

"Yeah, Jake."

"Father? It's me."

"I know who you are."

"Want to tell you something…I'm moving to San Francisco."

"So you're doing it. Well, I wish you luck as a writer. You going alone?"

"Yeah, driving coast to coast."

"Be careful, you hear."

"I'll call you when I get there."

"How will you make a living?"

"Oh, I'll find something part time, maybe driving a cab... could be interesting, fodder for my stories."

"You got to learn the streets first."

"I'll be fine."

"Thanks for calling, son."

"You're welcome, Father."

Robin hung up in bewilderment. He clenched his fists and glared at the ceiling. "GRRR!" Can't believe he planted that lie. So much for being a warrior! Even now, he craves Big Jake's approval. Oh well, maybe next time, for sure.

ASIAN FLU

SINCE HIS OFFER OF medical assistance, Blackwater had kept an eye out for his skinny neighbors. He learned their names from the mailbox on the first floor. No surprise that Grace and Henry thought him weird…been getting those looks most of his life. After the window was repaired, the two returned that "NO NUKES!" sign to its spot in the window overlooking the quadrangle. Their defiance made Niles uneasy. People could be weird. Saw it all the time in the hospital, especially on a full moon. When they replaced the nuke sign with "Peace on earth," he wrote their names on a Christmas card and followed it with "And good will to men. Your Neighbor, Niles." He slid the card under their door.

The next afternoon he rushed by Grace and Henry on the sidewalk in front of the building. He was wearing his scrubs and running late.

"Hey," she said.

Niles spun around. "Hello, Grace," he said.

"Thank you for the card, Niles…sweet of you."

Henry asked if he could bother him with some questions.

"I suppose…"

"Where were you when you heard the glass break?"

Grace rolled her eyes, not this again. Tired of this detective shit.

Niles said he was downstairs, watching Richard Boone on Medic. It was his favorite show.

"So I assume you heard the window break, even though you had the TV on."

"I have good hearing. Got to go..."

Grace hit Henry's arm lightly with her fist. "Give it a rest. This is becoming annoying."

"That guy's too weird to be true. I could see him throwing that rock just for the hell of it, appearing at our door with his medical bag, ready to save the day, like Richard Boone."

"Give it rest!"

As winter faded into spring, it became obvious to Blackwater that his neighbor was pregnant. Was she aware of the Asian flu? He had been tracking it since it surfaced in Singapore. By Memorial Day, this strain was popping up in East Coast cities, including Baltimore. It promised to be an infectious summer at Union Memorial ER, with sixteen-hour shifts if his colleagues caught the bug. The waiting room was like a petri dish. Everyone should wear masks.

The virus did fascinate Blackwater—how it spread, how it adapted, its origins. Prehistoric or mutated? He wanted to study the beast under a microscope. Had he a hero on this earth, it would be Jonas Salk, father of the polio vaccine.

Today was Marconi night for Niles. Grace happened to work there. Walked into the place two months ago, and there she was, taking an order. Been there every week since. He had reserved the solitary table next to the fish tank. He preferred watching angelfish to diners, but he did enjoy seeing Grace multitask, a real pro, never got flustered, no matter how many tables she had. It reminded him somewhat of the ER, where you had to be calm, organized, and efficient.

On this honeysuckle evening, he parked the Hudson out front on Saratoga Street. The maître d' led him to his table. Grace appeared, pencil and pad in hand. Most of the tables were taken, including a party of eight nearby.

"The usual, Niles?"

"Yes, Grace, H. L. Mencken lamb chops, blueberry pie with a scoop of vanilla, sprinkled with a chocolate chip cookie. And don't forget the mashed potatoes mixed with spinach," his late mother's specialty. He also asked to have all the courses, including dessert, served at once.

"Of course, sir."

Oblivious to the stares of children at the next table, he ate with great intent, shoveling food into his mouth till his cheeks bulged. Couldn't slow down, habit picked up in the ER. When Grace came by, he swallowed the mass and asked if she had "a purpose in life."

"What do you mean, 'purpose in life'?" She scraped the crumbs off the tablecloth with a knife and refilled his water glass.

Sipping black coffee, he took in her all-American demeanor, a natural blonde, straight out of the prairie, slender as a vine—except for the bump at the waist, cause for concern. Tonight he felt downright chatty. "I became a nurse to fulfill my purpose in life—to be a caretaker. What's your purpose?"

"Henry and I came to Baltimore to make a stand against nuclear weapons."

"My nickname at Union Memorial is 'Lurch,' after the character in The New Yorker cartoon."

"That's not nice."

"Not at all. Makes me feel human having a nickname. As a teenager, I felt like I was an alien from another galaxy. You should quit."

"Quit what?"

"This job."

"I'm perfectly capable, Mr. Blackwater, of working right up to the final month. We need the money, and I would go nuts just sitting at home. Uh-oh, just picked up another table. Hope they're big tippers. See you on the quad."

"You don't under—" No such luck. She disappeared into the crowd.

The next day he knocked on their door.

"What do you want?" sneered Henry.

"I want to talk to Grace."

"About what?"

"She should quit her job. The smoky room—"

Henry slammed the door shut. That didn't stop Blackwater. He scribbled a letter to Grace, telling her about the Asian flu, that it's nothing to be ignored, how a cough in Marconi's smoky room could threaten her and her baby. He put a stamp on the envelope and dropped it into the mailbox on the corner.

Evidently, that did the trick.

Now in her sixth month, Grace quit her job and halted her protests against nuclear arms. Suppose she had been arrested? Now and then this creep would turn up on Pennsylvania Avenue and talk trash about making a statement, such as setting the Pentagon on fire or kidnapping a general. Really? She sniffed a snitch, an FBI plant. Her nightmare over a miscarriage in a jail cell convinced her to stop. No more riding the train to Union Station to hold a sign in front of the White House. She hunkered down in an increasingly warm apartment. Henry was hardly home; he had picked up two more shifts, now working six days a week. Meanwhile, Grace was working her way through a pile of books, including a biography of the anarchist Emma Goldman.

Grace also pondered the future: How could she best contribute to making this world a better place for her child? In a long letter, she shared her concerns with her mother in Minot. She had made peace with her parents. Henry had not. He was barely on speaking terms with his bombardier father, who viewed him as a communist.

By mid-June, humidity had settled in, creating inversions of heat and pollution. Baltimore was a powerhouse in manufacturing, but it came at a cost. The air was filthy, burning the eyes—another reason to stay inside. Being from North Dakota, Grace wasn't used to this steamy climate. A couple of fans did little to circulate the air, and she showered several times a day, a quick in and out, heaven! With the shades drawn, she lived in her bra and panties, cooling her flushed cheeks with a paper fan while reading Poe's "Masque of the Red Death." It did not end well.

THE BURNING

BULLIES WERE A FACT of life on the quad, especially if you were a shrimp with coke-bottle glasses. Take Butch of lower Knollwood, a tub of lard who liked to sit on kids. He was also fond of tossing them around like rag dolls, practicing what he called "his judo moves." When Butch rolled through, better clear out of the way—unless you were Big Brother Glenn, who didn't take kindly to Butch mangling his little brother. Only he was allowed to pick on Miller. Glenn bloodied the younger boy's nose. He started to cry. That was the last we saw of that tub of lard. Yay, Glenn!

The following day, Glenn's crayfish, Penis, died in its watery cove in the terrarium. Days before, Miller and Glenn had watched the crustacean molting over a stretch of several hours…even as he ate the shell, maybe giving Penis a tummy ache.

Glenn wanted to find another crayfish in the stream where he found Penis, said this one should be a girl. He'd call her Pussy. "Don't tell Mom like before." Miller's revelation had forced Glenn to pretend Penis's name was Craig.

"I won't."

"You'll regret it if you do."

"Cross my heart and hope to die."

It was a rare day not to endure Glenn's ridicule. Big Brother was subdued after flushing away Penis. He'd had that crayfish for two years. On a mission to find Pussy, the brothers walked side by side through Whispering Pines. They crossed Burke Avenue and entered the woods at the top of the hill. At the bottom was the stream.

The temperature dropped several degrees in the shade. Miller imagined these woods as a haven where little people played among mushrooms and spirits sang when wind blew across the treetops. Glenn sloshed into the stream, hoping to find a crayfish among the rocks close to the bank. In cool, ankle-deep water, Miller closed his eyes and listened to the blue jays, cardinals, and mockingbirds fill the air. Word had it the woods would be cut down in the fall to make way for an apartment complex. Where would the animals go? The owls, foxes, maybe a bear or two. Because he hadn't seen one didn't mean there weren't bears in the woods.

Miller followed Glenn upstream, searching the sparkling pools. Dragonflies darted over the current. The boys spotted minnows, silverfish, tadpoles—but no crayfish. Then they came upon a greenish-brown bullfrog sunning itself on a white slab. Facing the water, it did not move during their slow approach.

"Guess he's waiting for a fly to buzz past," commented Miller.

"Hush," Glenn whispered. Like a cat, he crept along the facing. About two feet away, he made his move. The bullfrog sprang, but a second too late.

"Yahoo!" Big Brother cried. In his fist, he held his prize aloft. He showed it to Miller. "Isn't he ugly?"

"Not after the princess kisses him."

"That's a mushy story."

"I like fairy tales. Aren't you going to let him go?"

Glenn reached into his shorts, pulled out a black pocketknife, and handed it to Miller. "Open it."

"What are you doing?"

"I said open it. Now give it to me—not blade first, stupid, but butt first. That's it. Okay, here's your first biology lesson."

Glenn slit the soft, white underbelly. As he peeled off the membrane, the frog squealed. It was horrible, sounded like a baby. Amused by the look on his little brother's face, Glenn removed the rest of the skin. "That's the first step to dissection," he said, flipping the skin into the ferns. "I'd like you to remove the organs, but we don't have time, do we? We're looking for Pussy!" He spun the remains into the stream.

Miller hung back, felt squeamish. It brought to mind the morning after Hurricane Flossy, that black ant on the tiles, watching it swim through piss. Great fun, huh? This was a hundred times worse. And he helped make it happen. Had he known what Glenn was up to, he could have thrown the knife into the woods.

Glenn didn't catch crayfish that day. Goody, goody, gumdrops.

♦♦♦

Hot afternoons that summer drew Miller to the shade of the apartment building, where he would play chess with Sean. Wasn't too hard to checkmate him last fall. Even fell for the fool's mate, with the queen and bishop trapping the king in a few moves. But the kid was gaining ground as his health improved. Miller had given Sean a chess book. Sean studied the strategy of grandmasters, moving the pieces around the board. Their games became hour-long clashes that sometimes drew an audience. The Chowder boys, Gill and Tracy, were regulars. One rule, especially for Rusty: no suggestions or commentary. This was blood and guts.

"Ha, ha," intruded Glenn, "Baldy's growing fur."

"Shut up, poopyhead," said Sean, not taking his eyes off the board.

"When it gets longer, kiddo, get a flattop...like me," said Glenn, patting Sean's scalp.

"Leave him alone," said Rusty.

"You going to do something about it?"

Miller sprang at Glenn's ankles, knocking him off his feet. He threw himself on Glenn and hit his stomach as hard as he could. Glenn rolled on top of Miller. Rusty slammed into Glenn, and the three thrashed about on the grass.

"Fight! Fight!" cried the Chowder boys. From the playground and apartments around the quad, children streamed toward the conflict, including a pair of mothers—one from the West Building, a big woman wearing a paint-splattered apron, and one from the North Building, her flaming red hair in curlers.

"Enough!" bellowed Alice.

"Stop it, Rusty," said Mary Lou.

Sean's mother poked her head out the second-story window. "Sean, come in now."

"But I'm in the middle of a game."

"Now!"

Sean upended the board, scattering the pieces, and stormed off. Miller, Glenn, and Rusty rose from the grass, none the worse for wear. Miller adjusted his glasses, askew on his face. Children drifted away, including Rusty with his mother.

"Okay, who started it?" asked Alice.

"He did," said Glenn, pointing at Miller.

"That's a new one," said Alice.

"He was picking on Sean," Miller explained.

"I wasn't doing anything," said Glenn. "Shit—"

"Watch your words, young man."

"I'm glad Sean's feeling better."

That was the end of it, but not for Miller. He viewed Big Brother in a different light now, couldn't get that squeal out of his head, nor that weird look on Glenn's face, amused by the misery he caused, not only in the bullfrog but also in his little brother. When he tossed his cookies into the stream, Glenn laughed, calling him "a ninny."

Randy, Sacniete, Sean, and Miller celebrated Sean's eighth birthday with hot fudge sundaes at Read's Drugstore, "on the house," thanks to former streetcar man Mr. Sheer. Sean's gray pallor had faded away. His eagerness to return to school (he had lost a year) altered Miller's outlook. Maybe Immaculate wasn't so bad. Better than a hospital or being six feet under. Sean would be entering the second grade.

"You might be bored," said Randy. "You could easily handle third grade."

"I won't mind being the smartest kid in the class."

Then it happened, one Saturday night during *Gunsmoke*. As Marshal Dillon was showing some drunken cowpokes frontier justice in Miss Kitty's saloon, Miller's eyes strayed from the chessboard to watch them break up the furniture. When the Parliament commercial came on—"the most important quarter inch in cigarette history"—he turned back to the game. Sean's bishop had the potential to put him in a pinch. Had to cut him off. Miller moved his knight into enemy territory, threatening the bishop. Sean countered with his knight, landing it on the black square with emphasis.

"Check!"

Miller stared at the predicament. Phooey! How could he be so stupid, falling for that fork? Miller moved the king, and Sean captured the black queen. Plucking it from the board, he hopped about the room, waving the queen over his head. Miller tipped over the king and joined in the celebration, prancing and chanting like the Navajo medicine man he'd seen on *National Geographic*. The two spun around and around, faster and faster till they tumbled to the rug, giggling on a weave of blazing color and jagged lines.

The Fourth of July was closing in. What sort of mischief could he and Rusty get into? Be great to get their hands on some cherry bombs and hammerheads, like the ones they bought from a drape last New Year's Eve. Now their source was locked up in reform school for shoplifting a switchblade from Sunny Surplus. Had to look elsewhere.

As for Sean, he couldn't wait till the holiday. The three boys planned to follow the action at the top of Garden Drive, offering a view of the Towson fireworks as well as those in Baltimore.

Come the end of June, the Asian flu hit Whispering Pines, sickening Mrs. Minnow, their neighbor upstairs, Monica and Walter in the South Building, and, to the distress of many, little Sean Clover in the East Building. Miller and Rusty were turned away from the apartment. The boy was running a temp of 103.5. No visitors. He slept most of the time. Doc Howell visited Sean twice, checking the progression of the flu. After his second visit, Doc wanted to put him in an oxygen tent at Union Memorial. Miller learned from Mrs. Clover that Sean pleaded to stay in his own bed. If he went to the hospital, he believed he wouldn't return.

"What could I say, Miller? I had to give in."

Doc Howell gave Sean a shot of antibiotics. Miller wasn't much for prayers, except when he wanted something—such as the woods being preserved—but today he prayed with all his might for Sean's recovery, begging God not to take him. On the third of July, the fever broke. But the kid still had to regain his strength. Looked like he would miss those fireworks. Sometimes life was a shit sandwich.

Then Miller came up with an idea.

On the morning of the Fourth, Miller knocked on Mr. Blackwater's door, hoping the nurse wasn't asleep after pulling a night shift. Good chance he wouldn't answer the door. Pass him on the sidewalk, you'd be lucky to get a response. Strange bird, this nurse.

The door cracked open, revealing a gangly, unshaven man in blue boxer shorts. Blackwater undid the chain and adjusted his black-rim glasses. Checking the pinkish scar on the forehead, Niles said it would disappear before the year was out. He started closing the door.

Miller grabbed the doorknob. "Wait!"

"What is it?" he said, covering a yawn. "Did your friend fall off the skateboard?"

"Can I see your boat?"

"You woke me to see the Titanic?"

Was Mr. Blackwater annoyed or curious? Hard to tell. Miller said yes, and the nurse stepped aside. The boy pulled back the curtains. He wanted to see the Titanic in all its glory. The morning sun revealed four black smokestacks and colors painted on thousands of matchsticks. Miller did a slow 360 around the vessel. Lots of stick people on the main deck: musicians, waiters, loungers, dreamers, unaware of what lay ahead.

"You want it?" Niles asked.

"You mean it?"

"I have another project in mind…the Hindenburg. My work is done here."

"Would you be upset if I set it on fire? It is the Titanic."

"Long as you don't burn down Whispering Pines, I'd enjoy watching my creation go up in flames, yes, I would. Where do you suggest we burn the boat?"

"In the sandbox. So Sean can see it."

"He's doing well?"

"He has the flu."

"The flu…"

"Fever's dropped, but he can't come outside for the fireworks."

"Right, you present the Titanic. I'll light the sucker."

"I can put some glue on it."

"Make it burn pretty."

"Rusty and I did that with model airplanes—B-29s, coming in for a crash landing in England, wings on fire. Mayday! Mayday!"

"You have a good imagination. Are you a pyromaniac?"

"No, but I do like the look of fire."

"A blazing fire and no fireplace."

"What?"

"Let me grab some shut-eye."

Can't miss the Fourth of July parade down York Road. Standing on the curb in Towson, in shorts and a faded Donald Duck T-shirt, Miller wiped the sweat off his face with his forearm. Who cares if it's hot! An 1890 horse-and-ladder fire truck rolled by, followed by one of his favorites: fatty Shriners in funny hats doing figure eights on scooters. Bringing up the rear was the Towson High band playing "Dixie," just like every year, the way it should be. Too bad Sean couldn't see this.

He anticipated the burning, praying it wouldn't be a windy night. *Musn't share this with anyone*, especially his best friend, who was standing next to him, gawking at the majorettes. If Rusty blurted a single word about the burning to a sister, it'd be all over the quad by sundown. Mr. Eckert might find out and put a stop to the malarkey.

The long day crept by, marked by firecrackers throughout the neighborhood. Miller watched the setting sun transform the bricks of the East Building into gold that Scrooge McDuck would envy. What was it about time? When you're at the dentist, it passes too slowly. Be at the amusement park or the beach, and it passes too quickly.

A calm evening descended—less humid, welcome relief. Residents spilled out of their stuffy apartments bearing lawn chairs, ashtrays, and snacks. Kids were playing catch. Eckert was grilling a steak. Chess was being played on Big Guy's trunk.

In fading light, Blackwater appeared with the Titanic. He put it in the sandbox and stepped back, stroking his chin, not pleased with the position. Needed to be higher to show off the flames. Chuck Chowder, who was walking by with his boys, suggested placing it on a couple of trash cans.

"Great deal!" exclaimed Miller. Rusty and he raced off. Minutes later, they returned with two steel trash cans. They didn't tell what they did with the trash.

The Titanic was drawing a lathered crowd. When they heard of the nurse's plan, it was cause for more drink, for celebration. Alice and Ralph lugged a cooler across the quad. Everybody must have a drink.

Sean appeared at the window in his PJs, jumping up and down like a monkey to the applause below. His mother had to calm him down.

Miller stepped forward. "Hey, buddy, since you can't go see the fireworks, we brought something to you. Ladies and gents, I present the Titanic! Ta-dah!"

"Here, here!" cried Eckert. "Before you light the doomed vessel, let's have a toast to a brave lad. Here's to your health, Sean." Everyone added their voices, their encouragement.

Blackwater gave the order to "prep the ship." From stem to stern, Rusty and Sean squeezed glue onto matchsticks. Eckert opened the black case he had brought. Inside was a trumpet. He said he wished to play "Taps" while the fire burned…in honor of the military veterans at Whispering Pines.

It promised to be a glorious blaze, something to remember.

NO MORE STICKS

SEAN WAS FREE...FREE OF doctors, free of needles, free of fever, free of flu.

He was also free to leave home and explore the apartment complex. Free to spend hours on the quad playing chess or chasing a ball. Free to watch the green trash truck rumble into the parking lot, followed by Mr. Tony and Mr. Leon, who whistled, yelped, and emptied the trash cans into the back of the truck. Its big claw squished the garbage down the throat. "Feed me!" grinded the green monster.

"Hey, Little Man!" shouted Mr. Tony over the noise. "How you today?"

"Fine, sir."

"I feel fine too," said Mr. Leon. "See ya next time."

Those summer days belonged to Sean, with ball games in the morning and hide-and-go-seek in the dark. One half-moon evening, Rusty came with three glass jars that once held mayonnaise. Sean, Rusty, and Miller roamed the quad, capturing fireflies as they rose from the grass. Sean made it as far as the kitchen with his jar. "Look what I have, Maha." He showed her the fireflies crawling on top of one another. No, no, she said, he must free them outside. They had as much right to live as he. Sean had to agree. In the quad, he convinced Rusty and Miller to free their bugs. Together, the three boys opened the jars. They watched the lightning bugs take flight, like fairies into the night.

The following day an orange chemical truck appeared on Garden Drive. Out came a hose, spraying a white cloud over the quad. That did it for the lightning bugs. Sacniete refused to let her son play in the quadrangle until a thunderstorm washed away the poison. From her experience with the United Fruit Company in Guatemala, she understood the impact of DDT, especially on pregnant women. Monica and Grace should take care.

The rhythm of cicadas and crickets carried the season. Sean's skin returned to its natural shade of golden brown. Almost overnight he became the Maya prince, with black hair so shiny it reflected the sun. He had his late father's almond-black eyes.

From the dining room window, Alice set about capturing Sean and Miller in a watercolor. She sketched their postures: Miller on the grass, chin resting on fists; Sean sitting like a yogi.

While that game progressed, Rusty was tinkering in the basement with an old Schwinn, his first bike. He oiled the chain, inflated the tires, and wiped off the dust. Good to go. He carried the Schwinn on his shoulder up the stairs. Spreading his knees to avoid the handlebars, he rode across the quad. A tennis ball bounced off the back tire. Nine-year-old Tracy Chowder was rounding the cardboard bases.

"Bike's too small for you," said Miller, tipping over his king.

"You think?" Rusty stepped off the bike. "Heya, Sean…like this bike?"

"It's okay," Sean said with little enthusiasm. What did he care about someone else's bike? He vaguely remembered riding his tricycle before he got sick…before he came to this country. Lately, he had been dreaming of Paha. "*¿Dónde estás, Paha? ¿Cuándo te veré?*"

"*Pronto*," Paha answered. Soon.

"Want it?" Rusty asked.

"What?"

"The bike."

"Sure."

"You can have it for a hundred bucks."

"You tricked me."

"I'm kidding, Sean. It's free. Why don't you take it for a spin?"

"I don't know how to ride."

"I can fix that," said Rusty. "I'll put some training wheels on."

"We'll show you the ropes," said Miller.

"What's that mean?" asked Sean.

"It's a Navy expression...means we'll teach you."

In the days that followed, Sean rode up and down the sidewalks of Whispering Pines. The Chowder boys, Tracy and Gill, made fun of the training wheels, calling them "baby wheels," but Sean didn't care. He was moving. After three tries, he conquered Garden Drive, pedaling to the top, with Rusty and Miller egging him on.

"You're ready to ride," declared Rusty.

"I need more time." He was afraid of losing his balance. Could get hurt.

"You can do it," said Rusty. "Be with you the whole way."

"I have to ask Maha."

"Let's all go ask her," said Miller.

Over grilled cheese sandwiches, Sacniete listened to their plan. Against her better judgment, she agreed to it. That afternoon, Sean rode his bike on the sidewalk while the boys led on skateboards. On the edge of Towson High plaza, Rusty removed the training wheels. Sean positioned his foot on the pedal, ready to ride. Miller took off his leather helmet and put it on Sean's head, but it was far too large. "Okay, never mind. Ready...set...go!" Miller gave the Schwinn a shove. Rusty ran alongside, right hand on the fender, steadying the ride. Before Sean realized it, Rusty had released him. After an initial wobble, Sean gained control.

August arrived and shadows stretched earlier across the quad. Back-to-school ads for supplies, clothes, and lunchboxes reminded Miller that time was dwindling. He didn't want summer to end. A jingle for Jell-O circled Miller's brain: "...never too late to make Jell-O!" Soon he'd be eating Jell-O in that basement. He hated—no, double hated—returning to Immaculate Conception, chained to a desk for hours, eating baloney-and-butter sandwiches in "the dungeon," a regular James Cagney prison, no talking if you know what's good for you, then on to recess, barely time for a dodgeball game, then on to music with Sister Marietta, "Long Nose," who had a voice like fingernails across a chalkboard, so screechy it could make a dog cry. Made him want to put his head on the desk and cover his ears, like Pal the Wonder Dog in *Little Rascals*.

Twenty-four days till Labor Day and the end of summer. Something else bugged him. This morning he was supposed to meet Sean on the quad for their usual game of chess. Still hadn't figured out how to beat the kid. On Saturday, Miller checked out a book on chess at the Towson Library. Needed a fresh approach. When Monday arrived, he was anxious to test his new attack. The heck with controlling the center of the board. Choke him with pawns!

But Sean didn't turn up at nine a.m. Waving the gnats away from his eyes, Miller chewed on a blade of grass as the minutes clicked by on his Mickey Mouse wristwatch. Usually Sean arrived first. At fifteen past, he called up to Sean's bedroom window. Not a sound in return. He tossed pebbles at the screen, one after another, till one clipped a pane of glass. Mrs. Clover appeared at the window. She told him Sean wouldn't be coming down today.

"Is he okay?"

"He needs to slow down," she said, closing the red curtains.

Next morning, determined to have a game, he crossed the quad, chessboard under his arm. He tapped on Apartment 4D in the East Building, and the door opened. He smelled bacon. Mrs. Clover stood before him, wiping her hands on a towel. She was wearing an apron with woven parrots. Her clothes were always so colorful. Miller chose his words carefully. "Hi, Mrs. Clover, can Sean play a game of chess? We can play in his bedroom if he's too tired to play outside."

"That's very sweet of you, Miller," she said softly, "but I'm afraid we can't do that today. Sean's still a little tired. Another day of rest. Maybe *mañana*."

On Wednesday, the garbage truck came and went, still no sign of Sean. That afternoon, while skateboarding in the parking lot, Miller flagged down Mr. Knight's pickup.

"What's up, Miller?"

Miller stepped onto the running board. "How's Sean? See him?"

The big man turned off the engine. He shook a Camel from the pack, tapped it on his wrist, flicked open his USMC lighter, and lit the mule. Through the smoke, he looked the boy in the eye. "You want the hard truth?"

"What's wrong?"

"Cancer came back."

Had he heard right? Cancer came back? You sure? The plumber gave a slow nod. Can't they do something? Don't look good. Miller was trapped in an out-of-world reality, something from *The Twilight Zone*...couldn't take in the words...don't look good...can't be happening.

"You and Rusty been good for Sean. You let him be a little boy, not a patient. You did good, Miller. If you want to talk about it, I'm around. I'm hurtin' too. It's okay to cry, good for the soul." He started the Chevy; Miller stepped off the pickup. It left in a puff of exhaust.

He stared at the fading blue cloud. Did that mean Sean would lose his hair again? Maybe he could live with the disease...had a chance, right? He stashed the skateboard in the foyer. Crossing the quad, he aimlessly kicked a tin can. Instead of hitting the trash barrel, it bounced into the bushes. Squatting, he reached under the bush for the can...couldn't imagine his friend dead, stiff as a board.

On a slope behind the quad stood a cherry tree he had climbed many times. Miller swung his leg over the lowest branch and took his time getting to the top. He took in the robin's-egg sky, the swirling mashed-potato clouds, and the playground that appeared at his feet, full of kids, big and small, on swings, monkey bars, and seesaws—so healthy, so alive. A tear rolled down his cheek as he clung to the trunk. All along he assumed Sean would be fine, doctors would cure him. Kids weren't supposed to die. That's not how the movie ends. If he prayed really hard, vowing not to sin, to become an altar boy, would God hear his voice?

Word of the setback cast a pall over the quadrangle. For the first time ever, Miller had trouble sleeping, couldn't turn his mind off. After confession on Saturday, Miller dropped a silver dollar from his Christmas stocking into the poor box. With an Act of Contrition under his belt, this might be the best time to do it, while his milk-bottle soul was clear of smudges, venial sins. He lit a candle and knelt before the Blessed Mother, praying for a miracle.

Sean and Miller resumed their chess games on the grass but soon retreated inside because of the stares of children. Plus, the passing adults were polite to a fault. Their looks of sympathy made Sean feel like an animal in a zoo.

So they played on the kitchen table or, on bad days, in his bedroom. The Hopkins doctors were willing to try another bout of chemo, but they held out little hope, at best gaining a month or two. Miller was in the kitchen, staring at his plate of beans and rice, not knowing what to say or do as Sean begged his Maha to end the treatment: "No more sticks! No more sticks!" Mrs. Clover had no choice but to give in.

Sean's face paled and the cheeks hollowed. Miller dreamed that Nurse Blackwater had found a cure for cancer. Before he could tell Sean, he awoke to the same sucky reality. There would be no miracle. All the prayers in the universe wouldn't save his friend.

That morning Sean made a request. He wanted Miller to help him give away his toys: the steel cars and trucks, his holster and six-shooters, coonskin cap, his collection of US Army figures, his scooter, and various balls. They found homes with the Chowder boys and the Eckert girls. Miller kept the coonskin cap. Along the way, he was asked questions he could not answer. How's he doing?

asked Mrs. Chowder. Is he in pain? asked Shirl Eckert. Hard to speak when you have a lump in your throat.

Sean did hold on to the chess set and bike, took imaginary rides on that bike around the neighborhood, "pedaling to the moon." When Sean had no energy to sit up, he and Miller would play chess without pieces. While Sean kept track of every pawn, bishop, and knight on the board, Miller had no chance. After ten or so moves he was lost.

On a sticky afternoon, Sean lost the will to play chess in any form. The morphine made it difficult to concentrate. Sean's eyes blazed with intensity, as if he were seeing something Miller couldn't see. After receiving the last rites from Father Mamarella, Sean told Miller he had seen a red angel at the foot of the bed. "I'm not scared."

A few hours before he slipped into a coma, Rusty and Miller visited Sean for the last time.

"Save a place in heaven for Miller and me," said Rusty.

"We'll probably need your help getting there," added Miller.

Sean laughed through the congestion. "Maybe we can skateboard."

"Nah," said Rusty, "you'll have wings…."

After three days in a coma, Sean died on September 3, at 2:34 a.m. Alice broke the news to Miller the next morning. "Should've been there," he said, looking out the window. A sunny day, perfect for a ball game, a chess game, or a walk in the woods. The Chowder boys were tossing a football. Mrs. Eckert was hanging a sheet on a clothesline. Children were screaming in the playground. Life goes on. But not for Miller, not today. *Should've been there…when the red angel took Sean.*

In his bedroom, he ripped off the dates he had pasted on the wall since last October. He squeezed the newspaper strips into a ball and tossed it into the trash can. He saw no point in continuing to mark his escape from the Grim Reaper. Fuck him.

The Immaculate Conception funeral landed on the day after Labor Day, first day of school. Miller and Rusty had a dispensation to attend. Neighbors filled the pews in the chapel. Even Mr. Tony and Mr. Leon made an appearance in the back. The child had touched many lives. Rusty Eckert, Sr. organized the pallbearers: Niles Blackwater, Randy Knight, L. Wayne Sheer, Chuck Chowder, and Rusty Jr. Miller was deemed too small to carry the load. He resented the exclusion. Everything was a blur, too much to take in…the "Ave Maria," the changing of the wine and bread to the blood and body of Christ, Father Mamarella's homily, communion, closing prayers, Mrs. Clover's tears….

At the end of Mass, neighbors, one by one, laid a rose on the coffin. Miller clung to his mother. He was the last to approach. See you in heaven. He placed the rose in the center of the coffin.

MAYA MUSE

AFTER THE FUNERAL, AFTER the smiles, tears, hugs, and kisses, Sacniete retreated to her bedroom. She appreciated this outpouring of affection from neighbors and colleagues, but she had nothing left to give. Her soul was a dishrag, wrung out.

"Would you like me to leave?" Randy asked.

"As you wish," she said, closing the door. Sacniete lit a candle and sat on her heels before the shrine, an arrangement reflecting the gods of the Maya. She and Babajide had planned for Sean to learn Quiché, the indigenous language of the Guatemalan highlands. He would not grow up a slick city boy, cut off from the ancient culture. Their son would feel the pulse of their people by working the maize fields alongside his cousins, absorbing the wisdom of the village shaman, and hearing and speaking their five-thousand-year-old dialect. *El golpe*, the coup, ruined everything.

Though the Church forbade it, she would have her son cremated tomorrow. She planned to return to Guatemala and spread his ashes in the fields of her youth, an offering to their ancestors. Who's to say which life is richer? In a span of eight years, her child experienced the world's magic, even in a trash truck. Through his eyes, she saw her late husband, as good a man as there ever was.

She felt lost, adrift in a sea of strangers. Her heart ached for her village, her mother, sisters, brothers, aunts, uncles, and cousins—either dead now or in hiding. She longed to walk the lanes cutting through maize fields, to wake in a hammock to the call of a rooster, to smell Maha's tortillas, to gaze at the clouds ringing Santa María, a majestic volcano she took for granted when she was a bookish girl aspiring to go to the university in Guatemala City.

Her shrine rested on a low-slung table. Sacniete bowed to Ometeotl, Father of the Near and Far, the Formless One, represented by the zero, an India-ink calligraphy that once graced the mantle of their apartment in Guatemala City. She bowed to Mother Chicomecoatl, goddess of the earth, symbolized by a moonflower she'd found blooming on the side of the building. Between the gods was a photo of Sean, taken over the summer at Gwynn Oak Amusement Park. Her boy was in heaven, riding the Moon Rocket, Caterpillar, Ferris wheel, roller coaster, bumper cars, and merry-go-round. Between rides, he gobbled down cotton candy, pizza, and two hot dogs. She teased him for having "a wooden leg." On the way home in Randy's pickup, Sean rested his head in her lap, and she toyed with his beautiful hair. He said it was "the best day ever." Might have been hers too.

Through the afternoon, Randy scrubbed the bathroom and kitchen and mopped the floors. Had to keep busy…do something productive. As he wiped down the windows, television, icebox handle, and doorknob on Sean's bedroom door, he felt he was performing a cleansing ritual so the spirit did not linger. He stripped Sean's bed, washing the sheets and blanket and drying them on the line. He made the boy's bed as if he were back in boot camp at Parris Island: tight and balanced, not a wrinkle for the drill sergeant. He returned Sean's teddy bear to its proper place on the pillow.

A knock on the door. Now who could that be? In the hallway stood Lena Minnow, Miller's upstairs neighbor. Fixed a drip in her kitchen sink once. Gracious lady. Wanted to give him a tip, which he refused. Mrs. Minnow was cradling a green bowl covered with aluminum foil. "Brought you some pea soup," she said.

"How nice, Lena. Let me take it. Smells delicious. Thank you."

He tapped lightly on the bedroom door. "Mrs. Minnow brought us some pea soup. Want some?"

The door opened. Sacniete had shed the black dress for a huipil, a beaded garment with the colors of the rainbow. Beneath the fabric, he caught sight of her round breasts and dark nipples. Sacniete took his hand and led him to the bed. Their lovemaking was slow and silent, with sharp breaths and occasional sobs. At rest, on her back, her hand intertwined with his, she spoke of summoning Sean's spirit, his nagual.

"What's that?" he asked. A car rolled into the parking lot. Lights shone on the curtains.

"Think of a nagual as a guardian angel. It can take the form of a wolf, a hawk, a rabbit...depends on the alignment of stars and planets at birth. The nagual guides a soul through the dreamworld. I envision Sean's spirit as the quetzal, flying over the rainforest. It gives me comfort. He's now with his ancestors."

Someone entered the building. Footsteps. A door opened and closed. They made love a second time and had Lena's pea soup at midnight.

THE REST OF THE STORY

MY COUNTRY LET US walk together, you and I:

I will descend into the abysses where you send me
I will drink your bitter cup,
I will be blind so you may have eyes,
I will be voiceless so you may sing,
I have to die so you may live.

"Can't sleep," she said two nights later. The lament of Guatemalan poet Castillo spun in her head. Couldn't get it out of her mind.

"I'm awake. I know what we could do."

"*No ahora, mi hombre.* I would like to tell you the rest of my story."

"I've been waiting for what happened."

"Remember, Victor?"

"You mean the whore for the United Fruit Company?"

"He gave me two hours to pull everything together for the escape..."

Numb to the loudspeakers proclaiming a new day in Guatemala as well as the traitors cheering passing military formations, Sacniete strode across the plaza. She would have sprinted, but that might draw attention from the snipers manning the roof of the congressional building. She passed the body of an old man, a *campesino* draped over a bench, a victim of a bullet in the back. Would she ever see again the green tapestry of the Guatemalan hills? What of her cousins in the village of Chac? And Babajide's family in Chicomecoatl? Entering the apartment where she had spent the last five years, she saw the look of worry on the face of

Angelina, the university student who watched over Sean. Martial music was playing on the radio. Sean was napping on the sofa. Sacniete handed Angelina a wad of bills. Angelina thanked Professor Canul for her generosity.

"*Tengas cuidado*," be careful. No time for tears. Had to pack, what to take: passports, birth and baptismal certificates, Sean's teddy bear. She paused at the open closet. Her fingers touched Babajide's cotton camisa, a shirt showing the colors of her people. El hombre had an elegance that belied his roots as a "soil-grubber," what The Company called tenant farmers. Like her, he had won a scholarship, cause for a two-day fiesta in his village. Her village also had a fiesta, with a bit less pulque. The two were meant to meet on the boulevard during the '44 uprising. Destiny and democracy drew them together. The art on the walls of their apartment reflected the ideals they shared, beginning with a small wooden statue of Gandhi inscribed "Keep walking." Babajide found it in a flea market, said the phrase came from the salt strike in India against the colonialists: the struggle of the people is never-ending. She put the statue into her purse.

Twelve hours later, Victor, Sean, and Sacniete were on a Pan Am flight, descending over lights reflecting on the Potomac River. The sight of the Washington Monument and the Capitol ignited a stabbing pain in her gut. So far from home, family and village decimated…

How could this happen? At least they were safe and her boy healthy.

Victor had taken care of the particulars that allowed Sacniete and Sean to pass through customs. They were to apply for refugee status.

Randy interrupted the flow of words. "Why this spook, who helped instigate the slaughter of your people, take a sudden interest in you and Sean? Did he come on to you?"

"Never did. I was surprised. I thought he would want something in return, but no, he took good care of us, making sure our needs were met. He settled us in Whispering Pines. He lived in Washington. Once a month he would drive up the parkway in his fancy car and hand over a few hundred dollars. As for your question, I believe he had a guilty conscience, judging from his statement the day of the *coup d'état*: 'I didn't sign up for this.' Victor thought he was making the world safe from communism…don't think he expected genocide. No rallying 'round the flag that day. Had to get his ass out of the country fast. His blood work was done.

"Over coffee one evening, he revealed that he didn't care for the man he had become. How pathetic…*mierda total!* What was I supposed to do, give him comfort for his part in destroying democracy? Some deeds can't be forgiven. Live with it, Victor."

On Sean's behalf, she had to accept money. Impossible to dismiss the fear of cancer returning. Doctors gave no guarantees. Babajide was never far from her thoughts, especially at night, when she had nothing to distract her from the void in her heart. One restless night his spirit came in a dream, and love shone upon her soul, her yollotl. As a Maya, she was raised to perceive magic, especially during that time of transition from this life to the next. Maybe this was Babajide's way of saying farewell.

At the same time, she "couldn't muster the grit," as Victor might say, to tell Sean that his Paha was gone. Boy was learning English fast. After a month in the apartment complex, he was practically fluent. American television was changing how he viewed the world. He repeated advertising jingles…capitalist junk. He stopped asking about his Paha. Sacniete feared losing her son to this culture, this land of cheap bananas and coffee. In the newspaper, she read how the democratically elected government in Iran had been overthrown because the president wanted to nationalize the oil industry. Sound familiar?

Two years passed. Sean completed first grade at Immaculate Conception. Next year he would take first communion. Ironic she would send him to Catholic school, given the Church's cruel legacy in her country, but Sean needed structure and those Irish Franciscans tolerated no monkey business. As for herself, Sacniete had returned to the classroom, teaching two classes in the linguistics department at Towson State. The dean valued her expertise in Mayan and encouraged her to complete her PhD. Couldn't depend on Victor forever.

"How did you become Mrs. Clover?"

"It was a proposition I couldn't refuse."

"I don't understand."

"When the cancer returned, Victor offered to marry me so Sean could have access to the most advanced care at Johns Hopkins. The wedding took place in the Towson courthouse, just the two of us, along with a judge and a witness, Lena Minnow. For his wedding gift, he bought me a car, a 1949 Dodge Coronet, so I could drive Sean to the hospital for treatment. It was a challenge learning to drive, especially shifting gears. In Guatemala City, Babajide and I got around on motorbikes. With Victor, I drove around parking lots to get used to this big American car. He took me to the DMV for the learner's permit. Came up four weekends to help me practice for the test. Once I passed, we went our separate ways. 'See you in a month.' "

"How do you know he wasn't a bigamist?"

"Too much of a loner. I think he was married to the CIA."

For this nine-month bout of chemotherapy she dreaded making the journey alone, without Babajide to turn to for comfort and strength. She gave up teaching and pursuing her doctorate in linguistics. Like horses of the apocalypse, complications came in a rush, intense fever and loss of hair, including his eyebrows. His blood count fell, and he needed transfusions. She had dreams of driving, lost in the streets of Baltimore, unable to find the hospital.

Then, as if the gods were taunting her, Victor flipped his sedan in the median of the Baltimore–Washington Parkway. What happens now? How could she possibly afford Sean's care? The CIA asked for the body, and she signed the papers. He was buried with honors in Arlington. She did not attend the funeral. She was scanning the classifieds as well as the Food Fair bulletin board. Maybe she could clean houses. Or teach again. Two hundred dollars left for this month; half to go to rent in two weeks. They could end up on the streets, like those mothers who begged in Plaza Central.

A few days later, she received an official letter in the mail informing her of the benefits as Victor Clover's widow. The health coverage would continue. In addition to his insurance money and pension, she was the beneficiary of a six-figure bank account. *Gracias a Dios.*

Randy's snore ended the soliloquy. She shook one of his Camels free from the pack on the nightstand. She had been a heavy smoker at the university, quit the minute she learned she was pregnant. Gave up wine too, which was harder. Now there was no reason not to smoke. Cigarette in hand, she stood at the back window, gazing at the moon. Her future came to her in the moonlight.

The next morning, over breakfast, he asked about her plans. Maybe they could build a life together.

"With you?" she said with an incredulous smile. "Randy, you can't be serious."

"Why not?"

"Because I'm returning to Guatemala."

"Isn't that dangerous? I'll go with you."

"I don't think a Yankee with a USMC tattoo would be welcome. Babajide's cousins will protect me. I go in memory of my father, my husband, my village. I want to participate in the revolt. I may not carry a gun, but with the money I have, I can buy them."

"Listen to me, White Flower. My Uncle Jack was killed at Pearl Harbor. When I turned eighteen in '44, I joined the Marines out of spite. I wanted to kill Japanese in the South Pacific. Instead of becoming a sniper, however, I was assigned to the latrine unit. After the Japanese surrender, I was stationed in Japan. I was even in MaacArthur's parade through Tokyo. And you know who protected us? Japanese soldiers, who formed a wall, facing their own people."

"Why did they do that?"

"Because MacArthur understood the culture. He treated Emperor Hirohito with respect. As a country devastated by war, MacArthur knew the people had suffered enough. The Emperor could lead them on a path to peace and freedom. I was never so proud of the USA as I was then. But this, this atrocity you described, disgusts me. The CIA has become an instrument of evil. Let me go with you, Sacniete. I was a sharpshooter, the best on Parris Island. I know weapons."

"Like you know toilets. Sorry, had to say it." She patted his hand. "Randy, mi amor, you came into Sean's life at the right time. We needed you. You were a godsend. I must go home, without you."

"I could protect you."

She withdrew her hand. "Please…don't make it harder for me."

"I'm sorry, I'm just—"

"Shh!"

PARTING PASSAGES

BETWEEN CONTRACTIONS, GRACE PLANNED the next five years of her life. No more protests against nuclear arms, couldn't picture dragging her child to demonstrations...now pant...pain intensifying, too much, ah, a respite. Why not a lawyer? Hmm... Oh! Here it comes again; dear God, that was a big wave. Should I get an epidural? Henry has a good gig as head waiter...could care for the baby while she was in class at the University of Baltimore. Two years, bam, an associate degree—ouch! Breathe in, breathe out, get on top...law school for three years, then pass the bar. *Push!*

Grace screamed, and out slid a pudgy pink boy, three weeks late, making his presence known by peeing in the face of the obstetrician. Grace nearly split herself laughing. *Welcome to the world, Buster!*

About the same time, South Carolina Senator Strom Thurmond was filibustering against the civil rights bill, on his feet for twenty-four hours, breaking the record set by fellow South Carolina Senator John C. Calhoun in his defense of slavery and states' rights. Among the protesters outside the Capitol was Lena Minnow. Leaning on her cane, she matched the septuagenarian segregationist hour by hour.

For her effort, Gregorious gave his daughter a gift. "Want you to have this," he said, handing her an official document from the State of Maryland, framed and behind glass. She looked at the yellowed document, this Deed of Manumission and Release of Service. She read aloud the words:

"Whereas my slave, Isaac Shade, has enlisted in the service of the United States: now in consideration thereof, I, J. W. Wheeler of Baltimore County, do hereby in consideration of said enlistment manumit, set free, and release the above-named Isaac Shade from all service due me."

"Isaac was your great-grandfather. He built this house."

"Why didn't you tell me?"

"Because I viewed you as white."

"That's a helluva thing to say."

"Trying to be honest in my old age. Will you take this deed? You deserve it."

Lena hung the deed on her bedroom wall so her eyes would see it first thing every morning. Every protest, every march, every sit-in, she dedicated to Isaac Shade. In the words of the negro spiritual, "Freedom's been a long time coming!"

Robin Turnbaugh lost his father that month, a stroke at the police union banquet, face down in the chocolate mousse. "What a way to go," Mother said on the phone. He heard in her tone a hint of gloating, as if Father had it coming. In a North Beach chapel, he said a prayer for Big Jake. Never did have that conversation between father and son, the one where Robin would say the right words to make him understand. Whatever resentment Robin felt had dwindled to sadness over not making the SOB proud. God knows he tried, but ultimately Robin had to be his own man. Their last confrontation in the dance hall had freed him. He said his peace. He loved San Francisco, this city of writers, poets, and eccentrics. Here, he could be himself. Deep down, he believed Big Jake loved him and wanted the best for him… just couldn't get past his prejudice, a loss for both. That evening he toasted Father, wherever his soul might be. He and Michael clicked glasses. The pinot was superb.

After a bit of wavering (he would miss the action in the ER), Niles Blackwater, RN, accepted the Johns Hopkins University scholarship to study microbiology. On a whim, he had applied during the Asian flu pandemic—couldn't imagine a better job than being in a lab searching for clues through a microscope. He could relate to the scientific method. He had constructed his life in a similar fashion.

Rusty Eckert, Sr., decided to run for Congress and moved his family to Hereford so he could run as a Republican for the Fifth District seat. He would lose in the primary because of his support for civil rights. His opponent's slogan? "Your home is your castle."

Chuck Chowder, taking Eckert's advice, opened a private-eye office not far from the Towson courthouse. One of his first clients was Eckert himself, who'd launched a law practice down the street. He wanted everything Chowder could find on Van Cliffe—his taxes, investments, past acquaintances. In two years, the man would come up for parole. Eckert dedicated himself to ensuring that the murderer served the full sentence.

Pregnant with their third child, LuAnn, Chuck, and the two boys moved to Campus Hills, a housing development in north Towson. Robin's mother was their realtor.

Randy Knight drove Sacniete to the airport; they had one last kiss at the gate. After watching her plane take off, he decided to join the Merchant Marines. He drove to the harbor and joined the union. Two weeks later, he was on a freighter, bound for Sweden as an ordinary seaman.

Sacniete vanished into the jungle highlands of Guatemala. During the thirty-year revolt, *Madre Canul* achieved legendary status as a source for wisdom, strategy, and weapons. The CIA never made the connection between the late Victor Clover and the insurgent.

On Halloween at Union Memorial, a six-pound baby boy came into this world, born three weeks early. Monica and Walter named him Sean.

Serving a hot fudge sundae, L. Wayne Sheer was smitten with Sheila, a twenty-seven-year-old waitress at the Towson Diner. Had that Audrey Hepburn haircut, cute as a button as her spoon plunged into the chocolate…even gave him a wink. Had to ask for her phone number before the cutie escaped. She wrote her phone number on the back of the check. After a two-month courtship, the two married and moved to Ocean City, where they started a business running a tourist train up and down the boardwalk.

During the summer and into the fall, Margo Catalino went out with six different guys: Ed, John, Bill, Steve, Madison, and Byron. Three lawyers, two accountants, and a college student who came to her aid when she had a flat tire on Burke Avenue. Nice kid. Too bad Byron was only nineteen. Was a good kisser. Funny too. The other dates didn't click; Margo, given what she had gone through, had little patience for small talk.

Bottom line? She didn't have the energy or the will for a man in her life. Maybe it had to do with the hours of work during the week, sometimes stretching into the weekend. She loved teaching five-year-olds at Little Red Riding Hood, such a magical age, but the salary was too meager to live on. To fill the gap, she tutored eighth graders and high school students, preparing them for high school or college. She was working forty-five, fifty hours a week. On weekends, all she wanted to do was sleep. Couldn't get enough of it. Building a relationship took too much energy…at least for now.

As the leaves fell, Miller observed the turnover in the apartments: Nurse Blackwater moving to Fells Point; Randy to the Merchant Marines; Sean's mother to Guatemala; Robin in San Francisco. Hardest was Rusty leaving, moving to a place called Hereford, up north in the county. On the day of the move, beneath the cherry tree, Rusty and Miller pricked their fingertips and pressed them against one another. Blood brothers forever…

Never did become an altar boy. Couldn't do it…guess God didn't fulfill His part of the bargain…or maybe life wasn't like that, an exchange of favors. Nurse Blackwater said that microbes don't distinguish between good and bad people. Life was random. At times since the funeral, Miller felt like an adult living in a child's body. Mom told him to lighten up, be himself again. How could he not be himself? He searched the night sky for Sputnik, wishing Sean were here. In a sense, he was. Miller would carry Sean in his heart for all his days, using him as a beacon, lighting the way.

ACKNOWLEDGEMENTS

In the fall of 2019, I happened to be in Ireland with my wife, Denise. On a dusty shelf in an old bookstore, I came upon the last copy of *Dubliners*. I read it in graduate school, but I wanted a fresh look. On the plane, I read it cover to cover. So many secrets. So many festering lies. I owe a lot to James Joyce. I too would create a community full of secrets.

I wrote the novel during the pandemic, five hours a day, seven days a week, I was rolling. When I finished a story, I had the pleasure of reading it to Denise. She had a great ear for catching stuff that didn't belong in 1956. As a psychotherapist, she could dissect a character. In many ways, Whispering Pines is a journey through the mind.

Along the way, I tapped into the expertise of friends and family; Rick Bogdan on tanks; Stephanie Bolton on suturing a wound; Ken Whitaker on the .38, standard gun for Marines; Ralph Hoffschildt on the Army burn unit. Denise Bolton, Chris Lehner and Susan Lau were my first readers. Don Berger added poetic insight. Their feedback was invaluable. Ivy Pochoda, who edited Love Is Where You Find It, gave me the best advice on tension. It transformed the book.

I must thank Bill Loving, my old friend from the UMD days, for suggesting a title change. He introduced me to Tyson Cornell, publisher for Rare Bird. Tyson and I signed a contract a week later. It's been a pleasure to work with him. I commend him for his patience when I changed the name of the novel to *Donnybrook*; two days later I wanted it switched back to *Whispering Pines.*

I also appreciate Guy Inoci's editing. He had the right touch. And he cured me of my fetish for ellipses…

Then, of course, there's Jim Burger: His photo showed me at my best, full of life and laughter; Chris Standiford, plumbing; and Joseph Di Prisco for the thoughtful prepublication blurb.